Also by

Loki

Loki: Nine Naughty Tales of the Trickster

Sword of Lies

The Gnostic Prophecy

by

Mike Vasich

This is a work of fiction. Any similarities to persons, places, or events is entirely coincidental.

Copyright Mike Vasich 2013

Chapter One

Dr Russell Kellar stood in front of the Renaissance Hotel, turning over a folded piece of paper and fighting the instinct to get into his car and go home. The odds that Farouk actually had authentic scrolls from first century Palestine were so slim they might as well be non-existent. The best he could reasonably hope for were reproductions, but even those seemed like a long shot.

The most likely scenario would be Farouk trying to peddle fakes. He would try to pass forgeries off as authentic and rare, or maybe even ground-breaking, and he would play on Russell's desire to be the scholar who discovered the next Judas Gospel or Dead Sea Scrolls.

He should have just walked away—went home and worked on his book, which was in dire need of a new third chapter—but a lingering doubt remained. What if he walked away and the scrolls were authentic? He knew the answer already. They would be translated by someone else, and they would make that person's career. It would mean worldwide renown and respect, offers from prestigious institutions across the country, and more money than a college professor would see in a career.

What was the risk in seeing what Farouk had? He was already there, after all. If he wasn't convinced of their authenticity, he wouldn't make an offer. What would Farouk do? He wasn't going to shoot Russell and take his wallet. He'd just find another buyer who wouldn't be as discerning.

He shoved the paper into his pocket and walked through the front doors of the hotel. He'd see what the man had to offer and go from there. In all likelihood, he'd be back in his car in fifteen minutes or so, feeling foolish but satisfied that he had at least made sure. He tried to ignore the voice in the back of his head that reminded him how the Judas Gospel was discovered in almost the exact same circumstances.

The lobby was large with a high ceiling, stylish in a sort of absent way, with vast empty spaces between the few sitting areas and the front desk. There were few people there—a Thursday night in late April was probably not the height of the tourist season. His footsteps echoed off the marble floors as he walked over to the check-in desk.

A brunette with perfectly white teeth and a vacant smile greeted him. "Can I help you?"

"I'm here to see Abdul Farouk in the presidential suite."

Her smile didn't falter. "Your name, sir?"

"Dr Russell Kellar. He's expecting me."

She nodded and picked up a phone. After a short exchange with the person on the other end, she handed Russell a key card—the only way to access the presidential suite on the top floor—and directed him to the elevators.

Once inside, he slid the key card into a slot next to the tenth floor button. The elevator moved upwards smoothly, finally opening on a short hallway with two doors, one on either end. He walked to the door on the right and knocked.

It opened after a minute, and he found himself staring at a man about his age dressed in a well-tailored dark suit. His hair was extremely short and his face was angular and expressionless. His broad, muscular build was visible through the contours of his suit, and Russell guessed he was a bodyguard, although he had never met one as intimidating as this before.

"I'm here to see Mr Farouk. I'm Dr Russell Kellar."

The man did not reply, but instead stepped back and held the door open, gesturing with his free hand. Russell walked in and the door shut behind him. Before he could step further into the room the man was in front of him, palm out.

"Turn around."

His voice was cold and business-like, and there was no question in Russell's mind that he was used to having his orders obeyed.

The bodyguard's hands were all over him, from the bottom of his pant legs to the hem of his sleeves and everywhere in between. The search was not rough, but it was more thorough than it needed to be, the bodyguard searching in places where a gun could not reasonably be hidden. Did Farouk really expect a college professor to have a concealed weapon? He had never been frisked before examining artifacts.

He turned around when the man was finished. There was still no expression on his face.

"Satisfied?" Russell said, unable to completely hide his annoyance. The man did not respond other than to gesture towards the room. Russell walked past him, watching him out of the corner of his eye.

He stepped into a large sitting room and saw a dark-skinned man sitting in an armchair, facing him. He was dressed in an expensive suit as well, and his black hair was thick and well-coiffed. He stood up and held his hand out.

"Dr Kellar, it is a pleasure to meet you. Your studies of the New Testament are well-known for their insight."

Russell took his hand. "Mr Farouk, I presume?"

He nodded and smiled, gesturing for Russell to sit down.

"Would you like a drink?" Farouk picked up a glass of wine from the sofa table. "It's 1998 Petrus. A previous vintage was very popular with one of your presidents in the 1960s."

Russell dabbled in wine but was no expert. Even he, however, had heard of this famous Merlot. He vaguely remembered the price tag at being upwards of $2000 a bottle. He was tempted, but wanted to stay clear-headed for any negotiation.

"Thank you, but no."

He shrugged and took a sip of the Petrus.

"I must apologize for Zeev." Farouk nodded towards the bodyguard. "He is a jumper, and they tend to be very thorough."

Russell sat down on the sofa and glanced around the large suite while Farouk eased back into the chair. He tried to estimate how much the suite cost per night. $1000? More? As much as he enjoyed the privileges of being a highly-respected academic, he never saw lavish expenses like this. He wondered what other kinds of things Farouk sold besides old scrolls. How many antiquities dealers needed a bodyguard like Zeev?

"Do you meet many college professors who carry concealed weapons?"

Farouk smiled. "There are risks in my dealings, and I must take the utmost care that anyone I do business with is being forthright. I do hope that you understand."

"I don't generally carry a weapon."

Farouk chuckled. "Of course not. I hardly expected you to come in here and shoot me. But there are other considerations."

Russell waited a few seconds with eyebrows raised before realizing that Farouk was not going to tell him more without prodding. "Can I ask what you're referring to?"

Farouk leaned back in his seat and took a sip of his wine before speaking. "Despite your reputation, I could not be certain that you are completely free of outside interests that may not look fondly on my dealings in this country."

"Outside interests?"

Farouk leaned forward. "Oh come now, professor. Surely you aren't so naïve? You were invited here to look at an ancient scroll from the Middle East. Who might have an interest in such things?"

Russell nodded. "So there's a question of legality?" He assumed the scrolls were smuggled when he first heard about them from Lakaj, but he wanted to make it clear to Farouk that he was not some isolated academic with no real understanding of how the world worked.

The dealer merely smiled.

"And you thought I might have some sort of wire on me, is that correct?"

"I am certain now that you do not. Zeev is, as I have

said, very thorough."

Russell looked over his shoulder at the stone-faced man standing near the doorway. "You said he was a jumper," he said, turning back. "I'm not familiar with that term."

"He is a former Katsa. You have heard of Mossad, yes?"

"The Israeli spy agency?"

Farouk nodded. "A Katsa is one of those for whom Mossad training was not intense enough. They are sometimes called jumpers because they go from country to country, rarely staying for long."

Russell looked over his shoulder again. Zeev showed no reaction to any of the conversation, as if he hadn't even heard it. Russell felt a chill wondering how many people he might have killed in his career. He hadn't heard of Katsa before, but Mossad was infamously ruthless. Apparently Mossad was not ruthless enough for Zeev.

"But being a jumper is not as lucrative as one would expect," Farouk said. "One would think that putting your life in danger for your country again and again while eliminating its enemies would pay better than it does. Instead, they rely on love of country and fear of outsiders. It is the Israeli way, don't you agree?"

Russell didn't take the bait. "So he's your bodyguard?"

"That term makes him sound so brutish and dull. I prefer to think of him as my security coordinator."

"I assume you had to provide significant compensation to employ a man of his talents."

"Oh, yes. But it is worth the price to know that one is secure, is it not? What good is money if you must always look behind you and wonder who might stick a knife in your back?"

Russell shifted in his seat. He had dealt with antiquities dealers before, but never one like this. This seemed dangerous in addition to being illegal, and it was probably both.

"But enough of this talk. You are here to see the scroll, not discuss my business practices." Farouk stood up and motioned towards an oval conference table in front of a glass door to the balcony. The tall buildings and lights of downtown Raleigh were visible through the sheer curtain.

The table was empty except for one black Solander box, just the right size to contain a scroll. The case looked old, but appeared to be in good condition. Farouk had obviously been doing this for years. How many ancient documents had he peddled to millionaires who only cared about owning a piece of antiquity? How many priceless discoveries were ruined forever due to mishandling by amateurs?

He pushed his irritation down. Confronting Farouk about his practices would only make the man mad and would hinder negotiation. And it wasn't difficult to imagine Zeev actually assaulting him if Farouk felt truly insulted. The man exuded the arrogance of a petty dictator despite his friendly facade.

Farouk slid the box in front of Russell and released the latches. "I assure you that I have taken the utmost care with this document. There will be no incidents such as with the Dead Sea Scrolls."

Russell nodded. Farouk may be a smuggler, but he apparently understood how to preserve documents. Early handling of the Dead Sea Scrolls resulted in adhesive tape attaching fragments together and of some of the scrolls being trapped between window glass. Both practices had caused severe deterioration.

Farouk lifted the lid of the box and Russell leaned forward. The scroll inside was wrapped in tissue paper. Farouk pulled a small case from his jacket and took out a set of forceps. He pulled back the tissue paper before opening up the top flap of the scroll for Russell to examine.

It looked like it was made of vellum, and it was in excellent shape from what he could tell. There was some damage, but it looked remarkably well-preserved. The ink was distinctly visible, and there was minimal wear on the vellum itself.

Russell took out his phone and held it over the scroll. It was snatched from his hand almost before he realized it. He turned to see Zeev standing there, phone in hand.

"No pictures," he said.

"I'm sure the professor did not need his phone taken from him," Farouk said. "He is a reasonable man. All you needed to do was ask."

The expression on Zeev's face showed no regret.

"It would help if I could get a few pictures to provide some verification."

"I'm afraid I can't allow that, professor."

Russell frowned. "Can I use the forceps to open up a little more of the scroll?"

"Examine what you can see for now. If necessary, I will reveal more. I am sure you will be able to tell what the scroll contains from the preview I am offering."

Zeev handed the phone back and Russell slid it into his jacket pocket, annoyed but unwilling to pursue it further. Consigned, he pulled out his magnifying glass and bent over the table, careful not to lean too close to the scroll.

He was surprised to see that the writing was Aramaic. Some of the Dead Sea Scrolls were written in Aramaic, but most were in Hebrew. The Nag Hammadi codices were exclusively written in Coptic. It was rare to find documents in Aramaic, although not completely unheard of.

As he perused the scroll, he saw the phrase 'Son of Man' almost immediately. He also noted the word 'Sophia' repeated several times.

"Can I see more?"

Farouk unraveled the scroll carefully and Russell continued his examination. He saw the first two phrases again, and also saw something else that piqued his interest. If the hint of what he saw was a good indicator of the rest of the scroll, then Lakaj might have been right after all, although not exactly in the way that he had assumed.

He stopped the thought, unwilling to speculate before he was certain of anything. More study—much more study—was necessary.

"How do I know this isn't a fake? It will need to be dated and further examined before any offer can be made."

Farouk looked as if his feelings had been hurt. "Professor, my livelihood depends upon my reputation. If I were known as one who passed off forgeries, I would not long survive in this business. I assure you it is genuine."

"While I might personally believe you, I don't think my sponsor would be willing to pay without some assurance ahead of time. If I can take a small sample for testing, it will go a long way towards establishing authenticity."

Farouk reached behind him and pulled out a folder.

"I have taken the liberty of having it tested. As you can

see, it dates somewhere between 2200 and 1800 years ago. The inks and vellum support those dates, as I'm sure you'll agree." He handed the folder to Russell.

He skimmed through and noted—if the information was accurate—that Farouk's estimate was probably correct. That would place these scrolls about a hundred years before the Nag Hammadi codices. Even without considering their specific content, this was a groundbreaking find. If he was correct about what they contained, however, it would perhaps be the greatest archaeological find of all time.

He quelled his enthusiasm. There was no need for Farouk to know exactly how valuable this discovery might prove to be. While Farouk might be an expert in buying and selling antiquities, he was most certainly not an expert in Aramaic, which was a good thing since he would undoubtedly raise his asking price significantly.

Russell looked up from the scroll. "You're aware that a public university does not have overflowing coffers, I hope?"

"Please let us not play games, professor. I would not have had you invited here if you could only offer me funds from your university. We both know these scrolls are far beyond the meager means of public education."

Russell frowned. He had hoped Farouk wouldn't realize that he wasn't representing the university. His real sponsor could afford to pay more. And while it wasn't his own money, he wanted the leverage that came with a good price, a possible assurance that he could lead the translation effort.

"I can see that you recognize the value of these

artifacts. Can I assume you are interested in making an offer?"

Russell lowered his brow and stroked his chin, doing his best to make it look as if he was pondering the question. He wasn't sure he was entirely convincing.

"I need to talk to my sponsor and ask his opinion first. Is there somewhere I can call him in private?"

"Of course. Please step into the bedroom and close the door. Come out whenever you are ready."

Russell looked wary.

"I promise we will not listen in on your conversation, professor. You have my word."

Russell nodded and walked into the bedroom, closing the door behind him. He pulled his phone out and called the number, pacing the large bedroom while the phone rang. It picked up on the fourth.

"It's me," Russell said.

"Have you seen the scroll?"

"I just looked it over." He paused. "It might be the one you're looking for."

"Are you certain?"

"I need more time to examine it."

"How old is it?"

"Farouk had it dated. Unless the report is falsified—and I don't think it is—it dates back to 1800 years ago at the earliest. Based on the writing, I'd place it closer to about 2000."

There was a pause on the line.

"Are you still there?"

"So you think this scroll—"

"Was written during Jesus' lifetime. And it's in

Aramaic, which means it could very well be an original."

The voice on the line had a sudden urgent quality. *"Make an offer."*

"There's something else you need to know. I think it might be a Gnostic text."

"What? How could that be?"

"I identified certain phrases that would be much more likely in a Gnostic text."

"That's impossible!"

"I agree it's unlikely—I certainly didn't expect it—but it's not imposs—"

Russell was distracted by movement outside the window. He parted the curtain and saw a figure standing on the balcony. He didn't think it was Farouk or Zeev.

"Dr Kellar?"

"I'll have to call you back." He ended the call and stepped out of the room.

Farouk was sitting at the conference table with his back to the sliding glass door. Zeev stood next to him. Neither seemed aware of the figure on the balcony.

"Is everything all right professor? You look agitated."

Russell moved closer and kept his voice low. He could see a faint silhouette of the figure through the sheer curtains. "There's someone on the balcony."

Zeev had a gun in his hand instantly, although Russell hadn't seen him actually pull one out, and he positioned himself between the balcony and the conference table. Farouk backed away from the table and Russell did the same, his anxiety increasing exponentially.

"How did someone get out there?" Farouk asked.

Zeev's voice was tentative, as if he was processing

potential answers as he spoke. "I do not know. From the roof, perhaps. That would be the easiest way."

Farouk looked annoyed, the first time Russell had seen him lose his composure. "Go out there and take care of this!"

Zeev didn't move, content to observe for the moment.

"What are you waiting for?" Farouk said, his face contorted, furious that he wasn't being obeyed.

"He is only watching us."

"I want him gone from my balcony!"

"He is no government agent," Zeev said, more to himself, "or he would not have come alone."

"Get that man off my balcony!"

"He would have shot us by now if that was his intent. What does he want?" Zeev seemed to be musing to himself, curious more than reporting observations.

Farouk fumed, incredulous that Zeev merely stood there. But he stopped barking orders, perhaps realizing he could not force Zeev to do what he wanted.

Russell felt the hairs on the back of his neck rise. He could see the outline of the man on the balcony through the curtains, and he was as perplexed as Zeev about why he just stood there. The Solander box was still open, the scroll still visible.

Zeev moved slowly towards the sliding glass door. His gun was at his side, but Russell had little doubt that he could raise it and fire off the entire clip in seconds. He opened the curtains with his free hand and looked both ways, leaning in to reduce the glare. He finally turned back.

"There is no one out there."

"What do you mean there is no one out there? I saw

him myself!" Farouk said.

Zeev opened the sliding door and crouched down before looking up at the outside of the building. He scanned the area for long seconds before standing up and stepping out onto the balcony. He walked slowly from one end to the other, looking down on all sides, crouching down to check the floor and rechecking the roof.

He finally reentered the room and shut the sliding glass door behind him.

"No one is there."

"We all saw him!" Farouk said.

"Whoever was there is now gone. We should leave as well."

Farouk hesitated for a moment, indecision crossing his face. "I will not be chased from my room! This is what I pay you for!"

"You pay me for my expertise, and it is that which advises us to leave."

"I am not leaving this suite. You will simply have to be more watchful."

The tension was palpable, and Russell wanted more than anything to leave, but he could not will his legs to move. He was certain he had seen someone on the balcony, but he couldn't explain where he might have gone. He tried to convince himself that he had imagined the figure, that the shadows had played tricks on his eyes, but Farouk and Zeev had seen him, too. What was the likelihood that all three of them were mistaken?

"Mr Farouk, maybe we can continue this another day."

Farouk turned toward him, his face feral. "No. We will not be chased away by ghosts. And if it is not a ghost, then

Zeev will make it so."

Russell's eyes widened, and he feared what would happen if the shape on the balcony reappeared. He wasn't sure whether he was more afraid of the intruder or Farouk.

Zeev frowned, the only emotion Russell had seen on his face so far, and approached the door to the balcony again. He hadn't quite reached it when the glass door imploded, sending shards ripping through the room.

Russell put his hands up over his face and stepped back instinctively. The back of his legs collided with an end table and he fell, landing hard on his back and hitting his head on the floor. Farouk tried to scramble away and got his legs tangled in a chair, falling hard to his side.

Russell heard gunshots and lifted his head to see Zeev firing his gun, although the conference table blocked his view of the target. Zeev fired more than a dozen shots in rapid succession before pausing, a look of confusion on his face.

Russell pulled himself into a crouch with a nearby chair, both terrified and curious to see how badly mangled the intruder was after being hit with over a dozen rounds. He reached into his pocket and grabbed his phone, ready to call an ambulance.

As he saw the figure standing only ten feet from Zeev, he froze, unable to process what he was seeing. The boy looked no older than twelve or thirteen, small and thin with smooth, flawless features. His expression was blank and emotionless, and there was no sign of any injury on his body, which would have been impossible to hide since the boy wore no clothing whatsoever.

Even more shocking, however, was the complete lack of

any genitalia.

For a split-second, Russell wondered if it might be a girl, but he rejected that idea; the body shape seemed equivocally male with the obvious exception of the missing components. His brain fumbled for something to say, but before he could open his mouth Zeev fired off a dozen more shots at point blank range.

Terrified that Zeev was shooting an unarmed child, Russell took a step towards him, intent on trying to take his gun away, even though he knew he was no match for the man. He stopped suddenly when he saw that the boy still stood, staring placidly at Zeev. There was no indication that any of the bullets had struck him.

Russell glanced left and saw Farouk also watching with wide eyes, frozen with a mixture of fear and astonishment on his face.

"What the hell are you?" Zeev said, a look of disgust on his face. The boy stepped forward and pushed a chair up to the table as if he was a dinner guest replacing an item to its proper place.

Zeev put his gun into a holster under his jacket, and his hand came back out with a long knife that might be good for gutting grizzly bears. He got into a sideways stance and slowly approached the boy, who did nothing but stare.

Zeev's swing was almost too fast to follow, but Russell could have sworn that he saw the blade of the knife go right through the boy's neck. But instead of a fountain of arterial spray, there wasn't a mark on him, and he followed up Zeev's attack by striking him so hard with the back of his hand that the man flew across the room in the opposite direction. He landed against the far wall of the suite and fell with a resounding crash.

The boy turned to Farouk, and the dealer quickly positioned the large conference table between them. With one hand the boy grabbed the underside of the table and heaved the entire thing out of the way as easily as Russell would have tossed a newspaper aside.

The chairs went flying. Russell raised his hands to protect himself but was hit in the head and fell backward. He put a hand to his forehead and it came back wet with blood. As he groaned and rolled to the side he saw the Solander box—still closed—right next to him.

A frantic cry brought his attention back to Farouk. The dealer fumbled in his jacket and pulled out a gun, but before he could fire the boy grabbed his hand. Farouk threw his head back and screamed, attempting to yank his entire body away, but even his howls were not enough to drown out the sound of the bones in his hand snapping like brittle twigs.

The boy let go and the gun fell to the carpet. Farouk stumbled back against a wall and slumped to the ground, his face a contorted mask of agony.

Russell's intestines seized up when the boy turned and took a step towards him. He inched backwards, panic threatening to overwhelm him. He heard a grunt from behind and turned to see Zeev launch himself through the air.

The boy looked up in time to see Zeev flying towards him. But instead of falling back, he caught the large man by the throat, impossibly halting his momentum, and threw him to the floor. He held him down with one hand around his neck while Zeev struggled to break free.

Russell stared at the boy—who could not have weighed more than 100 pounds—choking the large man to death with only one hand and could barely contain his horror. As he scrambled to his feet, desperate to get away, his foot kicked the Solander box and he had a split-second of lucidity. He bent down and grabbed it before dashing towards the door, only turning back when Farouk screamed out, "Stop! Help us!"

The sound of Zeev's neck snapping made him nauseous, and Russell froze when the boy stood up from the body. He was able to move only when the boy turned to Farouk and advanced. He heard the dealer screaming as he ran out the door and into the hallway.

He rushed to the elevator and pressed the button repeatedly, terrified the boy would emerge from the suite at any second. When the doors didn't open, he glanced back and noticed the stairwell just across the hall.

He abandoned the elevator and flew through the stairwell door, the Solander box still tucked under his arm. He raced down the stairs, taking them three or four at once and lost his footing several times, only to be saved by desperate grabs at the railing.

Three floors down he stopped and looked behind him. The stairwell was empty and silent except for the reverberations of his own breathing echoing off the concrete walls. Trying to calm his rapid heartbeat, he looked up and listened for any indication that someone was following.

The tell-tale creak of a metal door opening several floors above sent his heart racing again. He stepped back and felt his foot slip down the first stair. He grabbed for the rail but he was off-balance and tumbled down the stairs to the next landing, hitting his shoulder hard on the cement floor. Terror fueling him, he ignored the pain and scrambled to the door. He yanked it open, the sound of the door handle hitting the concrete wall echoing in the enclosed space. He ran out onto the sixth floor of the hotel.

With a few long strides he made it to the elevator, and frantically pushed the down button while watching behind him. The elevator arrived just as the boy stepped out of the stairwell, his face expressionless and eyes vacant. Russell opened his mouth to say something—plead, maybe?, he wasn't sure—but he suddenly fell backwards when the doors opened, bumping into something before landing on the floor of the elevator.

"Watch it, asshole!"

A teenage girl stood half in and half out of the elevator, blocking the doors. She was wearing a skimpy bikini and had a phone in her hand and a bag over her shoulder. He must have fallen into her when the doors opened.

Russell got up quickly and pressed the button to the lobby. "Get in the elevator!" he said, realizing that in his panicked state he probably sounded like a lunatic, but knowing he had to do something to get her away from the boy.

"Fuck you, pervert!" She moved out of the door's path and turned, her face changing quickly from surprise to utter disgust. She backed away but the boy was faster. He reached out with an arm that seemed abnormally long and grabbed her by the throat.

Russell's back was against the wall of the elevator as the doors closed. His last glimpse was the girl's wide eyes and gaping mouth as the boy crushed her windpipe. The elevator lurched down and Russell bent over and threw up.

The elevator car stopped on the ground floor, but before the doors could open something hit the roof with a crash, the sound deafening in the small space. Russell crouched and looked up at the ceiling. The sound of wrenching metal was followed by sparks showering down as a hand with long, pointed fingers ripped through the top of the elevator and began peeling back the metal. The blank face of the boy peered down at him from the newly created hole.

Russell bolted into the lobby and ran full speed towards the front doors, bumping into several people and knocking down a woman bending over her suitcase.

As he made it through the first set of doors leading to the street a few screams erupted behind him. He didn't pause or look back as he rushed to the lot where his car was parked.

He fumbled with his keys and nearly dropped them, but was finally able to get the door open. He got into the car and slunk down in his seat as far as he could, trying to slow his breathing. He waited long minutes for something to happen, afraid that if he drove away the boy would see him. He fought down the desperate urge to peek out the window or look in the rearview mirror.

He set the Solander box on the passenger seat and reached in his pocket for his phone. He hit the speed dial and waited. It picked up after the fifth ring and went to voice mail.

"Dammit!" He inched up and looked back through the rear window. He didn't see anyone, but that did nothing to lessen his fear.

"... *after the beep.*"

"Cerise, it's me. I've found something important. Really important. It's a scroll and I think it was . . . I'm not sure, but it's maybe the most important text I've ever seen. I'll call you back when I can get to a safe place."

He hung up and put the phone back into his pocket before starting the car. He put it in reverse and then changed his mind, moving it back into park.

He reached over and opened the Solander box, carefully peeling back the tissue paper to reveal the text. He took his phone out again, switched it to camera and took a picture. He sent the file to his email address and also to Cerise's. She didn't know Aramaic as well as he did and it would be hard to read on a phone screen, but at least she'd have some evidence of the scroll.

He put the phone back in his pocket and shifted into reverse. He turned his head and froze when he saw a beautiful, terrible face looking in at him from outside the driver's side window, not more than a foot away.

Chapter Two

Cerise Davenport didn't notice she had a message on her phone until she was halfway to Chapel Hill. She'd woken up an hour later than usual due to a power outage in the middle of the night that reset her alarm, and she'd thrown all her school materials in her briefcase before getting out the door as quickly as possible. She would probably still be about a half hour late for her New Testament intro class, but there wasn't a lot she could do about it.

She saw the voicemail from Russell after she left a message with Janine, the department secretary, to get a TA to cover her class until she could get there, but she didn't listen right away. She had planned to get up early and prep for her lecture before she left, but since that didn't happen she wanted to mentally prepare on the drive in. It wouldn't be her most dazzling work, but after four semesters of teaching the class she'd be able to wing it pretty convincingly.

She made it to class in better time than she expected, although she was still nearly fifteen minutes late. Most of the students were still there, busily chatting or hammering away on their laptops. There was no TA there, and she wondered what might have happened. Janine was usually reliable, and Cerise wondered if the voicemail might not have been recorded for some reason.

She put the thought aside and jumped into her lecture after apologizing for being late. She was able to nearly finish Revelation, which only put her a little bit behind schedule. She'd be able to touch on common misunderstandings of the New Testament before doing a review for the upcoming final exam.

When class was over she headed to her office. Several students were waiting for her, some with panicked expressions on their faces. She dispelled one student's fear about failing the class because she got a C on a recent paper, helped two students better understand the symbolism in Revelation, and met with a graduate student doing his thesis on Paul's conversion. Two hours later she shut the door to her office and pulled out her phone.

She was confused about why Russell would send her a picture of an ancient text without any explanation. She called up her email on her computer to see a larger version of it.

It was written in Aramaic, although she couldn't really read it, and the texture and yellowing in the picture made it look like a piece of an old codex or scroll. She sat back in her chair and continued to stare at the screen while she listened to her voicemail, hoping there was an explanation.

She frowned. Russell sounded panicked and scared, and his comment about getting to 'a safe place' worried her. Was he in danger? She checked her phone for any other messages or missed calls, but there weren't any from Russell.

She popped out of her office and headed down the hall

to Janine's desk. Cerise paused when she turned the corner and saw two police officers talking to her. She wasn't sure if she should interrupt, but Janine waved her over.

"Dr Davenport, these officers are looking for Dr Kellar. Have you seen him?"

Cerise felt a wave of fear wash over her. "You're looking for Dr Kellar? Is he in some sort of trouble?"

One of the officers, a tall, thin man with a crewcut said, "We would just like to ask him some questions. Do you know where he might be?"

Cerise shook her head. "I haven't seen him since yesterday, here in the department." She wasn't sure why, but she decided not to mention that he had called her.

"If you do hear from him, could you please call us?" He handed her a card and she took it tentatively.

"Can I ask why you're looking for him?"

"Just some questions, that's all." His face didn't give away any information.

Cerise nodded, and Janine pointed the officers toward the department chair. "Dr Burgoyne's office is right over there," she said.

Cerise watched them go before turning back to Janine. "Do you know what that was about?"

"You haven't seen the news?"

Cerise felt a sinking sensation in her stomach. "Not yet."

Janine called up something on her computer and turned the monitor. A news story was running about a mass murder at the Renaissance Hotel in downtown Raleigh. Three people were killed and there was significant property destruction. The police were not releasing the names of the victims, but they did release a video of a man being chased through the lobby. The first man looked like it could have been Russell, but the image of the pursuer was so blurry that all she could make out was a vaguely human shape.

A desk clerk had verified that a man named Dr Russell Kellar was seen at the hotel, and a still photo from a security camera was shown on the screen, along with a notice that anyone with information about his whereabouts should call the police immediately.

"Russell," she whispered. She felt like someone had just punched her in the stomach.

Janine's brow creased. "I'm so sorry, Dr Davenport. I'm sure Dr Kellar is okay. He'll turn up."

Cerise backed away from her desk, her hands shaking. "Excuse me." She turned and walked back to her office, grabbing her phone out of her pocket as she went.

She shut the door behind her and leaned back against it, her eyes tearing up. She hit the speed dial for Russell's phone and put it up to her ear. She hung up after ten rings.

She sat down at her desk and listened to his voicemail again, desperate for something she might have missed the first time.

"I'll call you back when I get to a safe place."

Except he hadn't called back, and that meant he wasn't in a safe place.

She returned the call, hanging up again when she got voicemail. She went back to her computer and called up the scroll fragment, but after fifteen minutes of poring over it she couldn't find anything that might be a message or note from Russell.

She scoured the Internet for updates about the murders

at the hotel. Two victims were identified as an Egyptian and an Israeli national, although no other information about them was released. A teenage girl had also been found dead in the hallway on the sixth floor near the elevators. It was unknown whether there was a connection between the three murders.

No details about the cause of any of the deaths were being released, other than they were currently being investigated as homicides. Nothing was known about the identity or whereabouts of the second man running through the lobby.

She turned off her monitor, put her head in her hands and quietly sobbed.

Cerise stared down at her cup as the waitress refilled her coffee. Richard Burgoyne sat across from her, worry creasing his forehead.

"I don't think we should jump to any conclusions right now, Cerise. Just because we haven't heard from him yet doesn't mean anything bad has happened."

Cerise looked up from her coffee. "What was he doing at that hotel, Richard? He didn't tell me anything about this."

Richard glanced down at his own coffee before looking up. "So he didn't say anything to you?"

Cerise narrowed her eyes and stared at him for a few seconds before speaking. "What did he tell you?"

He took a sip of his coffee and pursed his lips. "Nothing really."

Cerise leaned forward. "Richard, if you know something . . ."

He sighed. "I was contacted by a Jesuit priest a few weeks ago who told me about a scroll that was smuggled out of Israel. It supposedly ended up in the hands of an Egyptian antiquities dealer named Farouk. I referred him to Russell."

Cerise was confused. "Why is that such a big secret?"

"It's not a big secret. I just think that Russell maybe didn't want you to worry."

"Why would I worry?"

"I looked up Farouk and he has been accused of smuggling artifacts out of the Middle East for years. I told Russell he should be careful, that's all."

"You think Farouk was the Egyptian national killed at the hotel?"

Richard didn't respond.

"So you knew he was some sort of international criminal and you sent Russell to him anyway?"

Richard raised his eyebrows. "That's not a fair characterization, Cerise."

"I'd be inclined to agree with you if Russell wasn't missing."

"I'm sure he's going to turn up. If he was hurt . . . I think something would've turned up by now."

She felt her eyes watering, but she wasn't sure if she was more upset that Russell was missing or more pissed off that he hadn't told her any of this.

"How do you know that, Richard? Just how the hell can you be so sure that whoever killed those people in the hotel didn't get Russell, too? Someone chased him out of that hotel, and now he's missing. He could be dead somewhere, and we wouldn't even know!"

He reached his hand across the table and took hold of hers. "I'm sorry, Cerise. I promise I'll do whatever I can to help."

She couldn't stop the tears from flowing. Richard came over to her side of the table and put his arm around her, and she buried her head in his shoulder.

Chapter Three

Cerise sped up her pace when she rounded the curve in the road and saw her driveway. She had run a few miles further than usual to put the stress and anxiety out of her mind, and she could feel the strain on her feet.

The extra miles had helped distract her, and she hoped she'd be tired enough to go to bed without obsessing about Russell's disappearance. She was afraid she wouldn't be able to sleep at all, and there was still no word about where he might be.

She ran past the huge oak tree near her mailbox and up the long, curving driveway, her house still not visible among the trees, and thought again how much she loved the seclusion in Cedar Grove. Not only were most of the houses nestled in the woods, but they were set far enough apart that you couldn't hear your neighbor yelling even if you were standing on your front porch.

She slowed down when she saw her car and finally stopped in the front yard, taking some time to stretch out her calves and thighs. The extra miles had tired her out, but now that her feet weren't pounding the pavement she found her thoughts drifting back to Russell and the murders.

Once inside she hung up her running jacket, her keys

and can of pepper spray clanking together as it swung on the hook. It was just after 8 pm and she wanted to take another look at the picture Russell had sent her before going to bed. She didn't usually translate original documents—the work was tedious and labor-intensive—but she hoped that working on it might tire her out, or at least provide a distraction.

She changed into her pajamas and opened her laptop. She called up her email, found the picture, and sent it to her printer. With a cup of tea in one hand and an Aramaic reference book in the other, she sat down at her desk to study the picture.

Two and a half hours later she straightened in her chair and stretched her arms out over her head, unable to stifle a yawn. It was a quarter to eleven and she had made decent progress, all things considered. Her Aramaic wasn't even good enough to be called rusty, but she felt like she had a tentative understanding of some words and phrases.

She easily recognized the words 'synagogue' and 'god'. It made sense that this was some sort of religious document, which was what she had expected. She was more excited, however, about deciphering what she thought was the word 'Sepphoris', which appeared twice in the fragment.

Sepphoris had been a major city in the Galilee region of Palestine. It was significant in ancient times because it was a major city with multiple synagogues, Roman baths, and theaters, and because it was only four miles from Nazareth. Some scholars thought it likely that Jesus might have learned his carpentry trade there, as well as how to read and possibly write.

It was a logical assumption. There wasn't much work or training to be had in Nazareth, a one-horse town if there ever was one. And Jesus would have learned much more about the tenets of Judaism in Sepphoris than he would have in Nazareth. The knowledge of the Torah he displayed in the Gospels was much deeper than a cursory understanding would have provided, and a cursory understanding would be all he would have received in Nazareth.

The strangest thing about the scroll, however, was the style in which it was written. A scroll like this was probably from anywhere between 300 BCE and 300 CE. Those dates would have to be checked, of course, but she felt fairly certain of them based on the writing. During that time period, most religious scrolls were primarily written as either 'sayings' or 'biographies'. Sayings encompassed common knowledge of the time, like the 'Sermon on the Mount' in the Gospel of Matthew. Biographies were usually written by someone who wasn't alive at the same time as the subject, and were based on earlier records and oral traditions that may or may not be accurate.

Cerise noted the first person pronoun as the subject in at least six places in the text, which meant the scroll was probably written in first person, an extremely unusual style for a religious text of this time period. Since the structure didn't seem to lend itself to sayings, she guessed it was probably an autobiography.

The author was unknown, or at least could not be identified from this one small piece. Even if the author named himself in another part of the text, there was no guarantee that he was who he claimed to be. It would not be unexpected for a writer in that era to adopt the persona of a significant personality of the time and write from that perspective. She was curious to find out the alleged identity of the author, but she'd need a lot more time with this text to figure that out, and it might not even be possible with the fragment she had.

She rubbed her eyes and got up from the desk. She didn't feel any better about Russell, but at least she felt tired enough to go to bed. She didn't have to get up until seven, which meant she could still get a decent night's sleep. She headed into the bathroom to get ready for bed.

While she was brushing her teeth she thought she heard a noise. She stopped and turned her head to listen but didn't hear anything. She spat into the sink and was rinsing it down when she heard the knock. She turned the water off and heard it again, a gentle, soft rapping.

She peered into the hallway at the closed door, wondering who would be knocking so late on a weekday. She grabbed the pepper spray from her jacket pocket and leaned close to the door.

"Who's there?"

The only answer was three quiet knocks.

She stood on tiptoes and looked out the window at the top of the door. She wished she had a peephole, but had never even thought about it until now. She didn't see anyone, but the window was high enough that someone could be crouching right up against the door and remain unseen.

"Whoever you are, I'm going to call the police."

She was most certainly *not* going to open the door, however. Her cell phone was on the coffee table in front of the couch. She took a few steps towards it, but then stopped when she heard another three knocks, followed by a quiet voice.

"Please help me."

Cerise turned around, eyes narrowed. It sounded like a kid. She went back to the door.

"Who is this?" she asked, before adding, "Are you all right?"

"I'm lost. Can you please help me?"

Cerise was sure it was a kid's voice, probably a little girl's. She didn't think it was possible for a man to imitate that voice so well. And if she was wrong, she still had a fistful of pepper spray, and she wouldn't be shy about giving whoever it was a full blast.

She cracked the door and peeked out, half-expecting someone to force it open. Instead, she saw a girl of about five or six wearing a pink t-shirt and jeans, shivering and looking pathetic. She had long brown hair and a smattering of freckles across her nose.

Cerise searched for anyone who might be hiding just out of sight before putting the pepper spray back in her pocket and opening the door all the way. She looked down at the girl, frowning. She probably lived nearby, but Cerise didn't recognize her. Cedar Grove only had a population of a few thousand, but that didn't mean she knew everyone, especially since she mostly kept to herself.

"Hi there," Cerise said. "You need some help?"

The girl nodded, her eyes wet with tears.

"You wanna come inside and get warm?"

She nodded, and Cerise stepped aside, motioning for her to come in. She shut the door and pulled a hooded sweatshirt off the hook, draping it around the girl's shoulders.

She crouched down. "What's your name, sweetie?"

"Amanda," she said through chattering teeth.

"Hi, Amanda. I'm Cerise. Do you wanna sit down?"

The girl nodded, and Cerise led her to the couch and sat down next to her.

"How'd you get here?" she said.

"I walked." The girl sniffed, and her eyes were red.

"Did someone drop you off somewhere and leave you?"

She shook her head.

"Did you walk here from your house?"

Another shake.

"Where did you come from?"

She shrugged.

Cerise crossed her arms and cocked her head to the side. "You don't know where you came from?"

She shook her head.

"Do you know your address?"

Another shake.

"How about your phone number? Or maybe your mom or dad's cell phone number?"

Nothing.

Cerise lowered her eyebrows, wondering how even a kid this young didn't know her own phone number.

"Did you walk a long way to get here?"

She nodded.

"How long did you walk?"

A shrug.

Cerise frowned. "Okay. Was it light out when you

started walking?"

She shook her head.

It had been dark for about four hours, but Cerise doubted that a little girl could have been walking on the road all that time without being noticed by someone. Then she realized she might not have been on the road.

"Were you camping in the woods with anyone?"

"No. My dad says camping is just people drinking beer in the woods, so we don't go."

Cerise put her hand over her mouth and stifled a grin.

"Were you walking on the road or in the woods?"

"On your driveway."

"Right, but what about before that? Were you walking on the road or did you get to the driveway from the woods?"

She shrugged.

Cerise was beginning to get annoyed. Why didn't this girl know anything? Or maybe she knew but wouldn't tell for some reason. Cerise glanced over at the door. It was locked, but she wondered if there was someone on the other side. Could this girl be part of a setup to rob her? It seemed ridiculous, but she couldn't totally rule it out.

Still, the best time to break in would have been when the door was open, and nothing had happened then. But why would anyone want to rob her house anyway? It wasn't like she had anything. It would be a lot of trouble and planning to break into a place with nothing of value.

"Are you thirsty?"

Amanda nodded, and Cerise got her a glass of orange juice and a plate of crackers and cheese. The girl drank half the glass in one sip and then eagerly went after the crackers.

"Can you tell me your parents' names?"

"They're not around."

"Okay, but could you tell me their names anyway? You want to find them, right?"

She didn't respond, but her eyes suddenly looked sad.

"Are your parents okay?"

"They're lost."

Cerise almost asked, "Where are they?" but stopped, realizing what a stupid question that was. She bit her lip, unsure of how to proceed. She'd already asked everything that would have been helpful, and wasn't sure what else the girl should be expected to know.

"Are you sure you don't know a phone number? Maybe we could call an aunt or uncle or family friend. Do you know anyone who might be able to help find your mom and dad?"

"I need to stay with you."

Cerise was taken aback. "With me? Why?"

"You need my help."

She sat back, uncertain what to say. The expression on the girl's face was one of complete certainty. It seemed as if their roles had reversed, and the girl was there to help her instead of the other way around.

"What do I need help with, Amanda?" She said it tentatively, almost afraid to hear the answer.

The girl stared back, eyes unblinking. "They're coming soon."

"Your parents?"

She shook her head.

"Who's coming?"

"Bad people."

There was a seriousness on the girl's face that hadn't been there before, and Cerise felt goose bumps rise on her arms.

"What bad people?"

Amanda shrugged.

"Why do you think bad people are coming here? Are your parents in some kind of trouble?"

"They want to hurt you."

Cerise felt chills wrack her body. There was something terrifying about hearing this from a little girl. Maybe it was the brutal honesty, the unwillingness to mince words. There was no doubt the girl was telling her the truth as she saw it, but what would make this little girl think that 'bad people' were coming? Was she a runaway who had been abused? She didn't think kids this young were usually runaways, but she wasn't an expert on the subject.

She looked at her more closely, searching for any evidence of bruises or other injuries. She didn't see any, but they might be hidden under her clothes.

"Did somebody hurt you?"

She shook her head.

"You can tell me if they did. I promise I'll help."

Another shake.

She was about to open her mouth again, but Amanda spoke up first.

"I know how to get to my house."

Cerise's eyes went wide. "You know the way to your house?"

"Uh huh."

She couldn't understand how this could be true. The

girl didn't seem to know anything; how could she know how to get to her house from here? She didn't think kids this young even had a concept of geographical directions.

"Do you live in Cedar Grove?"

A shrug.

"But you think you can tell me how to get to your house?"

She nodded.

Cerise sighed, contemplating what to do. She didn't believe that Amanda really knew the way, but what did it hurt to try? There was a chance that she really did know, but if she didn't Cerise could drive her to the sheriff's office and leave her there. That was probably an easier alternative to calling the police and trying to explain the situation over the phone.

"All right, Amanda. Why don't we get in my car and you can tell me where to go."

The girl smiled and got up from the table, leading Cerise to the front door. She stopped at Cerise's desk and grabbed the printout of the text she had been translating.

"What's this?"

"Just something I'm working on."

Amanda scanned the Aramaic text with a frown.

"What's this weird writing?"

Cerise tried to take it from her, but the girl moved it out of her reach. Trying to keep the annoyance from her voice, she said, "It's a very old language called Aramaic. Nobody has spoken it for a really long time. Now can I have that back, please?"

Amanda examined it again before handing it back slowly, almost teasingly. Cerise shoved it in her pocket, unwilling to put it back on the desk within reach of the girl.

Cerise grabbed her phone and her running jacket from the hook and opened the front door, and the two headed down the steps toward Cerise's car. Amanda hopped in the back and put on her seat belt, almost like it was her own car. Cerise slid into the front and put the keys in the ignition.

Before she could turn the key, Amanda said, "Don't turn it on yet."

Cerise turned around and looked at her, her eyes narrowed. "Why not?"

"They'll see us."

"Who'll see us?"

Amanda pointed out the back window towards the road. The porch light cast shadows across the yard and down the driveway, where they got deeper and darker until finally melding completely with the night. Cerise squinted but didn't see anything but trees lining the driveway. She started to turn to Amanda before catching movement from further down the driveway.

Three figures moved out of the shadows, almost seeming to emerge from the darkness itself. She couldn't make out any features, but they all looked the same size and build, and they moved eerily in tandem.

Cerise locked the doors, reached into her pocket and pulled out her cell phone.

"Don't move," Amanda said from the backseat.

"What?"

"If you move too much, they'll see us." Her eyes were wide, and Cerise could practically feel the terror emanating from her.

She whispered, "Who are they?"

"The bad people."

"What do they want?"

Amanda's stare was unblinking. "You."

"This is crazy," Cerise said, and yet she wasn't able to raise her voice higher than a whisper. "I'm calling the—"

"The police can't help."

Cerise had her phone in her hand but didn't press any buttons. It was ridiculous to be taking orders from a six year old who thought the boogey men were coming, but she couldn't deny that there was something terrible about these three figures, something unnatural.

"Amanda, you need to tell me what's going on right now," she whispered. "Is this some kind of joke?"

The girl stared out the window at the three figures advancing upon the house. They were very slight in build, and Cerise didn't think any of them were taller than she was. She thought they might be young teenage boys. When they were close enough for the porch light to illuminate them somewhat, Cerise was horrified to see that they were completely naked.

They passed the car without a glance, although Cerise didn't know if they hadn't seen her and Amanda or were just ignoring them. One walked up the front porch and another went towards the far side of the house. The third one passed right in front of her car, and Cerise recoiled when she noticed the smooth flesh where penis and scrotum should have been. He continued past the car and headed for the backyard, Cerise unable to prevent her face from contorting in disgust.

She wondered for a minute if the figure was a girl, but

she quickly rejected it. He was not built like a girl in any way, and she wondered if the other two also lacked genitals.

They must be members of a weird cult, maybe something that involved self-mutilation. She had heard of Islamic healers who slit their heads open during ritualistic frenzy, and there were other examples of self-mutilation in various cultures, although they didn't usually involve complete amputation of a major organ like the penis. But she knew that cult members could be compelled to do strange things like group suicide, so cutting off genitalia wasn't completely out of the question.

If they were cult members, however, she couldn't come up with any reason why they might be at her house. All her articles had been published in scholarly journals, and they were esoteric stuff for the most part. The only people who might find them controversial—or even understandable—were other religious scholars, a decidedly small audience.

Was it possible that Amanda's parents were in a cult? That would provide a reason for why they were there—and maybe even for why Amanda didn't know any basic information like her address—but that still didn't explain why they were interested in Cerise.

She felt like she was jumping to too many conclusions. She would have no evidence they were interested in her at all if Amanda hadn't told her. Was she really making decisions based on what a delusional six year old was telling her?

She should call the police, duck down low in the car, and wait. Or maybe she should drive away and then call the police. The 'cultists', or whatever they were, might get away, but she and Amanda would be safe. At least they didn't have any guns on them—one clear disadvantage to running around naked.

"We should go," Amanda said.

"We will. I'm just going to call the police first."

"They're gonna find us."

She could only see one of them; the other two were out of sight on opposite sides of her house. The one in front was standing on the porch, facing the door. He was completely still, almost frozen there.

Cerise pressed 911 on her phone, but hesitated to hit send. Something about the girl's warning resonated even though she tried to dismiss it. She kept the phone in her hand, ready to press send. She knew it was stupid, but she couldn't help her curiosity. There was something weird going on, and she wanted to know what it was.

As they watched, the one on the porch ripped the screen door off its hinges and tossed it aside before ramming his hand into the steel door. It flew open and slammed against the inside wall with a loud bang, splinters flying from the wooden frame.

Cerise gasped loudly. She had thrown the deadbolt in addition to locking the door, and he had ripped it open like it was made of cardboard. She put her hand over her mouth almost instantly, too aware of the volume of the gasp in the closed car.

There was no way he could have heard her all the way to the porch, but he turned anyway, locking eyes with her. Her blood froze, and she reached for the ignition as he leaped off the porch and dashed towards the car.

Almost simultaneously, the front bay window

exploded outward in a shower of glass and wood. The other two boys landed on the porch and launched themselves forward, right behind the first.

Amanda's scream startled Cerise into action, and she slammed the accelerator down, forgetting that the car was still in park. The engine roared but the car didn't move. She cursed in frustration and terror, her eyes wide as the three raced towards them.

She shifted into reverse just as they reached the car. She pushed the accelerator to the floor again, and the car lurched backwards, jerking her body up against the steering wheel. Dirt and rocks sprayed the underside, sending a chorus of grating clanks mixing with the breathless, high-pitched screaming of the girl in the backseat.

Cerise yanked the steering wheel to the right, attempting to evade them, but they were too close. One grabbed the hood, fingers sinking into metal as if it was made of wax. His muscles tensed and the car staggered to a halt, the engine still gunning and the wheels spinning madly on the dirt driveway.

The second one reached the driver's side door. He leaned his face close to the window and lifted the handle. The door was locked, but he continued pulling with increasing violence until it broke off in his hand.

Cerise leaned away as much as she could while still holding on to the steering wheel and pressing down the accelerator. The wheels continued to spin, sending more dirt spraying into the undercarriage, but the car refused to move.

Amanda's screams increased in intensity. Out of the

corner of her eye, Cerise saw the third one at the rear passenger door tugging on the door handle, his face pressed up against the glass. For a brief second, she was struck by how beautiful and flawless his features were. Despite the violence of the attack, his expression was calm, as if he wasn't experiencing any emotions at all.

Her attention was pulled back by the sound and spray of breaking glass. A hand grabbed her jacket sleeve and pulled her to the left. Her foot fell off the accelerator and the engine's roar died. Another hand grabbed the front of her jacket and began pulling her out of the window.

She flailed with her arms and jerked her body away instinctively, her terror hitting a fevered pitch. The fabric of her jacket tore in his hands, and she fell back towards the center console. He grabbed at her again, but she was able to get her foot on the brake and put the car into drive before shoving the accelerator down as far as it could go.

The car sprang forward, her assailant's head slamming into the door frame and then slipping out the window. Cerise looked up in time to see the one at the hood fall under the front of the car. She was jostled in her seat as one of the tires ran over him.

She tried to get to a full sitting position, which was difficult with the movement of the car on the uneven ground. She heard glass breaking behind her and Amanda's screams intensified. She risked a quick look in the back seat and saw the third one halfway through the rear passenger window, reaching for Amanda.

She swerved the car hard to the right and he was partially thrown out, but one hand held tight to the top of the door frame. She drove off the grass and onto the long, tree-lined driveway, turning the wheel with rapid jerks to dislodge him. He held fast to the door, however, and was able to step up on the window frame, completely ignoring the broken glass under his bare foot.

The road was close, and Cerise was afraid he would be able to climb all the way in once the car was on a smooth surface. The thought of what he might do if he got in the car fueled her desperation, and as the car reached the end of the driveway, she suddenly swung the wheel hard to the right.

The car lurched off the driveway, and she swerved to the left at the last moment, sideswiping the old oak at the base of the driveway. There was a thunderous crash, and Cerise was thrown to the passenger side as the car slammed to a halt against the tree.

She scrambled up and glanced in the back seat. He was pinned against the tree but was still trying to claw his way in through the window. She slid back into the driver's seat and hit the accelerator. The car screeched in protest as metal scraped against the hard bark of the tree, the wheels cutting into the dirt of the driveway as she gunned the engine. Finally it pulled free and she swerved out onto the road, the car speeding up quickly now that it was on asphalt.

The road was near to being pitch black, and there were no other cars in sight. Amanda's screaming had been reduced to dull whimpering, and Cerise risked a glance back. The boy was gone from the window, and she felt her entire body ease down in relief.

"Are you okay?"

The girl didn't answer, but Cerise didn't really expect her to. She felt like she was on the verge of hysterics herself;

she couldn't imagine how horrible it had been for a six year old girl. But it was over, and the sheriff's office wasn't too far away. She pulled her phone out and checked to see if it was still set to call 911.

"It's going to be okay. We just need to get to—"

There was a loud thump on the roof that shook the entire car, and Cerise cried out, turning the wheel hard and veering into the left lane. Amanda began screaming again, and Cerise tried to put the noise aside as she straightened the car out.

The car shuddered again, a sharper sound that came from right above her. Cerise cried out again, but she was able to keep the car in the lane. She looked up at the ceiling and saw the plastic liner bending in, as if the point of a dull knife was pressing down from above. It was followed by the sound of rending metal, and she felt her stomach drop.

She sped up and turned the wheel right and left quickly, hoping that whatever was on the roof—she was too terrified to admit even to herself what she thought it was—wouldn't be able to hold on.

The sound came again, louder this time, and a pale hand with long, pointed fingers suddenly burst through the plastic headliner, sending pieces of it down onto the front seat.

He peered down at her through the newly-created hole in the roof, his face as calm as it had been before. The wind was blowing his hair wildly, but other than that he didn't look as if the speed of the car was affecting him. He reached down and grabbed a jagged metal edge and pulled it up with ease, the screech of metal echoing inside the car.

He squatted down, putting his face into the hole, before

reaching in with one thin arm and grabbing for her. She screamed and pressed herself against the door, her head nearly out of the broken window, the cold wind blasting her in the face. He reached in further, his arm elongating, and grabbed a handful of her hair, yanking her up.

She screamed in pain as she was pulled out of her seat, fighting the instinct to grab at her hair by keeping her hands glued to the steering wheel. He continued pulling, the pain on her scalp intense, and the car slowed down as her foot was lifted from the pedal.

Knowing she wouldn't be able to hold on much longer, she let go of the wheel. The car ran onto the shoulder while she fumbled in her jacket pocket. Her head was pulled to the hole and brought within inches of his face.

Her fingers brushed the metal cylinder in her pocket. She grabbed hold and brought it up to the hole, pressing the nozzle down and spraying him point-blank in the face with the pepper spray.

He released her hair, both hands flying up to his face as he fell backwards, bouncing off the roof of the car and landing hard on the gravel shoulder while the car rolled on.

Cerise grabbed the steering wheel and floored the gas, gravel spraying behind her as she drove back onto the road. As she pushed the car to go faster she glanced in the rearview mirror. He was standing in the road, watching her drive away.

Chapter Four

Cerise pulled into the parking lot of an old family restaurant that had been closed down for years. The building was dilapidated, the parking lot deserted, and there was nothing else around. She drove the car between the building and the woods beyond so it wouldn't be seen from the road.

She killed the headlights and turned around. Amanda stared back at her from the darkness of the backseat.

"Are you okay?"

The girl nodded slowly.

"Did you get hurt at all?"

She shook her head.

Cerise paused, unsure what to say. She wanted to grill her for every bit of information she had—she was sure that Amanda was holding things back—but she was dealing with a little girl who had just gone through a terrifying ordeal and didn't want to push her over the edge.

"Do you want to get in the front seat with me?"

Amanda nodded and Cerise got out of the car, broken pieces of glass falling from her lap to the cracked asphalt. She opened Amanda's door and led her around to the passenger side before getting back into the car.

"I want to ask you some questions, would that be

okay?"

Amanda stared back but didn't indicate an answer.

"If you don't want to answer, you don't have to. But I think it would help if you did. Do you understand?"

She nodded.

Cerise decided she'd skirt the questions that couldn't be answered, like how the hell did one of them punch through the roof, or how did the other one sink his hands into the hood and stop her car from moving? She wasn't even sure she really wanted to know; the answers might include the possibility that she was losing her mind.

She decided to focus on things that were firmly in the realm of the real world, like why they didn't have any clothes on, or why they might be after her.

"Have you seen those boys before?"

"Sort of, I think."

Was this the kind of answer you got from a six year old? She had so little experience dealing with kids that she didn't know how they processed information. She only knew it was a different perspective than adults or even teenagers.

"Do you mean you've seen them but you don't know who they are?"

"I think I saw them somewhere. I don't know who they are."

"Do you remember where you saw them?"

Amanda scrunched up her face, what Cerise thought was an elaborate outward sign of mental processing.

After a minute or so, she said, "It was kind of a dark place. They were under me."

What the hell?

"Were you . . . high up on a building or something?"

"No, I was just floating."

"Floating? Were you in an airplane or . . . a balloon?" It seemed like a stupid question, but how else could the girl be floating?

"No. I was just floating."

"In a dark place?"

"Uh huh."

Floating in a dark place?

"Were you in a boat or in the ocean?"

"No, I was just floating. Kind of in the sky but not really."

Cerise felt her jaw clenching in frustration.

"Can we go to this place?"

Amanda scrunched her face again and stared so intensely at Cerise that she felt like she was looking through her. Finally, she said, "I don't think so, but you can go there with me."

"You can't take me, but I can go there with you?"

"Uh huh."

Cerise sighed. The girl was making no sense.

"Is it close? Or do we have to drive there?"

"I don't think you can bring cars there. I didn't see any."

"Can we fly there?"

She shook her head. "I don't think so."

Cerise sighed. "So how would we get there?"

Amanda shrugged. "You just have to want to go, that's all. I think you'll be able to go pretty soon, but you're not ready yet."

"Why not?"

Amanda stared at her again. "I don't know. But you're not ready. Maybe soon. Then we can go there together and you can see those bad boys and their boss."

"They have a boss?"

She nodded. "He's mean."

"Did he make those bad boys come here?" She finally felt like she was getting somewhere.

"Yeah. He wants to stop people from knowing stuff."

"What stuff?"

"Just knowing stuff, that's all."

"You can't tell me about this stuff?"

"There's really no stuff." Amanda folded her arms. "It's just knowing, that's all."

Cerise bit her tongue, fighting the urge to have an argument with a six year old.

"Is the boss in the dark place?"

"Yeah, but he's hard to see. He's sort of everywhere, I think. He's real mad. And he's got a funny name. Wanna hear it?"

Cerise nodded.

"His name is I Hold The Bath. Isn't that a weird name?" Amanda cracked a smile for the first time.

"Yeah, that is a weird name. Does he have a last name?"

"He's got lots of names, but I don't know them all."

"Do you know any of them?"

She thought for a minute before answering. "Sometimes they call him Yes We and sometimes they call him A Done Eye. Those are weird, too, but mostly they call him I Hold The Bath. I think he likes that one the best."

Cerise wondered if her original thought that this was

some sort of cult was near the mark. Cults did bizarre things—like run around with no clothes on—and were usually dominated by a charismatic leader who took on some otherworldly mantle of authority. They could become fixated on a perceived enemy and pursue that enemy relentlessly, sometimes figuratively and sometimes literally. There were definitely some cult characteristics here, but she didn't yet know enough to say for sure.

If this was a cult, it seemed entirely possible that Amanda might be involved with them, probably through her parents. That would explain a lot of things. Amanda's lack of knowledge might be the result of brainwashing, for instance. And all the nonsense about the 'dark place' might be more metaphorical than literal, although the girl herself wouldn't realize that. Maybe they even locked her in a dark room from time to time as an indoctrinating technique. It wouldn't be the most unusual child abuse she'd ever heard about.

But how could she ask Amanda about any of this? The girl would have no concept of a cult, especially if it was all she'd ever known. She might think of them as a large extended family, and any teachings of the cult would be so ingrained that she wouldn't be able to separate them from reality.

She decided that no good information would come from asking, and she might even provoke a bad response by inadvertently challenging some deep-seated belief. She knew too little about this girl to tell how she would react.

She needed to go to the police and tell them what had happened—with selective details left out so they didn't lock her up for being a lunatic. It would be enough to say that

Amanda showed up at her house and then three teenagers attacked. She'd omit the details about digging fingers into her hood and punching through her car roof. She'd just tell them that she and the girl had driven away when the boys broke into her house. It was dark enough that they'd believe she couldn't describe them.

She could leave Amanda with the police and go to Russell's house. She felt an ache when she remembered he wouldn't be there, but at least she would be safe. Those boys could still be at her house, and she wouldn't feel safe there anyway. Even if they had left, they might come back, and Cerise didn't know if the police would stay there for protection.

Would the police be able to stop them if they came back? Her car must have been going close to fifty when the one she pepper-sprayed fell off, and he had popped up immediately. Even though she'd only seen him in the rearview mirror, she was almost positive he wasn't hurt after falling onto the road. Any normal person would have been severely injured or maybe even killed, but he looked completely unharmed.

"I think we need to go to the police and see if they can help you."

Amanda's eyes got bigger. "I want to stay with you."

"The police will help you find your parents. I don't even know where to look. And they can keep you safe."

Amanda shook her head. "They don't want me. They want you."

Cerise narrowed her eyes and leaned in. "How do you know that?"

"They don't want you to know any more stuff. They're

afraid of you."

"Why would they be afraid of me?"

"Because you can hurt them."

Cerise didn't know how to respond. The girl knew so much more than she was telling, but Cerise wasn't getting anywhere with her questions.

"I think the police will help us sort this out."

Amanda shook her head. "I don't want to go to the police."

"Well, I'm sorry, but we need help and that's what the police are for. I need you to get in the back again."

Cerise got out of the car and stepped over to the passenger side. She expected the girl to refuse, but she willingly got out of the front and into the back.

After a quick search on her phone, Cerise found the nearest sheriff's office in Hillsborough, which was only about twenty minutes away. She considered calling, but thought it would be easier to explain in person. There was no emergency at the moment, and the drive there would give her time to get her story together so she didn't sound like a crazy person. She put the car into drive, pulled out of the parking lot, and headed out on the highway. In about a half hour this problem would be in the hands of the police, and then she could drive to Russell's house in Chapel Hill and worry about what had happened to him.

Chapter Five

After driving through the sleepy town of Hillsborough, Cerise pulled into the small dirt parking lot across from the Orange County Sheriff's Office. She shut the car off and turned around. Amanda wasn't happy about being there, but there weren't any alternatives.

"Are you ready?"

The girl stared back without responding.

"Everything is going to be fine. The police will be nice, and they're going to help you find your parents."

"They're lost."

"The police are good at helping people, Amanda, especially kids who can't find their parents." She added, "Are you sure you don't have any aunts or uncles or maybe family friends around? It would help the police out a lot."

"This is a bad idea." The look on her face was dead serious, something Cerise wouldn't have expected from a six year old.

"I know you're scared, but I promise it's going to be okay. The police help kids who are lost all the time."

Amanda looked as though she wanted to say something, but was hesitant. Finally she said, "I'm not lost."

"What do you mean you're not lost?"

"I mean I'm not lost. I was looking for you and I found

you."

Cerise narrowed her eyes. "That's not what you told me before."

Amanda looked down. "I didn't tell the truth."

Cerise glanced back at the police station. This new information didn't change anything. The girl might not think she was lost, but she was separated from her parents. That was enough. Cerise still had to turn her over to the police, especially since she had no one else to call. At this point she would have involved the police even if Amanda suddenly revealed she had an aunt who lived down the road. Things were just too weird to drop her off with someone and let it go at that. At the very least there was the possibility of some cult being involved. For all she knew, the police might have some information about this group, or maybe Amanda had been reported missing.

"I appreciate you telling me, but we still have to go talk to the police."

"I need to stay with you."

"I can't take care of you, Amanda. I have other responsibilities. And your parents are probably very worried about you."

"I don't need to stay with you for me, I need to stay with you for you."

"For me? Why?"

"I already told you. I can help you with the bad boys."

Cerise was feeling her patience strained.

"The police will be able to help. Now we need to go see them."

"They won't be able to help. They can't stop them."

"Amanda, those boys aren't coming to get you. They

probably went back to wherever they came from. They don't even know where we are."

"They're not people."

Cerise frowned. "I don't know what grownups might have told you, but monsters aren't real. They looked scary, but that's all. They're just regular people."

Cerise didn't believe it herself, but she didn't want to consider the unnatural elements of the attack yet. She'd analyze it when she wasn't scared and exhausted, when she could look at the events objectively. There'd be some sort of explanation.

"I know they're not monsters."

"Then what do you think they are?"

Amanda hesitated. She looked like she was deciding whether or not to trust Cerise. "You won't believe me."

Probably not, she thought.

"I can't promise I'll believe you, but I do promise that I'll listen."

Amanda's stare bored into Cerise, her face a portrait of indecision, then she looked over at the sheriff's office across the street. That seemed to make up her mind.

"They're angels."

"Angels? You mean like from Heaven?"

Cerise's doubts about a cult being involved were cut in half. She stifled her knee-jerk reaction to anything that had to do with God. It was often counterproductive and sometimes even disastrous to tell people you were an atheist, but she was usually good at keeping her mouth shut about it.

"They're not from Heaven," Amanda said. "They're from a bad place."

"You mean Hell?"

"I'm not allowed to say that word, but they're not from there. It's a dark place, and there's a lot of them floating around. And I Hold The Bath is there, too."

"Don't angels have wings?"

Strictly speaking, Cerise knew that was one of the silliest visualizations of angels, but it was the way virtually everyone imagined them.

"No, they don't have wings. But they're really scary."

Cerise had never heard angels described like that, but if Amanda thought those boys were angels, then she was right that they were scary. It was curious that she envisioned them without wings, since the traditional view was so pervasive that one could hardly turn on the TV or open a magazine without seeing some reference to winged angels.

"Why do you think they're angels? I thought angels were supposed to be good?"

"I think there are good angels. They're up above the dark place. They look like stars. But these angels aren't good angels."

"Even if they really are angels, we're safe from them here. They won't be able to find us."

"Yes they will. They know where you are. I think they're already coming."

Cerise pursed her lips. "Then I guess it's good that we're at the police station. They'll protect us."

"The police can't hurt them. They'll come here and do bad things just like at your house."

Cerise got a chill thinking about what had happened, but she wasn't ready to contemplate it yet.

"Amanda, I know you're scared, but nothing is going to happen to you here. We're going into that police station to talk to some policemen, and everything is going to be fine."

Amanda sighed and sank down into her seat.

Cerise got out of the car and opened the rear door. She expected Amanda to refuse or at least argue, but the girl got out of the car without a word or gesture of defiance and took Cerise's outstretched hand. They walked across the street towards the sheriff's office, the streetlamps making large pools of light in the inky darkness.

A few deputies were on duty, and Cerise and Amanda were directed to chairs around one of half a dozen desks. When she sat down, she immediately realized there was a problem she hadn't considered: she hadn't warned Amanda that she would not be telling the entire truth.

She glanced down at the girl in the chair next to her, suddenly afraid of what she might say. The deputy was certain to ask Amanda questions, and if she contradicted the story that Cerise told him, there was going to be a problem. She had no idea what that might be—he wouldn't believe anything ridiculous—but it would probably mean he would continue to ask questions, and Cerise had no idea where it might go from there.

The deputy who had directed them to the desk was walking over, so there was no time to prep her now. She had to decide if she was going to tell the story the way she originally planned or . . . what? What were the other options? She couldn't tell the real story. Maybe she and Amanda could just leave and go to another sheriff's office, figuring out a story that made sense on the way. She quickly abandoned that idea as the deputy sat down at the desk and smiled. It would look incredibly suspicious if they left now, maybe enough that he would even keep her from leaving.

"I'm Deputy Ayers, Miss . . . ?"

"Davenport. Cerise Davenport. I'm a professor at Chapel Hill."

He jotted a few notes down. "And this is your daughter?"

Cerise watched Amanda out of the corner of her eye, but the girl sat perfectly still and quiet.

"No, she's not my daughter. That's why I'm here."

He raised his eyebrows slightly and leaned back in his chair, his pen poised over his notepad.

"Amanda," she gestured towards the girl, "showed up at my door tonight asking for help. She told me she was lost, but she couldn't give me any information about her parents."

Deputy Ayers shifted his gaze to Amanda. "Is that right, Amanda?"

She nodded, her eyes wide.

The deputy shifted back to Cerise. "So you brought her in?"

Cerise took a breath. "Yes, but there's more. Three teenage boys showed up at my house—I live in Cedar Grove—and broke in. Luckily we were in the car at the time, so we were able to get away."

He nodded, his face looking more serious. "Are either of you hurt?"

They both shook their heads. "No," Cerise said. "They didn't see us until we were driving away."

"Do you know these boys? Have you ever seen them

before?"

"No, never."

"What about you, Amanda?"

Cerise felt her anxiety level rise. She avoided looking at Amanda, afraid that it would seem like she had coached her. But she dreaded hearing the word 'angel' come out of her mouth. That would torpedo the entire story.

Amanda shook her head, and Cerise mentally breathed a sigh of relief.

The deputy continued asking questions, and Cerise answered as fully as possible without revealing any elements that would make the story seem ridiculous. Each time she broached on something unexplainable, she held her breath, expecting Amanda to say, "A naked angel punched through the roof of the car," or "A naked angel stopped the car from moving." But the girl verified that what Cerise said was true, and the deputy didn't show any signs that he didn't believe the story as it was being told to him, although he was flustered that neither could offer any details about what the attackers were wearing or what they looked like.

"It was too dark to see anything, and we were both really scared," Cerise explained.

The interview took about an hour, and after it was done the deputy left them alone so Cerise could say goodbye.

"The police will help you find your parents, okay?"

Amanda looked back at her blankly.

"Do you understand, Amanda?"

"Yeah."

"You're going to be all right, and you can call me if you need to. The deputy has my phone number."

Amanda nodded half-heartedly. Cerise wasn't sure what she expected—maybe an emotional, teary farewell?—but a resigned stare was not it. The strange response did not, however, ease the guilt she felt at leaving the girl with the deputy. But there was nothing else that she could do. The police would take care of her, and it wasn't like she could take Amanda home with her even if she wanted to. If she had been abandoned by her parents—a distinct possibility—then she'd most likely have to go through the foster care system. It wasn't ideal, but it was the way things were.

Cerise stood up and gave the girl a tentative hug. She didn't hug her back. She considered saying something else but realized it would do nothing to change Amanda's mood. She smiled before heading towards where Deputy Ayers was watching.

"Are you going to be able to find her parents?"

He raised his eyebrows and shrugged. "It's tough to say. Maybe. But if we don't, we'll put her some place where she'll be taken care of."

"You mean foster care."

"If we can't find a relative who'll take her."

Cerise bit her lip. "Will she . . . be okay?"

"I'd say so. It won't be easy, but she'll manage. Kids are a lot more resilient than people think."

"I guess. It's just kind of upsetting to leave her here like this."

He nodded. "You'd have to be a sociopath to think otherwise, Dr Davenport. Of course it's upsetting. Most people's response to seeing kids in bad circumstances is to protect them. Perfectly natural. But you did the right thing bringing her here. I promise."

Cerise smiled. "Thanks. I appreciate it."

She turned and walked out of the sheriff's office, fighting the instinct to look back until she passed through the doors and into the early morning darkness.

Chapter Six

As Cerise approached her car she was horrified to see how mangled the roof and hood looked. She had seen them earlier, but she hadn't really processed the extent of the damage. The roof was peeled back like something had been ejected through it, and the hood had deep gouges where fingers had dug into the metal. It looked surreal, and she had no explanation for how they had done damage like this.

If she drove on a major highway, any cop she passed would stop her, and she had no idea what she would say. She could easily imagine being taken in for questioning, and the last thing in the world she needed right now was to be put into a cell for the night.

She got into the car and drove through the main strip of town until there were no houses or buildings in sight. She pulled off to the side of the road and got a crowbar from the trunk, then stepped up onto the bottom of the door frame, reached over, and pounded the metal strips down. After about ten minutes, they were flush with the rest of the roof. Anyone would be able to see the damage if they looked closely, but it could be missed in the dark as she was flying down the freeway. Or at least she hoped.

Satisfied that the roof wasn't quite as noticeable as

before, she got back into the car and drove off.

Cerise pulled into Russell's driveway around 3 am. His car was missing, and she felt a wave of despair. She had been able to put his disappearance in the back of her mind while she dealt with the more pressing problems of a lost little girl and attacks by lunatic cultists. Seeing his house brought it back to the forefront.

She turned off the engine, got out of the car, and walked up to the porch. She quickly located the key on her key chain and opened the door. There was a light switch on the wall to the left, but it turned the ceiling fixture on and she didn't want the room suddenly filled with light. Instead, she found a table lamp and clicked it on, creating a soft yellow halo that lit up the sitting area but left the edges of the room in darkness.

The room was exactly the same as when she had been there a few nights ago, with the exception of the missing occupant. The coffee table was half-covered with papers and books as usual, and she sat down on the couch and started looking through them. Aside from notes and articles about Gnosticism, she saw nothing of immediate value.

She jumped when she heard the knocks and reached into her pocket for her pepper spray. She crept over to the door, ready to pull out the canister in an instant.

Russell's front door didn't have a peephole, but the porch was visible from the bay window in the front. She considered sticking her head right up against it to look out, but she didn't want anyone on the porch to see her.

Three sharp knocks sounded again.

"Who's there?"

"Police, ma'am. Could you please open the door?"

She froze, suddenly feeling guilty.

"I'll show you my badge," he called through the door. "I'll put it in the window."

A hand held up a badge and she scanned it for a few seconds before throwing the deadbolt and opening the door.

He wore jeans and a sweatshirt, and looked like he hadn't shaved for a few days. He still had the badge in his hand, and he stuck it on his jean's pocket after she opened the door.

"Is there something wrong?"

"I don't think so. We've been looking for the owner of the house—Russell Kellar—for a couple days, and I noticed you enter. Do you live here?"

"No, Dr Kellar and I are friends, officer . . . ?"

"Detective. Dave Piedmont. And you are?"

"Cerise Davenport. Dr Kellar and I are co-workers at Chapel Hill."

He nodded. "I see that you have a key. Is it usual for you to come over so late?"

"No, but I hoped he might be here. How did you know I was here?"

"I'm doing surveillance duty on the house in case Dr Kellar turns up. I saw you drive past. Is he here?"

"No. I've been waiting for him to contact me, but I . . . I don't know where he is." She felt perilously on the verge of tears. "I guess it's stupid of me to think he'd be at his house, isn't it?"

"It's not stupid. We've been hoping he'd show up, too. We want to help him in case he's in danger. I suppose you've heard about what happened downtown?"

Cerise nodded. "Those murders. Do you know anything about who did it?"

He looked past her into the house. "A little. Could I come in for a few minutes so we can talk about it?"

She knew he was probably fishing for something that would let him search the place, but she didn't care at the moment. It might even turn up something helpful.

She opened the door wider and stepped aside. He walked in, casting wide glances throughout the room and sticking his head down the hallway and into the kitchen before settling down in a chair near the couch. He was situated so he could see anyone coming from the kitchen or hallway. She resumed her position on the couch.

"So do you know who killed those people?" She asked.

"We're still working on it. We have a few leads, but the suspect is still out there. That's why we're looking for Dr Kellar. We want to make sure he's okay. Do you know where he is?"

"No."

"Has he contacted you since last night?"

She pulled her phone out, called up the message and handed it to Piedmont. He put the phone to his ear and listened before giving it back to her, then he took out a small notepad and jotted something down.

"Do you know anything about this scroll that he mentioned?"

Cerise wavered for a minute, and she was sure it made her look guilty, but she didn't want to reveal the document to the police yet. She was afraid he would take her phone as evidence. Was it a crime to lie to the police? She wasn't sure.

"No idea. He sees a lot of ancient documents so it could be anything related to early Christianity." That was mostly true.

Piedmont squinted slightly. "Do you work in the same department?"

"Yes, I'm a professor of religious studies as well, but we have different areas of expertise."

"Dr Kellar's is in . . . " he flipped through his notes, "something called Gnosticism, is that right?"

"Yes."

"What is that exactly?"

"That's not an easy question to answer. It's a bit complicated."

He smiled. "It's 3 am and I'm on a stakeout. I don't have a lot of better things to do right now."

She smiled back. "I'll tell you what. I'll explain Gnosticism if you tell me what you know so far about those murders."

"Fair enough." He looked toward the kitchen. "Got any coffee?"

Ten minutes later they were sitting at the kitchen table, steam wafting out of white mugs.

"Are you a Christian, detective?"

"Call me Dave. And yeah, but I don't go to church very often."

"The best way to understand Gnosticism is to compare it to modern-day Christianity. There are lots of different denominations, but they're incredibly similar for the most part, far more similar than sects were in the first few centuries after Jesus was crucified. For the sake of a starting point, can you sum up the basic gist of Christianity as you understand it?"

"Hmm, I guess so. Jesus is the Son of God, and He sacrificed himself for our sins."

"So how do you get to Heaven?"

"Well, I think you have to be a good person—no murdering and all that—and you have to believe in Jesus and that he died for us."

"So anyone can get to Heaven?"

"I suppose so, as long as they believe and don't do evil things."

Cerise nodded. "The Gnostics had a different belief about how people get to Heaven. First of all, only a select few people could actually get there—those who were . . . special. These special people could get to Heaven by having certain knowledge revealed to them. The Greek word for knowledge is gnosis."

"I take it that's where Gnostic comes from?"

"Yes." She took a sip of coffee.

"So what made them special?"

"Let me see if I can condense this a bit." Her brow furrowed. "I guess I should start closer to the beginning.

"The Gnostics believed that the true God was an unknowable entity that lived in the spiritual realm. He had a daughter named Sophia—Greek for wisdom—and she tried to understand her father.

"Her failure to do so caused her pain, anguish, and other negative emotions. These emotions became personified as powerful entities, one of which was called Ialdabaoth. The Hebrews referred to him as Yahweh."

He leaned forward. "You mean God?"

"The God of the Old Testament, yes, but not the true God for the Gnostics. They thought that the anger, jealousy, and evil actions of the Old Testament God—Yahweh—was attributable to his formation from negative emotions."

"Did they think He created people like in Genesis?"

"Yes. According to the Gnostics, he is responsible for all the deeds in the Old Testament, including the creation of the universe and humanity. And of course all the really bad stuff, like plagues and the flood and so on. They thought he was a flawed being because of his negative origin. He made humans out of the matter of the universe, but because he was flawed, we are flawed as well. In fact, the material universe itself is a flawed creation, according to the Gnostics."

"But what about the Gnostics? Didn't He create them, too? They're people."

"Not exactly. The Gnostics thought that their bodies were just containers for Sophia's positive emotional leftovers. Yahweh made the material bodies, but not the spiritual essence. But being suddenly attached to a material body was so alien to them that they became confused and didn't know who they really were."

Piedmont nodded. "So the knowledge—the Gnosis—they learned was of who they really were?"

"Exactly. When they learned their true nature through gaining Gnosis, they would transcend their material forms once they died and ascend to the spiritual realm to be with the true God."

"What about Jesus? I don't see how He fits in here."

"Jesus was sort of a positive version of Ialdabaoth, also spawned from Sophia's positive emotions. He came to

Earth to spread Gnosis to those who could understand it."

"But only Gnostics could understand it, right?"

"Right. Only they could ascend. Everyone else was basically screwed."

"They went to Hell?"

"No, the Gnostics didn't believe in Hell. They thought that anyone who wasn't a Gnostic was like an animal—no spirit. When they died, they were just . . . dead."

"So if you were in the club, you got to meet God. But you couldn't just join the club, you had to be born into it."

"Basically. It was a way of legitimizing themselves as exclusive spiritual elites."

"What about Jesus' crucifixion and resurrection? If He was really just a leftover bunch of emotions—"

"Well, leftover from a goddess, so they wouldn't have considered it so trivially."

"Okay, but why wasn't He confused about who He was like the other positive leftovers?"

She smiled. "Because he had gained Gnosis!"

He frowned. "Wait a minute. So if somebody gains Gnosis, then they automatically get resurrected like Jesus? Is that what you mean?"

"Exactly! Gnostics thought Jesus was quite literally a model to emulate. Once they gained Gnosis they would be equal to Jesus!"

He sat back in his chair, frowning and stroking his beard.

"Jesus was important to the Gnostics not because he was the Son of God, but because he represented what they could achieve. A Gnostic would in theory be equal to Jesus in every way once he gained Gnosis.

"They viewed his material body as artificial. The real Jesus—the Christ part of him—was all spirit, and when they crucified him all they did was release the spirit. Hence, the resurrection. The body was just a container.

"Obviously I'm simplifying a lot of stuff here. There were many sects and variants of Gnosticism that differed on this point and that point, but those are the basic tenets that I think most Gnostics would agree on. Keep in mind this isn't my area of expertise."

Piedmont sat back in his chair and folded his arms. "I never heard about any of that in Sunday School."

Cerise smiled. "Of course not. Orthodox Christians of the time stamped them out of existence."

"And you're not an expert in this stuff?"

Cerise laughed. "Hardly. But Dr Kellar and I have had plenty of discussions about it. He's probably the world's foremost Gnostic expert, so the info tends to trickle down. Plus, I'm interested in different aspects of Christianity." She paused. "Now, how about your end of the deal?"

"Okay. What do you want to know in particular?"

"Do you know who killed those people?"

He looked away for a minute. "It's kind of strange."

"Nothing could surprise me after tonight."

He eyed her curiously before continuing. "We have video of Dr Kellar being chased out of the hotel, but the image of the pursuer is blurry."

"I saw that on the news yesterday."

"Eyewitnesses who saw the man swear that he was not wearing clothes."

Cerise paled.

"Are you all right?"

"I'm fine. I was just . . . surprised." It couldn't be a coincidence; there had to be a connection. She wanted to analyze it, but she couldn't suppress her chills. She took a gulp of coffee to warm up and mask her reaction.

"But there's more weird stuff. When we canvassed the scene, we determined that Dr Kellar was chased from the elevator. When we checked out the elevator itself, the roof had been ripped open, like someone had gotten in there with the jaws of life or something."

It was all she could do to sit still. "Do you have any theories about how that happened?"

"None that make any sense. We didn't find any equipment or tools that could do that kind of damage, and there's no evidence on the video of the suspect having anything on him—like I said, lots of witnesses thought he was naked. There was no explosive residue or burn marks, so it couldn't have been an explosion either."

It was the same ones who attacked her; nothing else made sense. But what was the connection? Why would two college professors be attacked by cultists with—she hated to admit it—some sort of supernatural strength? There was no other explanation at the moment for ripping through metal with bare hands.

She wanted to tell Piedmont what had happened to her, how one of the cultists had ripped her car roof open. Even though he had seen evidence he couldn't explain, it wasn't the same as actually watching it happen, and she knew he wouldn't believe her.

"What about the victims?" she asked.

"Two were connected. One was an Egyptian businessman and the other was an Israeli national who apparently worked for him. Both of their necks were broken. There was a third victim—a nineteen year old girl—who was found dead near an elevator, also with a broken neck. We don't think there's any connection between her and the other two victims. It's possible that she just got in the way of the killer."

"Do you have any idea why these people were killed?"

"The Egyptian was rumored to be a smuggler, so it could be a deal gone bad or something like that, I guess."

"You don't sound convinced."

"Yeah, I guess I'm not. The way they were killed, with their necks broken, is weird. Why not just shoot them? Or stab them? And the Israeli—he must have been some sort of bodyguard. The guy was all corded muscle. Whoever broke his neck must have been incredibly strong. It's hard enough to break a normal person's neck, but a guy like that?"

"Did he have a gun?"

"Yeah, and shots were fired. A lot of shots. We found casings all over the place, but no sign of blood other than what was on or near the victims."

"He could have missed, right?"

Piedmont shook his head. "No way, not at close range like that. Not someone who was trained, and I'd bet anything that guy was highly trained. Anybody he hit would have been splattered all over the place, especially with the number of shots he got off. But nothing. It's really weird."

"Could the killer have had a bulletproof vest or something?"

"Yeah, that's probably it, but then you'd think that some shots would have hit an arm or neck or something.

Even if all the shots hit the vest, the guy would've been incapacitated."

"The vest wouldn't have stopped them all?"

"It would've stopped them from penetrating, but they still hit with incredible force, enough to break ribs. I've been shot while wearing a vest before. It hurts like hell. A couple dozen shots from a powerful handgun? It's hard to believe anybody could survive that, even with a vest."

Cerise stared down into her half-empty coffee cup. "So do you have any theories?"

He laughed. "None that wouldn't get me committed."

Cerise smiled but couldn't suppress the terror creeping over her. "Do you believe in God, Dave?"

He sat up. "That's kind of a non sequitur, isn't it?"

"I haven't been to church since I was a teenager, and even then I only went because my parents forced me. It all just seemed so . . . made up. No offense."

"None taken. But yeah, I do believe. I don't go to church very often—mostly Christmas and Easter—but I believe in Jesus and all that. I guess you don't?"

"I don't believe in anything that doesn't have the potential to be proven." *Or at least I didn't until last night,* she thought.

"I think that's okay. I hate to sound all churchy, and I know some people would say you'll go to Hell and all that, but I don't think God would send anyone there unless they really deserve it. He'll judge you based on your actions."

"That's not exactly church doctrine for most Christian denominations."

Piedmont shrugged. "Just because the Pope wears a funny hat doesn't mean he knows everything. He's human just like the rest of us."

She smiled and drained the last of her coffee. "Thanks for talking. I appreciate you telling me what you know."

He stood up. "No problem. If you hear from Dr Kellar, give me a call." He reached into his pocket and produced a card. "We want to make sure he's safe, and anything he can tell us about the killer will help."

Cerise took the card and set it in front of her on the table.

"I'll see myself out. Thanks for the coffee."

After he left, she pulled out the paper with the scroll fragment and unfolded it on the table. She studied it for a few minutes before heading to Russell's study. Five minutes later she returned with an armful of reference books and set them down on the table. She knew she wouldn't be able to sleep, so she might as well get some work done.

After an hour of further translation, she sat back in the chair with her brow furrowed. It was definitely written in first person, although she couldn't identify the author yet. She had, however, translated the words for knowledge, Torah, and journey. It was tempting to extrapolate and make some hypotheses, but it would take dozens of hours more work to even begin to understand the basic contents of the scroll. She didn't know if more than this fragment even existed at this point.

She was jarred from thought by shouting from outside. She pocketed the paper and ran to the front window. There were three pale figures on the lawn, completely naked and staring right at her.

She gasped and covered her mouth, the fear hitting her

like a kick in the stomach. They stood only a dozen yards away like perfectly aligned marble statues, looking directly at her as if they knew she would open the curtain and see them at that exact moment. Their pale skin nearly glowed in the darkness as the light from the window fell on them.

Cerise was sure that these were the same ones from before, although she didn't see any sign of injuries. There was no emotion on any of their faces, and like before there was no evidence of any genitalia.

Detective Piedmont was in the street, walking towards them and shouting. He had a gun in his hand, but it was down at his side. He reached the curb and stopped, pointing his gun at them and barking an order. They didn't respond or even acknowledge that he was there.

He took a step closer and shouted again, the look on his face intense. One of them turned to face him. Cerise saw Piedmont recoil slightly, but he stood his ground and yelled something like, "Get down on the ground!"

Instead, the one began walking towards Piedmont with deliberate purpose, not quickly but with no hesitation or fear. The detective shouted again, louder this time, and held his ground, although he looked increasingly nervous.

When he got within twenty feet or so, Piedmont shouted one last time for him to stop before firing. There was no visible effect, not even a slowing of his pace, and the detective fired off five or six more shots before the man reached him.

Cerise was positive that every shot had hit its target, but there was no sign of injury. Piedmont tried to backpedal but the cultist was too close. He reached up and grabbed the detective's hand. Piedmont fell to his knees and screamed, his face contorted in agony. The cultist held his other arm up, his fingers growing longer and thinner, and then he plunged them down into Piedmont's face.

The screaming stopped abruptly, and before she could turn away the cultist's arm jerked back. Something was clutched in his hand, something small and amorphous and wet. He dropped the detective's crushed hand and Piedmont slumped forward. Cerise caught a last glimpse of what was left of his face—a pulpy, unrecognizable mess—before he hit the ground.

The cultist turned back to her and she scrambled away from the window, bile rising up in her throat. Before the curtain closed completely she saw all three advance towards the house.

She ran through the kitchen to the side door. Her car was just outside in the driveway. If she could get there quickly, then maybe she could get away like before.

She grabbed the handle of the side door and almost pulled it open before quickly letting go; one of them was just outside. She moved back and tripped on the three steps going up to the kitchen. A loud crashing sound came from the living room, quickly followed by breaking glass from the other side of the house.

The stairway to the second floor was just around the corner from the kitchen, and she got to her feet and ran there. She flew up the stairs three at a time and headed towards the bedroom at the front of the house. Once in the room she shut and locked the door, realizing how futile a simple door lock would be in keeping them out.

The only window in the room led to the roof and looked out on the huge willow tree in the front yard. She heard more sounds of breaking glass from downstairs and ran to the window. She tried to push it up, but it wouldn't budge. Panicking, she pushed harder, putting her entire body into the effort, but it refused to move. She glanced back at the door, terrified they would break through at any second, before trying the window again. She started to push it up once more, hoping her fear would give her the strength to move it. She paused suddenly, reached up and flipped the lock, and then pushed the sash up easily.

The night air wafted in and she stepped out of the window quickly, scraping her head on the bottom of the sash. The roof was wet and her foot slipped out from under her, but she caught herself on the window frame. She crouched down and moved toward the edge of the roof.

The willow was old, and its branches hung down over the house in long trails that brushed the roof. She stood up slowly, the height making her nervous. A fall to the ground wouldn't kill her—at least it probably wouldn't—but she could easily break a bone or worse. And the broken bone would be the least of her worries if they caught up to her.

She reached for the lowest branch that she thought would hold her weight, its tiny leaves just brushing the tips of her fingers. The sudden sound of wood splintering startled her, and her foot slipped on the edge of the gutter. She fell, her abdomen full with the sickening sensation of gravity exerting its power. Her arms swung wildly, desperate for anything to grab, but all she found was open air.

She hit a branch on the way down and tried to grab at it, but she was too terrified to get a solid grip and instead bounced off and hit the ground on her side with her left hand out, instinctively trying to break her fall. An audible snap accompanied fiery, stabbing pain in her wrist, and she yelled, tears instantly welling up in her eyes.

She gritted her teeth and rolled to her right side, knowing she didn't have the luxury of waiting for the pain to subside before they would get to her. With her good hand she pushed herself up to her knees and got to her feet. Her car was only a few dozen feet away and she ran for it, cradling her injured hand against her torso.

She couldn't remember if she had locked it or not, but she didn't want to stop to get her keys out. She reached the door and tried the handle; it opened smoothly and she slid in, breathing a sigh of relief. Her right hand went to her jacket pocket, and her stomach sank when she realized she didn't have it on. She could envision putting the keys in the right pocket after she opened Russell's door, and then she had hung her jacket on the rack near the front door. She hadn't thought to grab it before she ran towards the back door.

Panic threatening to overwhelm her, she looked over to the front porch. The door was wide open, and she could see the splintered frame where it had been forced. Her jacket was just inside. All she had to do was run inside, grab it and turn around. It would only take five seconds.

She popped the door open and was about to step out when she saw two of them drop down from the roof, almost exactly where she had fallen. Eyes wide, she slammed the door shut and locked it before realizing that she was now trapped.

They approached slowly, and out of the corner of her eye she saw the third one exit the side door and walk towards the front of the car. There was no way she could get out and away from them before they reached her, and she had nothing to fight them off with. The pepper spray that had worked before was still in her jacket, along with her keys.

She reached over to the glove box and began rifling through it for anything she could use as a weapon. All she found was a pack of old gum, a worn and folded map, and the manual to the car. Before she sat back up she saw an old pencil on the floor of the passenger side and grabbed it. It wasn't much but it was better than nothing. It could work as a shiv, but even if she was able to stab one of them—which was probably unlikely—the other two would have her before she could use it again. Or maybe the pencil would just break into useless pieces, and then they'd rip her face off like they did to poor Detective Piedmont.

She looked over her shoulder and saw his bloody remains on the lawn near the street. She turned away before she could fully register his mangled corpse.

They drew closer and spread out, forming a triangle; one on her side, one in front, and one heading towards the back. Cerise flipped down the visor, dug through the coins in the center console, and reached down under her seat, each move sending a stab of pain through her arm, but she found nothing that could help her. As they moved closer her fear spiked and she turned the ignition, willing the car to start.

The engine came to life.

She stared down at the keyless ignition for a second, unable to believe that the car was running, and then adrenaline took over. She shifted into reverse and slammed down the gas pedal. The wheels screeched, and she was pressed into the steering wheel as the tires caught the concrete and the car flew down the driveway.

She heard and felt it strike the cultist behind her, but she only pressed the pedal down further, careening into the street. The two still standing were just beginning to move, probably as surprised as she was that the car had actually started. She turned the steering wheel hard, and the car spun and then roared forward as she shifted into drive and floored the pedal.

She could see the three of them in the rearview mirror, standing in the middle of the road watching her drive away.

Chapter Seven

Cerise pulled into the empty parking lot of an office building complex and turned off the lights. She closed her eyes and put her forehead on the steering wheel while tears dripped down her cheeks.

She had no idea why any of this was happening or why Russell had disappeared. Even worse, she had no idea what to do about any of it. Aside from the police—who would think she was a lunatic—she couldn't think of anyone who could help her.

What did those cultists—if that's what they were—want from her? She wondered if they had caught Russell and maybe he had told them about her. But why would they even care who she was? The scroll fragment *might* be controversial, but she didn't know anything about it until a few hours ago, and what she did know amounted to practically nothing.

It could have been a coincidence—that they had shown up at his house at the same time she had been there—but she didn't think so. Why would they go there in the first place? Russell didn't have anything of value, or at least she didn't think so. The only thing that made sense was they wanted her because of the scroll.

If they did have him, they had probably seen the text

he sent her with the picture of the scroll fragment. It wouldn't have been hard to track down her address from there. And if Russell had told them about their relationship, it would make sense that they would check his house after she got away from them the first time.

But she was skirting the things that terrified her the most, the things that made no sense: they could rip through metal with their bare hands, and they completely lacked any human expression. Amanda's insane notion that they were angels seemed less insane by the moment.

She picked her head up and wiped the tears from her face. She tilted the rearview mirror so she could check out how horrible she looked. She nearly had a heart attack when she saw the face staring at her from the backseat.

"Jesus Christ! How long have you been back there? You scared the living hell out of me!"

Amanda frowned. "I'm sorry. I didn't mean to scare you."

Cerise put her hands on her face and tried to calm her rapid heartbeat. When the panic in her chest died down, she turned around in her seat.

"I thought I dropped you off at the police station."

"I didn't want to stay there. I wanted to stay with you."

Cerise stumbled for what to say. "How . . . how did you get away from the deputy?"

Amanda shrugged. "I sneaked out when he wasn't looking."

"But . . . you must have been right behind me. How did you get in the car without me noticing?"

She shrugged again, but didn't otherwise answer.

Cerise felt a chill go through her. Her story wasn't

impossible, but it was so unlikely that it might as well be. The chance of Amanda sneaking away from the deputy was hard enough to fathom, but apparently she had also gotten out the front door without being noticed, followed Cerise across the street to her car, and somehow gotten into the backseat without being seen or heard. And she had remained invisible and silent for the entire trip from Hillsborough to Chapel Hill. How could a six year old—or anyone, for that matter—do all that?

And yet there she was. Cerise had never imagined that a little kid could be so utterly terrifying.

"Where are we going now?" Amanda asked.

Cerise had no idea what to say. Should she take her to another police station? What would she say this time? Would there be a record of her dropping the girl off at the sheriff's office? And if so, what did that mean if she showed up with her at another police station? She didn't think it would go over very well, and she thought she might even be arrested this time. If those cultists showed up while she was in a cell, there'd be no way she could get away again.

"I think . . . I'm not sure." Cerise needed time to think. She couldn't take this girl with her, and if she was being honest, she didn't want to be anywhere near her. The child scared the hell out of her.

"Is your wrist okay?"

"How did you know I hurt my wrist?"

"I saw you fall off the roof. It looked scary. You looked like you hurt your wrist pretty bad."

"It hurts a little." It hurt more than a little, but she had been so pumped up on adrenaline that she hadn't noticed the pain too much after the initial break.

"You can fix it."

"I could wrap it, but I'll need to see a doctor. I think it's broken."

She glanced down at her wrist, noticing for the first time how much her arm had swelled.

"You don't need a doctor. You can do it yourself."

Cerise narrowed her eyes. "Some things need to be fixed by a doctor, Amanda."

The girl cocked her head. "You know where it's broke, right?"

She felt like she was being lectured to. "I think so."

"Close your eyes."

"What?"

"Close your eyes."

Cerise felt dread in the pit of her stomach. "Why do you want me to close my eyes?"

"It'll be easier that way. Don't worry."

She felt an impulse to get out of the car and run, but in her current state she didn't think she could outrun the girl. What was she going to do when Cerise closed her eyes? She decided she was more afraid of what might happen if she didn't. With a glance around to make sure no one was there, she closed her eyes, hoping the girl wouldn't stab her or do something equally horrible.

"Try to think about where it's broke, like a picture in your head."

Cerise was still waiting for something to happen, but she conjured up the image of her broken wrist anyway.

"Now get really close to the broke part. Almost like you're inside your arm."

She mentally zoomed in until she could see an image of

the fracture. She was surprised that she could imagine the break with such clarity, as if she was seeing the actual injury and not just an image of it.

"Now try to think about fixing it."

Cerise almost opened her eyes, but then she felt warmth in her wrist from the inside. She closed her eyes tighter, losing herself in the image.

The fracture went all the way through the ulna, but the broken pieces were still in place. She willed herself closer to the break until it loomed in front of her, a massive chasm between two enormous cliffs. As she stared at it, red tendrils began to grow from either side, hesitantly at first, but then more quickly. More and more sprouted, each one winding its way to the other side, joining the two walls of the chasm until a forest of red filled the space.

From either side a white lattice began to grow over the frame of the tendrils, building in layer upon layer until she could only see the red tendrils in isolated spots. The lattice thickened and the individual holes began to close up, eventually covering the entire network of vines. Seconds later, the chasm between the cliffs was completely filled, and she couldn't tell it had been there at all.

She opened her eyes. Amanda was still sitting in the backseat, calmly smiling at her. The warmth in her wrist was fading, and the pain was gone. She flexed it carefully, not really believing what she had seen. When she felt nothing but the smooth workings of her wrist, she moved it around in a circle, the swelling visibly retreating while she watched.

"What did you do to me?"

"I didn't do anything."

"My wrist . . . it's fixed. How did you . . . ?"

"I didn't do it. You did. I just showed you."

Cerise's head was spinning. "Amanda, what is going on?" She felt like she was near hysterics. There were too many things that made no sense. Was she going insane?

"You just know more stuff now. That's all."

"What does that mean?" She wanted to scream, and only the sight of the extraordinarily calm six year old in the backseat prevented her from doing so.

Amanda shrugged.

"Do you know how the car started?"

"You knew it would start, so it did."

In that instant of terror, she *had* known. The fact that she didn't have the keys had been completely shut from her mind in her desperation for it to start.

What was happening to her?

Cerise turned back around and stared out the front window into the darkness, afraid that she would see pale white forms suddenly appear. They first appeared after Amanda showed up at her house. At Russell's, Amanda had apparently been in her car when they showed up again. What was the connection between them?

Cerise turned back around. "Amanda, do you remember how you told me that those bad angels were after me, not you?"

She nodded.

"Does that mean they will leave you alone?"

"I think so. They don't know about me, not really."

Cerise frowned, confused. What did that mean?

"If we weren't together, would they still show up where you were?"

Amanda scrunched her face up. "I don't think so." She furrowed her brow more before continuing. "Do you ever see moths?"

"Moths? Sure. Why?"

"You know how they like to fly around lights in the dark? They're kind of like that."

"The bad angels are like moths?"

Amanda looked down and folded her arms, appearing to be deep in thought. After a few seconds, she looked back up.

"You turn on a light and they see it. It's not really a light, but it's like that. They don't see me. They just see the light."

Cerise looked back out the window. "Am I the light?"

"No."

"Are you?"

"No, it's something else, but I don't know what."

What was the connection between the two attacks? Her eyes went wide and she felt the outside of her pocket for the folded up piece of paper. She wanted to dig it out, but she was terrified that she might be right.

"Amanda, do you know anything about a scroll?"

"What's a scroll?"

"A rolled up piece of paper. A really old piece of paper."

"I don't think so. Is it important?"

"I'm not sure. Maybe."

She had been working on the scroll when Amanda showed up at her house, and then again when she was at Russell's. Was it only a coincidence that so-called angels showed up each time she tried to translate the fragment?

It was ridiculous. There was a rational explanation for

all of this, something that would withstand scrutiny. She wouldn't suddenly start believing in angels just because she couldn't explain a few things. She might as well start believing in vampires or zombies.

She couldn't explain Amanda yet, either, but an explanation existed. The safest place for her was the police station, but Cerise didn't think that was an option anymore, at least not at this point. She did, however, have an idea of where she could take her.

"I need to call somebody, okay?" She pulled out her phone and scrolled through her contacts. With some hesitation she hit Richard Burgoyne's number. He was the only person beside Russell that she felt she could trust, and he wouldn't ask a lot of questions that she couldn't answer.

After eight rings, a voice thick with sleep answered.

"Hello?"

"Richard, it's Cerise. I'm so sorry to call you like this, but I desperately need your help."

Chapter Eight

The wide, tree-lined street seemed to swallow up the little car. On either side of the road huge houses were set back on massive lots with finely manicured lawns and extensive landscaping. Many houses could only be partially seen from the road due to long driveways and tall trees that filled the front yards.

"Who lives in these houses?" Amanda asked from the backseat, eyes wide as they drove slowly down the street.

"People who make more money than me," Cerise said.

"How much money do you make?"

"Enough so that I'm comfortable."

"How much money do the people in these houses make?"

Cerise steered the car up a curving driveway leading to a large, Tudor-style house set amongst sweeping oak trees that must have been over a hundred years old. She switched the engine off and turned around in her seat.

"Millions and millions of dollars."

Amanda moved closer to the window and looked up at the house. "Who lives here?"

"A friend of mine. His name is Richard."

"Does he have a lot of money?"

Cerise sighed. "His wife does. Her family started a

business a long time ago."

Amanda looked back up at the house, twisting to take it all in.

"Are we going to stay here?"

Cerise didn't answer. Instead, she got out of the car and opened the back door.

"Come on out."

Amanda crossed her arms and leaned back in her seat.

Cerise frowned. "What's wrong?"

"I don't want to go in there."

"Why not?"

Amanda didn't respond, but remained in the car, her lower lip puffed out like a cartoon character's version of a pout.

"We're just going inside to see my friend. He's really nice."

"You're leaving me here!"

"Amanda, will you please just get out of the car? I promise I won't leave you right away. I need to go see someone and I want you to be safe."

She shook her head and refused to budge.

Cerise considered dragging her out of the car, but knew it would be better if she could be coaxed. She was asking a lot from Richard, and if the girl was going to be difficult she would feel incredibly guilty for leaving her with him. She knelt down to the child's level and said, "All right, you can stay in the car. But don't go anywhere, okay?"

Amanda relaxed but the pout remained.

Cerise shut the door and walked up the cobblestone path to the front of the house. The large wood door opened before she could knock. Richard Burgoyne stood in the doorway in a black robe, his gray hair looking disheveled but otherwise seeming wide awake.

"Hi, Cerise."

"Thanks so much for helping me out, Richard."

Richard smiled. "It's no problem, really. My grandchildren come over all the time, so I'm used to watching little ones. Where is she, by the way?"

Cerise rolled her eyes. "She won't come out of the car." She looked back and didn't see Amanda. "She must have slumped down in the back seat."

"I'm sure she'll come in soon. Kids don't usually hold out too long."

"If you say so."

"So you said she was dropped off at your house by a neighbor who had an emergency?"

That was the best story Cerise could come up with on short notice. Richard was too smart to really believe it.

"Yeah. She was in a bit of a jam and I told her I'd help out. But then this thing cropped up with my parents and I don't think it'd be good to have her along."

Another ridiculous story that Richard wouldn't believe, but he didn't show any sign of skepticism. He either believed her—unlikely—or was being a really trusting friend.

"I'm glad you called me. I've been wanting to try out some of my new tricks for the grandkids. This'll give me a chance to have a test audience."

Cerise smiled. "I should be back tomorrow, and I'll call Amanda's mother to let her know she's okay."

Richard nodded, and Cerise was relieved he didn't ask any other questions or seem bothered about the weird circumstances. She hoped he'd be good for one more request.

"I have one more favor to ask."

"Yeah, I bet you do." He was looking at her car. "That's some kind of damage. What happened exactly?"

"I'm not sure. Amanda and I left the house after I got the call from my dad, and my car was gone from the driveway. I walked down to the curb and saw it parked down the street. It was like this when I found it. Whoever took it must have done that to the roof, but I have no idea why they would do something like that."

"But you didn't call the police, right?"

"No, I, um, I knew it would take a while for them to come out and my dad said it was important that I get there, so . . . ."

"So you just left right away."

"Yeah."

"Makes sense." He looked back at her, his eyebrows raised as if he expected some sort of explanation. When he didn't get it, he held up a finger and retreated into the house. A few seconds later he emerged with a set of keys and handed them to her.

"Take my son's car. It's the blue BMW parked in front of the garage. A little old and beat up, but it runs great."

She sighed in relief. "Thanks so much, Richard. I'll take good care of it." She took the keys and handed him hers.

"I guess you should get going," he said.

She turned but then stopped, reaching into her pocket for a folded piece of paper. "Can I give you something?"

"What is it?"

"I'm not entirely sure, but I think it's important."

Richard unfolded the paper and scanned it, his brows furrowing.

"Is it Hebrew?"

"Aramaic."

He nodded. "Where did you get this?"

"Russell sent it to me the night he . . . before he disappeared."

"Did he say what it was?"

"No, just that it was important. I've transcribed some of it, but it's really slow going." She hesitated, not wanting to sound like a conspiracy theorist. "I think it has something to do with his disappearance."

He pursed his lips. "It's intriguing. Too bad it's not in Latin so I could transcribe it for you. Can I make a copy of this?"

"Sure."

He ducked inside the door and Cerise looked back over to the car. Amanda was still hiding in the back seat. She hoped she wouldn't give Richard a hard time.

Richard popped out of the door and handed the sheet of paper back to Cerise. "I'll go over your notes and see if there's something I can help with. Maybe I can do some research."

She thanked him again and gave him a quick hug before heading to the car and opening the back door. Amanda was crouched down on the floor.

"I have to go, but I'll be back for you tomorrow, okay?"

She turned her head away from Cerise.

Realizing there was nothing she could say to help the situation, she shut the door and headed towards the garage. She got into the blue BMW and pulled out of the driveway, passing her torn up car and the little girl she was leaving behind. She couldn't dismiss the feeling of neglect as she pulled away, but she had a long drive to DC and she had something new to worry about.

She hadn't seen Jack Horner in twelve years, and her nerves were on edge just thinking about contacting him. He was the only person she knew who wouldn't think she was insane. And even though he probably hated her, she was still sure that she could count on him to help.

Chapter Nine

Richard watched his son's BMW disappear down the driveway, his face etched into a frown. Cerise was in some kind of trouble and it was probably related to Russell's disappearance, but there wasn't much he could do if she wasn't willing to tell him what was going on.

He wanted to press her, but he didn't think she'd tell him. Even worse, she might get defensive and not accept his help at all, which meant this little girl would be sucked into the trouble. Better to keep the child out of it and let Cerise try to work things out on her own. If she wasn't back tomorrow he'd call the police. For now he'd keep his fingers crossed.

He stepped down from the porch and walked over to the car, forcing a smile. There was no sense in worrying Amanda; she was probably already scared and anxious after being dumped with some strange old man she didn't even know.

He was curious to know who she really was; Cerise's story was obviously fabricated. She might be a neighbor, but he was sure there was more to it than Cerise had said. It could be an abuse situation, which made it even thornier, but he trusted Cerise's judgment. She was one of the sharpest young professors he'd known in thirty-five years of teaching, and he would give her the time she needed to sort things out.

Thanks to his grandchildren there were a lot of things around the house to engage the girl. Maureen would be surprised in the morning to see a new kid in the spare room, but she'd be fine with it once her grandmotherly instinct kicked in. They'd have some big, kid-friendly breakfast—pancakes and sausage or maybe french toast—and he'd let her pick some stuff from the garden. His grandchildren always loved doing that.

He gazed into the back window and frowned. He'd expected to see her huddled down on the floor but the backseat was empty. There wasn't anyone in the front seat either.

He walked around the car and looked through all the windows, hoping that maybe he'd missed her in the dark and a new angle would expose her, but it was clear that she was not inside. He dropped down to his hands and knees and looked underneath, but there was no one there either.

He didn't see anyone in the yard, but there were a lot of trees, bushes, and landscaping where a little kid could hide. It was strange that he hadn't seen or heard the car doors open. Could she have slipped out of the car while he was looking away?

"Amanda? Can you come out, please?"

There was plenty of room between houses so no one would hear him shouting, and their bedroom was in the back of the house on the top floor so Maureen wouldn't hear him either. He scanned the yard on both sides of the driveway but didn't see any movement.

He hoped she was still near the car, but it was possible

that she'd made her way to the backyard where there were many more places a small child could hide. He'd spent hours playing hide and seek with his grandchildren back there, but it would be a lot more difficult to find a girl at night who didn't want to be found. His granddaughters couldn't help giggling if he came close to their hiding spots.

"Amanda?"

No response.

He jogged out to the road and looked right and left, afraid that she might have tried to follow Cerise, but the street was empty both ways. He thought it was most likely she was close by; beyond a big yard the world looked like a pretty scary place for a little kid. He just had to find her.

The big oaks with their low branches were good candidates for hiding spaces. There were about a dozen of them scattered on both sides of the house so he started on the side closest to the driveway, thinking that would be where she might go first. He weaved in and around, the wide trunks creating pools of deep shadows. He craned his head up where the branches were low enough for a small girl to climb, hoping she hadn't actually scampered up. One slip could send her to the ground, and even if she stayed low she could end up with a broken arm or worse.

He exhausted the hiding places on the near side, his eyes open for movement in case she decided to dart from one place to another, but he didn't see any sign of her. His worry increased with every minute that he didn't find her, and he was afraid he'd have to call the police soon.

His eyes caught something stir on the far side of the house. It might have been a deer—there were a lot of those around—but it also might have been a small girl. He hurried to the other side, his slippers soaked from the wet grass.

He reached the closest tree and stopped, his eyes alive for any motion. "Amanda? Are you over here?"

Something moved in his periphery. He circled the trees and shrubs, eyes alert in case she made a sudden dash. He wasn't exactly fast, but when he played hide and seek with his grandchildren he could nearly always catch them if he really wanted to. Youth gave them speed, but old age gave him longer legs and the ability to use geometry to cut them off.

If there had been a deer it would have bounded out when he got close, but he saw no movement. He was certain Amanda was behind one of the nearby trees. He probably wouldn't have to call the police.

He ran more quickly through the shadows and the low-hanging branches, his eyes darting here and there for any sign of her. She wouldn't be able to escape being seen forever.

"Amanda! I know you're out here," he sang out, his voice playful. He hoped to hear giggling, but aside from his own labored breathing and the constant chirp of crickets, he couldn't hear anything.

He stopped and leaned his hand against an oak, bent over to catch his breath. He couldn't believe that he hadn't found her yet. His grandchildren couldn't stay hidden for more than five minutes after he found their general location.

Resting against the tree, he reached into his pocket and pulled out the copy of Cerise's fragment. He couldn't read it in the dark, but he could see numerous scribblings in the margins. He was suddenly curious to examine it a little closer, but wouldn't be able to do that until the morning. After he finally found Amanda, he'd be too tired to do much of anything other than plop down in his armchair and turn on the TV to wind her down and get her ready for bed.

He folded the paper up and shoved it back in his robe pocket. He was looking forward to talking with Cerise and Russell about its contents. If they found something important, it could have a ripple effect on his own studies. He pushed aside a twinge of worry that Russell wouldn't turn up. There were enough police looking for him that they were bound to find him soon.

He turned around, hoping he'd see the girl sneaking away from behind a tree, but the yard looked as empty as before. He wondered if he could entice her with some cookies from the house. Maureen had some sitting on the kitchen counter. He could get them and then make a show of eating them. He had a hard time believing a six year old could resist such a tactic.

He turned towards the house, looking forward to the excuse to have a few more cookies, but suddenly froze. A pale white figure stood directly in front of him.

His first impression was of dark hair framing the most beautiful face he had ever seen, flawless and unlined, with nearly pure white skin. The boy had the appearance of a teenager, but there was the unmistakable air of something ancient about him. When he noticed the lack of genitalia, however, he felt a shock of revulsion.

He thought immediately of the *castrati*. The absence of the scrotum and the accompanying long limbs were reminiscent of those unfortunate young boys who fell prey to the church during the Renaissance. But it was a ridiculous comparison. A *castrati* would have his scrotum removed to prevent deepening of his golden voice, but the penis remained intact, and this boy—was it a boy?— had no penis. He was equally sure that this was not a female; the musculature and shape were not right.

He took a step back. "Do you need help?"

The boy did not respond other than to continue walking forward.

Panic began to swell in Richard's chest. He turned toward the house, visualizing the panic button on his alarm console just inside the front door. It was certainly time to call the police now.

He stopped in mid-step.

There was another naked youth, this one standing between him and the house. And as he looked toward the street, a third appeared.

They were not identical, but they so resembled each other that he was sure they were siblings of some sort. All three were terribly beautiful and bizarrely sexless, and all three advanced on him slowly.

"Please," he said, feeling fear creep into his gut. "I'll give you anything you want."

The neighbors were too far away to hear his cries as they fell upon him with expressionless faces and outstretched arms.

Chapter Ten

Jack Horner spun his chair around and looked through the tenth story window of the HMDL Security headquarters, wishing he could block out the voice of his attorney, Christina Alford. His defense was the last thing he wanted to talk about. In fact, he didn't want a defense at all; he would rather just plead guilty and go to prison, but his boss and friend, Mitch Kirkland, wouldn't hear of it.

He stared out at the Washington Monument, just barely visible across the Potomac on a clear day, and half-listened to Christina.

"Jack, we need to focus."

He didn't turn his head. "I'm focused. Go on with what you were saying."

Christina sighed. "I know this is extremely difficult and painful for you right now, but it doesn't serve anyone to put you in prison."

"I don't know about that. It would at least prevent me from killing anyone else."

"Jack, could you turn around and look at me?"

Jack slowly turned his chair to face her. She was in her mid-thirties, but her Kewpie Doll cuteness made her look ten years younger and belied an aggressive litigation style that had won her a reputation as a hard ass. Mitch hadn't spared expenses to get one of the top defense lawyers in

DC.

She said, "This is not a complicated case, and it's going to be pretty straightforward to show that this was just a tragic accident."

Jack sat with his shoulders hunched, his hands folded in his lap. "It wasn't an accident. Accidents aren't the result of criminal negligence."

Christina tensed and then relaxed. "I understand that you feel guilty, but there's a difference between moral responsibility and legal responsibility, Jack."

"I know. I went to law school, too."

"Your background isn't criminal law."

Jack shrugged. "I remember some bits and pieces. *Actus reus* and *mens rea* and all that."

"Look, Jack, I can't take away the guilt—and I'm truly sorry for what happened—but I *can* tell you that going to prison won't give you the resolution you're looking for. All it will do is cause you more pain. You need to keep yourself out of prison so you can get help and rebuild your life." She paused before adding, "I'm sorry to be so blunt, but I think you need to hear more than just sympathy right now."

He stared at her for long seconds before answering, replaying the same scene in his head that had been running almost constantly for a week.

"Do you have kids, Christina?"

"No, I don't have kids, but—"

"My daughter was finishing her first year of kindergarten. When I came home at night she would tell me all the things she did at school, then I'd chase her around the house before telling her a story and taking her to bed.

"Sometimes when I tucked her in at night she would

tell me she was afraid of monsters in her room. I would go through the room and kick out all the monsters and tell them they weren't allowed to come back. I'd grab them by the scruff of their necks or by their tails and I'd drag them across the room and boot them out. She'd laugh and tell me that I missed one, and I'd have to go find him and drag him out of hiding before tossing him out of the room. She'd look at me like I could protect her from anything.

"We had top security on all the windows and doors, cameras at the entrance, all the stuff you need to keep the shit of the world out of your home. My wife thought it was overkill, but she went along with it. We had the money, and if it gave me peace of mind, it made her feel safer, too.

"It's ironic, isn't it? If somebody had assaulted my family on the street, I wouldn't have hesitated to shoot them. But it was me who they most needed protection from, not some random druggie out to score some cash for a quick fix."

"You need to stop doing this to yourself. It wasn't your fault."

Jack sat up in the chair and leaned forward, his eyes flashing. "Are you fucking kidding me? Whose fault was it if it wasn't mine?"

Christina didn't flinch. "It wasn't anyone's fault. It was an accident."

"It wouldn't have happened if I hadn't been drinking!"

"You don't know that."

"We both know that's bullshit. If I hadn't been drinking, I would've seen that car coming."

"Your blood alcohol level wasn't above the limit."

He laughed humorlessly. "Yeah, that's right. I was one

hundredth away from being legally intoxicated. What a hero. Except that doesn't make a goddamn difference and you know it! I knew I shouldn't have been driving, but I drove anyway. And look what happened!"

"I understand that you feel morally responsible. Anybody would in your situation. But we can't view the facts of your case through the lens of your guilt. That's one of the reasons why defendants should never represent themselves; they can't be objective about their cases."

"Fuck being objective. That doesn't make—"

She cut him off with a wave of her hand. "Look, Jack. You don't know for sure whether you would have seen the other driver or not. He was going fast, probably too fast. And you're probably overestimating the length of time that you weren't looking at the road. If it was only a few seconds you wouldn't have been able to avoid the car, you just would have seen it coming. You wouldn't have been able to get out of the way in time."

"You don't know that. You weren't there."

"You're right, I wasn't. But do you really think that you can look back on that instant and say with 100% certainty that things would've been different if you hadn't had a couple of drinks?"

Jack narrowed his eyes at her. "Fucking lawyers."

"Yeah, but this fucking lawyer is going to keep you from doing something stupid that you'll regret later, like letting yourself go to prison."

He clenched his jaw. "You don't know what I'm going to regret."

"Neither do you." She crossed her arms and leaned back in her chair. "Now do you want to continue this pissing contest or do you want to get some work done?"

Jack couldn't decide if he wanted to throw her out the window or laugh. It was rare that he couldn't intimidate someone—it was a skill he had honed to perfection since he had earned his first black belt. The fact that he was facing down a woman who weighed half as much as he did and barely came up to his chin made it even more amusing.

He unclenched his jaw and smiled. "Sorry. I don't mean to take it out on you."

She smiled back and leaned forward, sliding a manila folder over to him. "It's fine. You think you're the first client to give me grief? You're Mr Rogers compared to some of my clients."

He laughed. "I can't see you watching Mr Rogers. That polite niceness didn't seem to rub off."

"My dad was a fan—he's the nice one. Now are you ready to get down to work?"

He nodded, feeling as powerless to prevent his defense as he was to prevent the deaths of his wife and daughter. It made him sick to realize that he was too important to the company to go to prison, which was why Mitch hired a lawyer as good as Christina in the first place. Would he have such good representation if he was just some ordinary guy?

The question was stupid and obvious, and he put it out of his head. He wasn't going to prison even though he deserved it, and he'd have to live with the fact that he'd killed his wife and daughter for the rest of his life.

With any luck, that wouldn't be much longer.

Chapter Eleven

Jack closed the door behind him and walked into the loft. He set his phone on the kitchen table and sat down, still clutching the bottle in the brown bag. He unscrewed the top and took a drink, grimacing as the whiskey went down.

He pulled his 9mm pistol out and put it next to the bottle. The apartment was empty, the lack of noise both welcome and maddening. He grabbed the neck of the bottle and took another long swig. Bottle in hand, he walked over to the wide expanse of windows that stretched thirty feet up to the ceiling of the loft.

The view of Washington was fantastic, especially at night. It was the reason they had bought this particular loft rather than the one they liked on the other side of the building. This one was more, but they both agreed that it had been worth it. Besides, what good was all the money he was making if they didn't spend it?

He took another drink, whiskey spilling onto his shirt and tie, but he barely noticed. He wiped his mouth with his shirt sleeve and walked down the hallway to the closed door at the end. He leaned his head up against it and stayed like that for a minute before reaching down and turning the handle.

The door opened slowly and he stared inside. The canopy bed was ridiculous and clichéd, but it fit the room with its lacy yellow curtains, flower print wallpaper borders, and white furniture. He glanced around, taking in the stuffed animals and dolls, the row of small shoes lined up against the wall, the pile of picture books next to the bed. He clenched his jaw and slammed the door hard enough to send a framed mirror hanging in the hallway crashing to the floor.

He picked it up and stared at his face in the cracked glass. The bruises on his face were yellowing, and the four inch cut on his left temple was healing. It had bled profusely and taken nineteen stitches to close, but was otherwise superficial. It was a visual reminder of how minor his injuries were from the crash, at least compared to his wife and daughter.

He sent his fist, still clutching the bottle, into the mirror. Whiskey and broken glass splashed him, and his hand started burning. Shards of glass were stuck in his knuckles, and the back of his hand was coated with a fiery mix of blood and alcohol. He dropped the broken bottle and mirror and walked back towards the kitchen, his shoes grinding the glass on the wood floors into a wet, jagged mess.

He sat down at the kitchen table and picked the shards out of his hand. Once most of the glass was out he grabbed a stack of napkins from the middle of the table and pressed down on the bloody mess he had made of his hand.

He continued to press down while he stared at the gun on the table, imagining the feel of the grip in his hand. It would take less than a second, and he couldn't think of a reason in the world not to grab it, shove the muzzle in his mouth, and squeeze the trigger.

As he reached for the pistol his phone vibrated with an incoming text. It was probably Christina or maybe Mitch checking up on him. He grabbed the gun but didn't lift it from the table. His eyes lingered on the phone.

He couldn't think of a single person he wanted to hear from, or a single thing of importance that the text might contain. And yet, he let go of the pistol and picked up the phone instead, for some reason compelled to know who might be texting him at the very moment he was about to blow his brains out.

He didn't recognize the number, and whoever sent it was not in his contact list. He called up the text and frowned, lingering over it before finally putting the phone down and picking the gun up. He sat at the table holding the gun in front of his face as dusk turned to night, wondering why he didn't just pull the trigger.

There was no redemption in that text. There was nothing for him at all, nothing but painful memories from the past. He had no desire to see her again, and even less to help her. Besides, any kind of crisis she might be having paled in comparison to what he was going through. And what kind of help could he possibly offer her even if he was willing?

He shoved the gun up against his eye, finger on the trigger. One quick pull and a 9mm bullet would fly through his right orbital and blow his brains out the back side of his head. More than anything he felt a sense of relief that it would be over and he wouldn't have to think about how he had killed those who had meant the most to him.

He opened his eyes and let the gun fall down to the table. He picked up the phone, scanning the text once more before finally hitting the call button.

The phone only rang twice before Cerise picked up.

Jack walked into the diner and did a quick glance around before spotting Cerise. He walked over and she stood up, both unsure how to greet the other.

"It's been a long time," he said.

"Yeah. Ten years, right?"

"Give or take."

She motioned to the booth and they both sat down and stared at the table for long seconds. A waitress came by with a coffee pot and filled their cups. Cerise cradled hers while she tried to think of what to say.

"What happened to your hand?" she said, noting the gauze around his right fist.

"Ran into some broken glass. No big deal."

"With your hand? How does that happen?"

"My fist ran into it."

She dropped it, not wanting to know more.

"You look good," she said. "Different from when I last saw you. More . . . something."

"Old?"

"Yeah, but not in a bad way. More mature, I guess."

"I've done some growing up, I suppose. Maybe more than I wanted. What have you been doing?"

"Teaching at Chapel Hill."

"Just like you wanted. Religious studies, right?"

She nodded. "I finished my doctorate in early Christianity. Got promoted to full professor a few years ago."

"Congratulations."

"Thanks."

She felt antsy, like this small talk was wasting time that could be better spent looking for Russell, but she didn't know how to transition into *'I was attacked by naked angels after my professor boyfriend was kidnapped and sent me a cryptic email. Oh, and a weird girl showed up on my doorstep who knew the attack was coming. Any suggestions?'*

"How about you?" she asked.

"I'm one of the vice presidents of HMDL."

"The security corporation?"

"Yeah."

She nodded, putting aside all that she knew about HMDL's dark history providing 'security forces' in Afghanistan and Iraq. There was no sense in provoking an argument about the shady dealings of his employer, but she couldn't help wondering how involved he was in such things.

After a long awkward pause of staring into her coffee cup, she finally said, "Look, Jack, I don't know how to broach this, but I really need your help."

"Why me?"

"What?"

"Why do you need help from me specifically? I haven't seen or heard from you in ten years, and all of a sudden you're asking me for help. I'm guessing you're in trouble and you're desperate. Is that about right?"

He wasn't disguising his annoyed tone, but she expected it after the way their relationship ended.

"I'm sorry about how we . . . left things. I didn't mean

to hurt you."

"I'm not talking about that, but since you brought it up, I think I deserved better than a phone call."

"I'm sorry. I . . . I was young, and I didn't really know how to tell you." She didn't add that she had been terrified to see him again after the incident.

"You at least could've told me to my face. The last time I saw you was at the bar when that guy grabbed you."

She wished she could forget that night. Jack had to be peeled off a drunken frat boy by three bouncers, and he'd spent the night in jail. The kid—his name was Chris Clarents—had to be taken to the hospital with a broken nose, concussion, and two broken fingers. She'd visited him in the hospital and he'd come out okay, but he was too terrified to make a police report.

"What you did . . . you didn't have to do that."

"Do what? Stop that guy from groping you? I would think you'd be glad I was there to—"

"You beat him to a pulp. He was just a stupid kid. He didn't deserve that."

For a second he looked like he was going to argue, and Cerise braced herself. She had gotten into many arguments with him in the past, and none of them had been pleasant. He was quick-witted, confident to a fault, and stubborn as hell; qualities which had served him academically, but had been a burden on their relationship.

But the expression on his face suddenly softened, as if all the fight had left him. In three years of dating she had never seen him back down from a confrontation.

"You're right. I was a hothead. But you could've at least let me see you to apologize."

"It wasn't just that night. You . . . you were angry a lot, and when you were drinking it was like . . . like you became a different person. And there was a lot of drinking."

"I never would've hurt you."

She looked down, unable to meet his eyes.

"You were afraid of me, weren't you?"

She looked up and raised her eyebrows the slightest bit.

He leaned back in his seat. "Yeah, I guess that makes sense. For whatever it's worth, I'm sorry."

"It was a long time ago." She sipped her coffee. "I appreciate you meeting me like this. I thought you might not be willing to see me."

"I'm not sure what you think I can do."

She sighed and put her face in her hands, trying to come up with a way to explain what had happened that wouldn't make her sound like a lunatic.

"I couldn't think of anyone else to call. You were right, I'm in a lot of trouble. I . . . I think some people are trying to kill me."

He paused. "Are you serious?"

She nodded.

"Why not go to the police?"

"They wouldn't believe me."

"Why not?"

She took a deep breath. How was she going to explain this? It was insane to think that he would believe her. Any connection they had was long gone. She knew virtually nothing about him anymore. She might as well be talking to a stranger.

And what would he say to her story? What could he say? Trying to put it into words only reinforced how crazy the story would sound—how crazy it *was*.

She started to slide out of the booth. "I can't do this. I'm sorry."

He reached out and grabbed her wrist.

"Wait."

Even though she hadn't seen him in ten years, the expression was unmistakable. She had never seen such a look of utter defeat on his face. It was like he had aged twenty years in the last thirty seconds. She sat back down.

"Jack, is something wrong?"

For long seconds she didn't think he was going to say anything. As he stared down at the table she noticed his appearance for the first time: he was unshaven and wearing clothes that looked like they had been slept in, though he didn't look like he had actually slept for a while.

"I'm being arraigned in a week."

She was afraid to ask what for, wondering if his temper had gotten the best of him and he'd killed someone. She didn't want to believe it might be true, but the image of him beating that student conjured itself up again. If Jack hadn't been pulled off, she had no doubt he would've beaten him to death.

He looked up, the expression on his face blank.

"A few weeks ago my wife and I were at my boss' for a dinner party. I had a couple drinks, but I didn't feel anything other than a slight buzz. Nothing that I hadn't driven on before.

"We left late, maybe around three, and stopped at the babysitter's house to pick up our daughter. She was asleep so I carried her out, put her in the backseat, and buckled her in.

"The streets were empty and I approached an intersection. I was—I don't know, maybe a hundred feet back?—and my daughter said something from the backseat. I turned to look at her . . . "

He stopped talking.

Her eyes got wide and she felt her stomach sink.

"I didn't see it, but they tell me a truck ran into the passenger side of the car. I felt the car lurch and I was thrown around. My head smashed into something." He fingered the jagged cut on his temple.

"There was a horn blaring, but other than that I couldn't hear anything. My first reaction was to check on my wife and daughter."

Cerise didn't need him to continue. "I'm so sorry, Jack."

"Aside from this," he pointed to the cut again, "and a few bruises, I was fine. The passenger side of the car was wrapped around the front of the truck."

She hesitantly reached her hand across the table and put it on his. "It's not your fault."

"You're wrong. It was my fault. I must have closed my eyes for a second or two when I looked back. I went right through the intersection."

Cerise didn't know what to say.

"When the police arrived they gave me a breathalyzer. I was just under the limit. They arrested me anyway, and took me away while I watched the paramedics pull what was left of my family from the wreck."

"But it was an accident."

"If I hadn't been drinking I would've seen that truck coming."

"Jack, I . . . ," but what could she say? This was not the

man she had been with years ago. This was a man who had lost everything.

"Do you have a lawyer?" It was a stupid question, but she couldn't think of anything else to say.

He nodded. "My boss doesn't want one of his vice presidents going to prison."

"Do you . . . does your lawyer think—"

He pulled his hand away. "I don't care what happens to me. If you hadn't called me, I'd be dead right now, so I figure maybe there's something I need to do for you."

She recognized the resolution on his face; he was done talking about what had happened to him and there was no point in asking any more questions. She swallowed her pity. He would hate that most of all, and it would only make him feel worse.

"I wish there—"

"Tell me why you can't go to the police."

She took a breath, feeling selfish in the face of what he'd told her, even though her problems weren't exactly trivial. She had to tell him now; he'd been more open with her in the last few minutes than he had in their entire relationship. She closed her eyes for a second, considering how to begin.

"I've been seeing a professor in my department for a few years. Russell Kellar. He's an expert in a certain area of Christianity called Gnosticism."

She scanned his face for a reaction but didn't see any.

"He met an antiquities dealer at the Renaissance Hotel in Raleigh a couple nights ago."

He looked down for a second, eyes narrowed in thought.

"Why does that hotel name sound familiar?"

"Three people were murdered there that night, one of them the dealer Russell met with."

Saying the words out loud made her sick to her stomach.

Jack nodded slowly. "Was Russell . . . ?"

"No. At least his body hasn't turned up. He was seen on a security video being chased through the lobby."

"The police don't know where he is?"

"No one does."

"So you want me to help you find him, but I'm guessing he was involved with something illegal with that dealer, right?"

"God, I wish it were that simple."

She took a long sip of her coffee, the cup rattling in her hand as she put it back on the table.

She reached into her pocket and pulled out her phone, calling up the picture before sliding it across the table.

"Russell sent me this the night he disappeared."

Jack picked it up and looked at the picture.

"What is this?"

"I think it's a piece of an ancient scroll, and I think it's really important."

"What does it say?"

"I don't know exactly. I made out a few words and phrases but I'm really only guessing."

"I take it he didn't contact you again after this."

She shook her head.

"Would it be worth a lot of money?" he asked.

"It depends on what it says. But I can't imagine something like that would be easy to sell. Its value is probably more scholarly than anything."

"We still haven't gotten to why you can't go to the police."

"I know. It's . . . it's hard to talk about."

He nodded. "Take your time."

She took another sip of coffee and stared into his eyes, again feeling guilt for asking for help from him.

"Around ten last night a little girl knocked on my door. She said she was lost, but she couldn't tell me anything about her parents, where she lived, how she got lost, or anything useful. While I was talking to her, she suddenly just blurted out that she knew the way to her house.

"I didn't think too much of it at the time; I was just glad that she knew something and that I wouldn't have to take her to the police. But now that I think about it, it was like she was warned about something.

"We got into the car, and three . . . men . . . walked up my driveway. They didn't see us in the car, but one of them heard me gasp when he . . . "

"When he what?"

She hesitated before speaking. "He was on my porch and he . . . he just ripped the screen door off the frame."

"He broke down the door?"

"No. He ripped it off the frame and tossed it aside like it was made of cardboard. And then he broke down the steel door with his bare hands. I know it sounds insane, but I saw it happen."

Jack narrowed his eyes. "Cerise, you know that people can misremember events when they're scared."

"Have you ever known me to exaggerate, Jack?"

He thought for a moment. "No, I guess not. Is it

possible he had some kind of tool that you didn't see? It was dark, right?"

She shifted in her seat. "They didn't have anything on."

He frowned. "Like tools?"

"No. I mean they didn't have *anything* on. They were completely nude."

"Nothing? Not even shoes?"

"Nothing. And there's more." She gauged his expression before continuing, wondering if he thought she was crazy yet, but it was neutral. She had no idea what he might be thinking. "They were . . . they didn't have any genitals."

"What?"

"They were sexless."

He sat back in the booth. "Their genitals were cut off? Are you sure?"

She folded her arms and stared at him.

"Right, you're sure. Sorry, it's just a bit much to take in."

She relaxed slightly. "I know. But there's more."

He raised his eyebrows but said nothing.

"When they saw me and the girl—Amanda—in the car, they came after us. I tried to drive away, but one of them grabbed hold of the hood and held the car while another one smashed my window. I eventually got the car loose and got onto the road, but one of them was on the roof. He punched through and tried to drag me out. I had some pepper spray in my jacket and I managed to get him with it. He let go and fell backwards onto the road."

He stared at her for a minute, saying nothing.

"It sounds insane, I know, but I—"

"Is the car outside?"

"What?"

"Your car. Is it parked outside? I'd like to see the damage. Maybe I can make something out of it."

She shook her head. "I swapped cars with a friend. I was afraid the police would pull me over if they saw how damaged it was."

She told him her theory that some sort of cult might be involved, and how she had dropped Amanda off at the sheriff's office before heading to Russell's house. He listened patiently while she recounted Detective Piedmont's murder and how she had gotten away, only to find Amanda in the back seat.

"How did she get there? She couldn't have sneaked away from the deputy so easily."

"I have no idea. She was just there, and I didn't even notice her until I pulled into a parking lot. She scared the hell out of me. I dropped her off at a friend's and then came to you."

He didn't say anything for long seconds, and Cerise was afraid of what he might say. She knew he wouldn't dismiss her outright, but the story was beyond belief, and she wouldn't blame him if he thought she was having a mental breakdown.

"I can see why you don't want to go to the police. At the very least, they'd detain you."

She breathed a sigh of relief. Even if he was just humoring her, at least he hadn't dismissed her story outright.

"How come they don't have wings?"

"What?"

"The girl called them bad angels, right? Assuming she's right—"

"Are you serious? She's just a scared little girl, Jack. She's making something up to try to understand the horror of her situation."

"Is the idea that they might be angels really any crazier than what you've told me?"

She didn't know what to say.

"So let's just assume for a minute that they really are angels." He held a hand up to halt her objection. "Why don't they have wings?"

"Okay, assuming they are angels," she wanted to add, *which is ridiculous*, but he was right that her story was just as insane, "the development of angels with wings was added around the Renaissance, and is probably a result of artists' infatuation with Greek and Roman culture. You know Cupid, right?"

"Of course."

"Cupid is the Roman equivalent of the Greek god Eros, and both are depicted with wings. Renaissance artists used elements of Greek and Roman culture—especially mythology—in their depictions of Christianity, and angels got wings as a result of their association with Cupid and Eros."

"What about in the Bible? Does it give any descriptions of angels?"

"Not really, and certainly nothing with wings. The word angel comes from a Hebrew word that means messenger. It makes sense to give them wings since Heaven was thought of as up above before we knew what really was up above."

"What about the lack of genitals? I assume the Bible doesn't say anything like that, but I don't remember Michelangelo painting angels without penises."

She smiled slightly. "I don't recall ever seeing any traditional depiction of a Christian figure without genitals, not even God.

"But if we're still assuming they're angels—which is absurd—I would think that the lack of genitals would be more accurate from a common sense perspective. Angels are created whole by God. They wouldn't be born and they wouldn't be created by sexual intercourse. They also wouldn't have any need to urinate or copulate, so the notion of divine beings with genitals is pretty silly."

He stroked his chin. "If a little kid thought angels were after her, wouldn't she think of them with wings? Instead, she thinks that angels are skinny, naked white guys without their wee wees. It seems weird that she'd consider them angels in the first place."

"We don't know anything about her past. It's entirely possible that a fundamentalist cult would reject the concept of angels with wings, and maybe their literature shows them sexless as well."

"Assuming a cult is involved."

She narrowed her eyes. "That's a hell of a lot more likely than the idea that I'm being stalked by angels."

"What about their unnatural abilities? Ripping doors off frames, punching through car roofs? How would your cult hypothesis account for those?"

"Just because I can't explain it doesn't mean there isn't an explanation. Are you seriously asking me to believe that angels are after me? Do you realize how many other things would have to be true for that to happen?"

"I'd guess that some things you don't believe in might have to be true, right?"

She leaned forward. "Listen, I appreciate you not dismissing my ridiculous story. It's a lot more than anyone else would have done. But I can't accept that God is after me."

"I'm not saying that God is after you. And I'm not saying that God is even real; I have no idea one way or the other. But there seem to be supernatural elements in your story—at least if it happened the way you say it did."

She smoldered but didn't say anything.

"Think about it from a scientific perspective. One of these guys punched through the metal roof of your car. Was there any blood?"

She blinked, recalling the image in her head.

"I don't think so."

"So how could someone—even someone incredibly strong—punch through sheet metal without getting any kind of injury? He would've broken every bone in his hand, and the metal edges would have shredded his skin. But not only was he not bleeding, he was apparently still able to yank you out of your seat by your hair. That would be impossible with a broken hand, even if he wasn't feeling any pain."

She didn't know what to say.

"So that's the problem," he said. "If they're just crazy cultists, we have a real problem explaining how they can do those things."

"That doesn't mean that they're angels."

"Maybe not—probably not—but what other theories do

we have? We've got some evidence—the girl's statements that they're angels, along with their apparently incredible abilities—and we have no competing theories to explain the things they've done."

"We might as well assume they're vampires!"

"I know you're just being a smart ass, but think about it for a second. Did these guys exhibit any characteristics of other supernatural beings you've heard of?"

Her first instinct was to object to this idiotic line of questioning, but she forced it down and instead went through the catalog of boogey men in her head. They didn't seem like vampires, werewolves, zombies, ghosts, aliens, or anything else she could think of. That didn't mean they were angels, but she decided not to argue for the moment.

Jack said, "The only other plausible explanation—for now—is that it didn't happen the way you think it did. Which route should we pursue?"

"It's not just a simple dichotomy."

"I know, but we need a starting point. We can modify the theory as we get more info."

She bit back a sarcastic reply, realizing that his questioning meant that he would help her.

"Okay, we can go ahead assuming they're 'angels', but I'm not going to accept that. There's another answer, we just have to find it."

"Maybe we will. But at least we have a direction."

She leaned forward. "Jack . . . thank you for helping me. I know this must be hard right now. I really don't know why you're doing this."

"I'm not sure myself. I hated you for a long time, and I had all these things I was going to say if I ever saw you again. After I met my wife—and especially after my daughter, Lauren, was born—all my anger just left. Not right away, but eventually, and I realized I had . . . made mistakes. With them gone, I don't even know what to do. But I need to do something or I'll sit in my apartment with a gun in my hand, wondering why I don't just splatter my brains across the wall."

"Jack, I—"

"Let's just focus on your problem for now. I'll be fine."

She looked down. He wasn't fine, but there was nothing she could do about it.

"Okay, where do we start?" she asked.

"My place. I need to pick up a few things."

Chapter Twelve

Cerise followed him to his loft and waited in the car while he parked and went up. He came back down about fifteen minutes later with a big overnight bag over his shoulder. He'd also changed into jeans, t-shirt, and a beat up leather jacket that she thought she recognized. He put the bag in the backseat of the BMW and got into the passenger side.

"I can't believe you still have that jacket," she said. "How old is that thing?"

He smiled. "Old. And it's more surprising that it still fits, although I seem to remember it being a little looser when I first got it."

"I know the feeling." She glanced down at the clothes she had been wearing since last night, wishing that she could change. She hadn't gained any weight as far as she knew, but she couldn't deny that her body now was not the same as it was when she was twenty-five.

"So what now? I have no idea what to do or where to go," she asked.

"I think we should start with Russell's cell phone. Let's see if we can figure out where he is."

"How do we do that?"

"Stingray."

"What?"

"Head off to the freeway and I'll explain."

Three minutes later Cerise pulled the car onto the freeway and felt the BMW speed up to 75 with no problem whatsoever. Richard had been right; it was old, but it was still a BMW.

"So that thing can locate a cell phone?"

"It's called a Stingray, and yes it can, so long as the phone is on."

"I've never heard of anything like that before."

"Cops like to keep it quiet. They don't want perps to know they can be found via their cell phones or they might start turning them off."

"How does it work?"

"It basically tricks a cell phone into thinking it's a tower. Once I have the number, all I need to do is connect a laptop and triangulate the position. When we get closer to Raleigh you'll drive around and I'll try to find the phone."

"So how did you get one of those things?"

Jack smiled. "I've got some resources."

"Meaning it belongs to HMDL?"

"Not officially."

"So if you get caught with it, it's a personal item and not something associated with your company?"

"I can neither confirm nor deny."

Cerise glanced at the bag in the backseat for a second. "How much does one of these cost?"

"Probably more than your house."

Her eyebrows went up. "Would anyone really believe that you personally own this thing and that it's not on loan from your company?"

"Probably not, but that's why we have lawyers."

Jack opened his laptop as they passed Fredericksburg.

"Wouldn't the police have already tried finding Russell like this? He's a witness in a highly publicized triple murder, they've got to be doing everything they can to find him."

"Yeah, probably."

"Then wouldn't they have already found him?"

"It depends on where they looked. The Stingray doesn't have an unlimited range, so if they're looking in the wrong general area they won't find the phone. I'm hoping we'll get lucky."

"What are the chances that we can find it if the police haven't so far?"

Jack looked over at her with eyebrows raised. "Do you want the truth?"

She nodded.

"Slim to nil, but this is as good a starting point as we have so far."

"What if Russell's phone is off? Will the Stingray work if his phone isn't on?"

"No, it has to be on. If we don't pick up anything, we'll head to the crime scene and see if we can find out something there."

Cerise drove on, unwilling to break the silence while Jack continued to fiddle with his laptop.

They drove for a half hour without a word before Jack finally broke the silence.

"Can I see the picture of that fragment?" Jack asked. Cerise reached into her jacket pocket and handed over the printout she had used for translating.

Jack examined it, frowning. "Why would someone get killed over a scroll? Is it worth a lot of money?"

"It depends on what it says. If it has something of historic value, then maybe."

"How much would it be worth if that was the case?"

"A few years ago the Judas Gospel sold for somewhere in the vicinity of half a million initially, and resold for maybe two million, but it was one of the most revolutionary religious finds of all time. This would have to be something comparable to be worth money like that."

"Wasn't the Judas Gospel in National Geographic a few years ago?"

"Yeah, it was a big deal. Lots of major scholars were involved."

"What does it say that's so revolutionary?"

"It portrayed Judas as the reluctant hero of the Jesus narrative. The betrayal is part of the overall plan, and Judas is opposed to it. He finally agrees to it at Jesus' bidding because it will lead to the Crucifixion and Resurrection. Essentially, Judas is the lynch pin of the plan, and he is literally doing God's bidding."

"The plan included Jesus being nailed to a cross?"

"According to Judas. It makes sense if you consider God to be omniscient. Without Judas' betrayal, there's no Christianity."

"Did the Judas Gospel change anything?"

"Yes and no. We know a lot more about early Christianity because of it, but it's a non-canonical Gospel that we knew about before, we just didn't have a copy of the document. It was probably written later than the four

New Testament Gospels, and it tells us more about a sect of Christianity that didn't survive—the Gnostics—than it does about orthodox beliefs of the time."

"That sounds pretty significant to me. Why isn't it a bigger deal?"

"It *is* a big deal, but because the Judas Gospel is not part of the canon, it's not considered dogma. And because the date of its writing was later than the four Gospels in the New Testament, its insight into the historical Jesus story is suspect, to say the least. Like I said, it tells us a lot about the Gnostics, but its value otherwise is less clear."

"So you don't think anyone would be killed for something like that?"

"As far as I know no one *was* killed for the Judas Gospel, so no, I don't think so. The topic was really more esoteric than practical, and usually only scholars are interested in that kind of stuff."

"If there was a discovery that would be important enough to kill for, what might it be?"

Cerise considered it. "I suppose it would have to be something that would challenge orthodox belief in some legitimate way, but that would be highly unlikely to be discovered."

"Why?"

"Well, it's rare to find even partially intact documents from the ancient world as it is. To find something of that magnitude would be like finding one random sentence in the Library of Congress. The odds are just against it."

"How did you know about the Judas Gospel?"

"It's referenced in some old texts, but prior to around 1983 no one knew an actual copy existed."

"Are there any other documents like that? Ones that you know existed but don't have?"

"A few. The big one would probably be the Q Gospel. It's a hypothesized source for the first three Gospels."

"Hypothesized?"

"How familiar are you with the New Testament?"

"Only what I learned in Catechism and Sunday School."

"Do you remember the order of the Gospels?"

Jack paused for a minute, thinking. "Matthew, Mark, Luke, and John?"

"Yes. And that would lead you to believe that Matthew was written first, but Mark was actually the first of the four Gospels, followed by Matthew and Luke, and then John."

"How do you know the actual written order?"

"There's lots of evidence, but here's a basic piece. Mark has some problematic grammar and language in it. In places, it's just sort of . . . clunky. Matthew and Luke have many of the same stories, but the language in those stories is smoother. If Mark came later, why would the writer have made the language clunkier?"

"How does that tie in to the Q Gospel?"

"There are incredible similarities between Mark, Matthew, and Luke, things that can't be accounted for by just passing the same stories down by word of mouth."

"Like what?"

"Entire passages copied word for word from one Gospel to another."

"So whoever wrote one of the Gospels had to have access to a written copy of one of the others. I'm guessing that Mark was the source for one of the others."

"Probably, but there's a problem. Some passages in Matthew and other passages in Luke are copied verbatim from Mark, but those passages almost always differ from each other."

"Why does that matter?"

"If the writers of Matthew and Luke—separated by about twenty years—both had the Mark Gospel in front of them, why are hardly any passages copied from Mark the same between Matthew and Luke?"

"So maybe Luke had Matthew and Mark in front of him and didn't want to repeat stories from Mark that had already been told."

"But Matthew and Luke also have identical, word for word stories that don't appear in Mark. What's weird is that in each case, they appear in a different place in the narrative. It's like they had an extra source aside from Mark and just plugged in that material wherever each of them saw fit, since Mark didn't give them any indication about where they should go."

"So this extra source—"

"Is the hypothetical Q Gospel. It's likely a source for Matthew and Luke in addition to Mark. Nearly everything we find in Matthew and Luke from the Q Gospel is sayings attributed to Jesus, although we can't really know what else it might have contained."

"How do you even know it existed as a document? Couldn't it have been handed down orally?"

"How much agreement would you expect if these stories were strictly word of mouth over twenty years?"

"The basic gist would stay intact."

"Maybe. But in these cases, Matthew and Luke agree

nearly word for word. What are the chances of that happening unless there was a written document to copy from?"

Jack nodded. "So finding Q would be a big deal."

"Earth shattering, at least in religious and academic circles. I don't know what kind of effect—if any—it'd have outside of those domains. Probably not much, to be honest."

He held the paper up. "Could this fragment be part of the Q Gospel?"

She shrugged. "It could be anything, quite frankly. I just don't know enough to say. We could be looking at Jesus' autobiography for all I know."

He looked over at her strangely. "Jesus had an autobiography?"

She laughed. "Hyperbole. But that *would* be something people would kill for."

"It would've been hard to hold a quill after getting nails shoved into His hands."

"Very funny. But the author of an autobiography in the ancient world might not necessarily be the same person as the subject."

"Then how could it be an autobiography? Doesn't auto mean 'self'? If the 'self' didn't write it, isn't it just a normal biography?"

"Nowadays, sure. But people in the ancient world didn't have the same sense of truth that we do."

"What does that mean?"

"We tend to see truth in stark terms; either something happened or it didn't. That's an oversimplification, but you get the point. Nobody but the person himself could write an autobiography now.

"Historians in the ancient world, however, would accept oral stories about their subjects without questioning whether they were 'true' or not. The stories were true in a sense, and they didn't worry if the events didn't literally happen.

"Like Jesus feeding the multitudes with bread and fish. If you are only looking at the historical Jesus, the notion that he multiplied the food he had to feed all those people is absurd. However, the point of a story like that is partially to portray him as a provider to the masses, although the bread and fish could be considered symbolic. In that sense, the story is 'true' in that it shows Jesus' nature and his relationship to the people. An ancient historian wouldn't fret over whether it 'really' happened or not."

"So the document this fragment came from could be revolutionary."

"Maybe."

"Let's assume it at least has some information that these angels don't want us to know. So far, the people we know who came into contact with it are either dead or missing, is that right?"

"I guess so."

"If Russell is still alive, what might they want him for?"

She could tell that Jack thought he was probably dead, but she didn't want to think about that.

"I have no idea why angels would want a college professor."

"Humor me."

She sighed heavily, wishing they would pursue some other avenue. Jack knew damn well that she was an atheist;

she wondered if he was getting some kind of perverse pleasure from taunting her. But then she remembered why he was there with her and instantly felt guilty.

"Russell is probably the world's foremost Gnostic scholar, so maybe there's a connection there."

"Why might angels want a Gnostic scholar?"

She rubbed her forehead, thinking. "If the scroll is Gnostic, I guess they might want an expert in that area. But if they're angels, why would they need a human anything?"

"Maybe God isn't omniscient."

"Maybe God doesn't exist."

"Or maybe they're acting independently. Maybe they're rebels, like Satan."

She could barely stand to listen to this, but she kept her comments to herself. Indulging in the belief that God was real was bad enough, but the notion that Satan existed was beyond absurd. Not only was the devil a vague and changing concept in the Bible itself, it was so obviously a tool of the religious hierarchy that she couldn't understand how any educated person could believe it was real.

"I'd rather assume they were angels than demons."

"I'm not sure what we call them really matters. But back to the question: what use would they have for a Gnostic scholar? Could there be information in the scroll they need?"

"I suppose, but it's hard to believe they wouldn't know the language themselves."

"Would God need them to be able to read and write? Is there anything in the Bible about angels reading and writing?"

She had never thought about it before, and she couldn't

think of any instances where an angel read or wrote anything. That didn't mean there were none, but it would make sense. She couldn't come up with a reason why reading and writing would even exist in Heaven; there had to be more effective ways to communicate with God.

"It really depends on your concept of God and Heaven. Is Heaven an ideal Earth-like place like many people assume, or is it totally alien to our limited human understanding? If it's Earth-like, then reading might exist because language exists. If it's alien, then I would guess reading would be unnecessary. It would probably be more like instant telepathy; everything God thinks, people just know."

"Our angels seem like they probably belong to a more Earth-like place, don't you think?"

She didn't answer, but contained her eye-rolling.

"But you said they never made a sound when they attacked you, is that right?"

"They were totally quiet. And their expressions never changed, almost like their faces were carved from stone."

"Is it possible they might be mute?"

"If we're assuming angels are real, then I guess anything is possible. But if they're supposed to be messengers, then I would think they'd have to talk."

"Fair enough. So maybe they didn't talk because they didn't need to give you any information."

"Trashing my car and yanking me out by my hair was a pretty clear sign of what they wanted."

"Was it?"

She looked at him strangely. "Can you think of another reason they attacked me twice other than trying to kill me?"

"These angels are really powerful, right?"

She glanced at him sideways, wondering what he was getting at.

"If they really wanted to kill you, how come they didn't succeed?"

"Because I got away!"

"True, but think about how they might have killed you. One of them stopped your car while the other tried to pull you through the window. When you got out to the road, the one on the roof tried to lift you out."

"What's your point?"

"If it was me and I wanted to kill you, I could think of a lot of ways to do it other than trying to grab you or pull your hair."

"That doesn't mean that they weren't!"

"Think about it, Cerise. You're remembering the terror of the situation, but you know damn well that we tend to view things differently under extreme stress.

"Try to put yourself into an observer's point of view. If the angel on the roof wanted to kill you, why not just reach in a little further, grab your throat, and choke you to death? Or maybe just hit you really hard on the head? If he can punch through metal, he can sure as hell punch through your skull."

She wanted to argue, but couldn't think of a reasonable counterpoint.

"Later at Russell's house, they had no problem killing that detective—an armed, trained police officer—but they couldn't manage to get a lone, unarmed college professor? Does that really make sense?"

"But Detective Piedmont didn't know what to expect! I

knew what they could do, that's why I was able to get away."

"Do you really think beings with this kind of power—three of them, by the way—wouldn't be able to compensate for your awareness of them, at least the second time?"

"So if they didn't want to kill me, why were they after me?"

"For the same reason they came after Russell. To capture you."

Her eyes went wide with the realization that Russell might still be alive.

Chapter Thirteen

It was 5 am and they were halfway to Raleigh—just outside of Richmond—when the Stingray made a beeping noise.

"That's surprising," Jack said.

"What is it?"

"Looks like we got a reading."

Cerise's eyes were wide. "Does that mean you know where Russell's phone is?"

"Not yet. We need two more pings to triangulate a position."

"So what do we do?"

"Just keep driving. We'll probably hear another one soon."

Within the next ten minutes there were two more pings.

"Did you find it?" Cerise could barely keep her eyes on the road.

"Just worry about driving. I'll worry about this."

Jack fiddled with the laptop for a minute or two before smiling. "I think we found it. Take the next exit and go north."

Once they got off the freeway, Jack directed her to the parking lot of a strip mall.

"Is it here?"

"No, but I want to show you the map before we get there. It's about ten miles further up. Here, take a look."

He showed her the map on his laptop. There was an icon indicating where the phone was.

"It's there?"

"Yeah."

"So what now? Do we call the police?"

"Wait. Look at the street view."

The image changed to a view of a large building that she instantly recognized.

"That's a Catholic church."

"Yep."

"Why would Russell be in a church?"

"We don't know if he's there at all. All we know is that's where the phone is."

"So what does that mean? Whoever kidnapped him is in church right now?"

Jack shrugged. "Maybe. It's worth a look." He called up the church's website. "We're in luck; there's an early Saturday mass going on right now. We can blend in with the crowd and stay pretty much unnoticed."

"Shouldn't we call the police?"

"Maybe. But there's a risk that they might not find the phone and whoever has it. They probably won't go in with any kind of stealth, and then our link to Russell will be gone. Anyway, it'd be hard for the police to find that one phone in a crowd."

"What do you think we should do?"

"Let's go there first and check it out. That way we'll be able to give the police additional information when we finally call them, and maybe they'll have a leg up on finding the phone and whoever has it."

Cerise frowned. "What if we go in and someone recognizes me?"

"I don't think we'll see a lot of naked guys in there."

"Don't be a smart ass. It's possible that someone might be working with them or in charge of them. We could still be dealing with a cult, and cults have leaders."

"For one thing, no one is expecting you, but it's easy to disguise you a bit. Besides, you'll be with me and no one knows who I am. If it looks like there might be a problem, we'll cut out and call the police, but it's your decision. I'll do whatever you want."

Cerise stared at the laptop screen. Why was the phone at a church? It seemed the least likely place for Russell to be. But Jack was right that it might just be his phone. So whoever had the phone was probably involved with the attacks, but what would they be doing at a church at mass? Attending services?

"Let's go check it out. But please promise me that nothing will go wrong."

He half-smiled. "This is what I do for a living, Cerise. I promise we'll be careful."

"Okay. Before we go let me make a call." She pulled her phone out of her pocket and began scrolling through the contacts.

"To who?"

"I want to check on Richard and see how he's doing with Amanda."

The phone rang five times before it was answered.

"Hello?" It was a woman's voice, shaky and weak.

Maureen Burgoyne.

"Maureen, it's Cerise Davenport. Can I talk to Richard?"

There was a stifled cry, then someone else got on the line.

"Who is this?" It sounded like a young man's voice. Daniel Burgoyne, Richard's son, was seventeen. Cerise had only met him a couple times, but she thought it was him.

"Is this Daniel?"

"Who is this?" He sounded angry and impatient.

"It's Cerise Davenport. I work with—"

"I know who you are." His voice hadn't warmed up. "If you're looking for my dad, you're too late."

She didn't want to prolong the conversation any longer than she had to. Daniel was obviously furious about something, and she didn't want to poke her nose where it didn't belong.

"When he comes back, would you just tell him that I called?"

There was a pause on the line, and Cerise imagined him scowling on the other end. She was about to tell him never mind when he finally spoke.

"My dad is dead. He was murdered last night."

Her hand went to her mouth and her eyes went wide. "Oh my god! How . . . ?"

"On our front lawn. He was ripped apart." He paused, the rage in his voice just barely contained. "Is there something else you want?"

She didn't know how to ask, but she needed to know if Amanda was okay.

"I'm so sorry, but I . . . I need to know if Amanda is all

right."

"What?"

"Amanda—the little girl your dad was watching for me. Is she all right?"

There was no response.

"Daniel? Are you there?"

"I don't know what the fuck you're talking about. There's no little girl here."

She nearly dropped the phone, her eyes wide and her face pale. "I'm so sorry for your family," she managed weakly before hanging up. She turned back to Jack, who was staring at her with intense concern.

"What is it?"

"Richard Burgoyne—my friend—he was killed last night."

"What about Amanda?"

"She's not there. Richard's son didn't see any little girl."

Jack put his arm around her shoulder. "She could be fine. Don't jump to any conclusions."

"It has to be related, doesn't it?" She strained to fight back tears. "Daniel said that his dad was ripped apart. Just like Detective Piedmont. Please tell me these angels wouldn't hurt her."

"We don't even know if they have her. She might have run off on her own. I'll send an anonymous message to the police to be on the lookout for her. That will at least get things rolling, and maybe she'll turn up hiding in somebody's shed or something, completely unharmed. If she could get away from a sheriff's office without anyone knowing, she could get away from anybody."

Hot tears flowed down her face. "Why is this

happening, Jack?"

"I wish I could tell you. But listen, if they just wanted to kill her they would've done it already. I think it makes more sense that they want to capture her, not kill her."

"Sense? We're talking about fucking angels! None of this makes sense!"

He took her hand. "I know it's upsetting, but I promise you we'll do whatever we can to find her."

Her temper abated and she wiped her face with her hands. "Why would they even want a little girl?"

"I don't know, but we'll find her. She's somewhere, and whoever has the phone will be able to fill in some of the blanks, I'm sure of it."

Cerise sighed heavily and sunk down into the seat, her face in her hands. "This feels impossible."

"I know it does, but that doesn't mean it is. Think of it like a dissertation; one step at a time till the thing is done."

She nodded. It was hard to put aside her fear for Russell—and now Amanda—but Jack was right; it wasn't something they could solve all at once. She'd have to be patient. Panicking and sobbing wouldn't get them any closer.

"Are you okay to keep driving?" Jack said.

She wiped her face and nodded.

"Let's head to the church. We don't want to miss the service or we'll have to try to find the phone again, and whoever has it might shut it off. Or the battery could die, and then we'd really be out of luck."

"How will we know who has the phone? There might be a lot of people there."

Jack grinned. "We'll just have to call it and embarrass

the hell out of somebody."

They pulled up to the St Michael the Archangel Parish about halfway through mass. The church was a towering, red-bricked, vertical structure that looked like it might have been built in the early 1900s. A massive cross at least fifteen feet tall topped the building just above the rose window. It was enveloped in scaffolding, probably to repair the cracks in its decaying edifice.

They approached the large wooden doors and paused.

"What are we going to do exactly?" Cerise pulled down the sunglasses Jack had given her to help her stay unnoticed. She had also put her hair up, although neither one of them could do much about the fact that they were dressed in casual clothes and were likely to stick out in a congregation of well-dressed church-goers.

"We sit down in the back, call Russell's number, and hope we can identify the person who has the phone before they shut it off. My guess is they'll be fairly obvious considering the circumstances of the phone; nervous or agitated at least."

"My name will come up on Russell's phone when we call. Is that a good idea?"

"We'll use my phone. All that will show up is the number."

"So if the phone rings, what then? Do we call the police?"

"Yeah, I think that's a good bet. But we'll need to keep an eye on this person in case he—or she, I suppose—leaves."

"What if they see us?"

"We'll make sure they don't."

"That's not much of a plan."

Jack smirked. "Trust me."

She narrowed her eyes. "So you sneak around in churches and try not to be seen? Is that what you do for a living?"

"Glad to see you still have the sharp tongue. But to answer your question, it's not what I do on a daily basis, but yes, I have done covert work."

"If they do see us—on the off-chance—what then? I mean, what if they have guns or something?"

"I don't think that's likely. But even if they do, they'll be more focused on getting away quietly than making a huge scene that will draw the police." He put a hand up to stifle her objection. "If a gun comes out, I'm prepared." He tapped his jacket just under his left arm.

"You brought your gun?"

"Would you rather I'd left it behind?"

"I think I would on principle. But I guess I'm glad you have it at the moment."

Jack grabbed the door handle, but Cerise reached out and stopped him from opening the door.

"What if those angels are there? Not in the congregation, but maybe somewhere in back?"

He patted his jacket where his pistol was holstered.

"I can't believe I'm asking this, but if they really are angels, do you think your gun will do anything to them?"

"Cerise, they're not really angels."

Her face fell for a moment, but he held his hand up and continued.

"I don't know *what* we're dealing with here, but angels

is probably the best way to describe them for now, especially since that's what the girl called them. But even if they're unnaturally strong, they're still made of flesh and bone, and I've seen what hollow-point bullets do to flesh and bone. It'll stop them. I guarantee it."

"I saw a detective shoot them, Jack. They didn't even flinch."

"Then he missed." He held up his hand to forestall her argument. "It was dark, wasn't it?"

She nodded.

"Despite what they show on TV, it's not that easy to hit someone with a handgun, especially in the dark. And it's even harder when your adrenaline is pumping. He missed them, Cerise, but in the heat of the moment, you couldn't tell the difference. I guarantee it."

The look on his face convinced her, and she was relieved to hear him say that he didn't really believe they were angels. He was going along with this incredible story too easily, and maybe he thought she was crazy and was just humoring her.

Whatever the case, there was no turning back at this point. If she didn't hallucinate the whole thing—and she was certain that she hadn't—some answers might be inside this church.

"Ready to do this?" Jack said.

"I'm ready. I just hope we aren't too noticeable when we head in."

Cerise grabbed the door handle and pulled. The unique mixture of furniture polish and mildew greeted them as they stepped inside. They could hear the muffled sound of someone speaking from the sanctuary, followed by the louder, mumbled response from the congregation.

The sanctuary was large and the pews were half filled, with those at the back empty. A priest was at the lectern, his voice projected on speakers strategically positioned above. Cerise and Jack slid into an empty pew on the far left side.

Cerise leaned over and whispered, "Are you going to call now?"

Jack didn't answer, instead scanning the congregation. After about five minutes, the priest called for a silent prayer and Jack pulled out his phone. He dialed the number and hit the send button, and Cerise held her breath, dreading and anticipating a ring tone in the empty space of the sanctuary.

Minutes later, the priest ended the prayer. Neither one of them heard any ringing.

Cerise leaned over and whispered, "What now?"

"We'll try it again."

As the service neared closing, there was another moment of silent prayer. Jack tried the phone again. They both strained to hear the faintest sound while scanning the pews for any sign that someone might be reaching for a vibrating phone. Then the priest began talking again, and neither of them had any idea who might have the phone.

When rows began to be called up for the Eucharist, they slipped quietly out and walked about thirty feet away, just off to the side of the church.

"Is there some other way we can tell where the phone is?" she asked, already knowing the answer.

"Aside from checking every person in there, not really."

Cerise's shoulders sagged. "What do we do? The service is nearly over."

"We don't panic, for one thing. The ringer might have been turned off for church, and it's possible that it'll get turned back on again when the congregation leaves. We'll try again as people are heading out, and it will probably be easier to spy potential targets."

"How are we supposed to do that?"

"For starters, ignore the women. Chances are that a man has the phone."

"Chances are? That's a hell of a risk to take. What if you're wrong?"

"Dammit, Cerise, I'm not a miracle worker! But if I was looking for a security risk and I had no idea who it might be, I'd use known profiles to narrow my search. One of those profiles would say that the perp is in all likelihood a male. Yes, there's a risk that it isn't, but we can't possibly cover all bases."

She unfolded her arms. "All right. So we ignore the women. That still leaves a lot of—"

She was interrupted by her phone ringing. She pulled it out of her pocket and gasped when she saw the screen.

"It's from Russell!" She held the screen up so Jack could see it. "What do I do?"

"Answer it! I'll listen in." She held it up to her ear, but Jack gently grabbed her hand before she could press the button. "It might not be him."

She nodded and put the phone back up to her ear.

"Hello?"

There was a pause on the line before a weak voice said, "Cerise? It's me."

She glanced at Jack, her eyes wide. "Russell! Are you all right?"

"I'm . . . fine. I need to see you. Can you meet me somewhere?"

"What the hell is going on? Where have you been, and why haven't you answered your phone?"

"I can't explain right now, but I'll tell you everything when I see you. Are you home?"

Jack pulled his head away from the phone and nodded quickly.

"Yes. I just got up a little while ago." That would have been true on a normal Saturday.

"I need you to drive to Richmond. There's a church there—St Michael the Archangel. Can you meet me there at noon?"

Jack nodded again.

"Yes, I can be there. Are you in some kind of trouble?"

"No, everything is fine. I'll explain when you get here."

The line disconnected and Cerise pulled the phone away from her face, her forehead creased with worry.

"We've got about five hours," Jack said. "Let's go somewhere and figure out a plan."

Chapter Fourteen

Cerise shuddered as the thick wooden door closed behind her. The sanctuary felt colder than when she and Jack were there earlier, and she wondered if it was the lack of warm bodies or only her imagination. Jack was in a pew off to the side, head down in fake prayer. He'd gone into the church an hour ago to investigate under the guise of praying, while she'd sat in the car, anxious about what would happen.

She avoided looking at him, trying to pretend he was just some guy in a church that she didn't know, but she couldn't completely resist glancing over as she passed. He kept his head down and his eyes closed, apparently oblivious of her presence, although she doubted that was really true.

She passed an old man walking the opposite way down the aisle and sat in the front by the altar. She glanced around, her stomach fluttering nonstop. There were two older women praying in nearby pews, but neither paid her any attention.

Her watch said 11:59. Russell was never late, so she thought he would show up any second. She heard the thud of the front door shutting and turned around, but there was no one there. She turned back around and felt her heart jump suddenly.

Russell stood near the doorway leading to the back of the church. She stood up as he walked over, wrapping her arms around him. He returned the hug stiffly before pulling away and guiding her down to the pew. He held her hands and looked around nervously before meeting her gaze.

Cerise pulled a hand free to wipe away tears. "Are you all right?"

"I'm fine. Just a little tired. I've been working on something."

She shot him a strange look. "Working on something? You make it sound like you were on a retreat. Everyone was under the impression that you were either kidnapped or dead."

"I . . . it's complicated, and I can't really speak freely right now."

She folded her arms. "Why can't you speak freely? You need to tell me what's been going on. Why didn't you answer any of my calls?" Her relief was quickly turning to anger.

"I'm sorry. I was working on something extremely important, and I couldn't get away from it. There were . . . circumstances that I couldn't control."

"Like what? What was so goddamn important that you couldn't even let me know you weren't dead?"

He put a conciliatory hand on her knee and she fought back the impulse to push it off.

"Cerise, this scroll that I've been translating . . . it's the most important ancient document I've ever seen. I can't even begin to tell you how—"

He stopped suddenly and glanced over to the doorway from where he had emerged. The priest who had delivered the sermon stood there staring at them a few seconds before stepping back out of sight.

Cerise asked, "What was that about?"

"I need you to meet someone." He stood, trying to pull her up with him.

She pulled her hands away and folded her arms. "I'm not doing anything until you tell me what the hell is going on!"

"Cerise, please. I promise that everything will make sense if you just come with me."

"Dammit, Russell! I deserve an explanation for what you've put me through! People are trying to kill me, and I think it has to do with this scroll and whatever else you're mixed up with!"

He sat down next to her and took off his glasses.

"Cerise, you're safe now. I promise."

"Fine. If I'm safe, then you won't mind telling me what's going on."

He glanced nervously back to the doorway. "I can't explain everything, but Father Lakaj can. He's just back there in his office. If you could—"

"He can come here and talk to me. I'm not going anywhere."

Russell opened his mouth but didn't say anything. He put his glasses back on and frowned.

"You're not being reasonable."

"I don't care about being reasonable right now. You have no idea what I've been through, in addition to being terrified that you were dead. But instead of telling me what's going on, you're playing this secretive game. You want me to meet this priest? Fine. I'll meet him right here and you two can tell me the whole story. And then we can call the police so you can tell them what you know about those murders."

"No! You can't call the police!"

"Why not?"

He looked flustered and terrified at the same time; she had never seen him like this.

After long seconds of indecisiveness, he finally sighed. "All right. I'll bring Father Lakaj out. Will you stay here?"

"Are you kidding?"

He nodded before heading back through the doorway.

Once he was out of sight, Cerise turned around and looked over at Jack. He was in the same place, his head still down. She caught the two old women looking in her direction, but they quickly averted their eyes. She turned back around, positive that Jack had heard everything Russell said. She wanted to talk to him and ask him what he thought, but that would have to wait.

After a few minutes Russell walked back through the doorway, the priest from before right behind him, his mouth set in a thin line.

She stood up as they approached.

Russell said, "Cerise, this is Father Miklos Lakaj." He turned to the priest. "Father, Professor Cerise Davenport."

He held out his hand and Cerise took it briefly.

"Dr Davenport, it's a pleasure to meet you." He had a faint accent, Eastern European she thought. "Dr Kellar has told me about your expertise with Aramaic translations."

She shot a look at Russell and his eyes widened for the

briefest of seconds. She had no idea why Russell would tell anyone that she was an expert in Aramaic. Given a stack of reference books and plenty of time, she might be able to provide a rough translation of a document, but nothing definitive.

"I don't mean to be rude, but why is Dr Kellar telling you anything about me?"

He smiled in response, but it didn't touch his eyes.

"It would be best if we could talk in my office. What I need to share with you is very sensitive, and it would not be helpful to have this information out before it is properly vetted."

"Vetted? You make it sound like this is top secret."

"I don't want to sound melodramatic, Dr Davenport, but it *is* 'top secret', although it is not a government concern."

"So it's a church secret?"

Father Lakaj gestured back towards the doorway. "Please, if we could discuss it in my office?"

Cerise bit her lip. What was so important about that scroll that it needed to be treated like a state secret? She thought of what she had read about the translation of the Judas Gospel. Those scholars would most certainly have been this secretive before the document was fully translated. Lakaj and Russell were probably just being overly cautious. Probably.

But what would Jack do once she was out of his sight? Would he duck out and call the police? Wait until she got back? Listen at the door of the office? She had no idea, and she wished she could talk to him before deciding what to do.

"All right. We can talk in your office."

She let Father Lakaj lead her through the doorway, fighting the impulse to look back at Jack.

Father Lakaj's modest office had a small couch, and Cerise was surprised to see someone sitting there already. She was even more surprised when she noticed he was wearing a large pectoral cross and had an Episcopal ring on his finger. He smiled and stood up when Cerise entered.

"Father Lakaj, I assume this is Dr Davenport?"

"Yes, Most Reverend. As you requested."

"Wonderful." He extended his hand to Cerise, and she took it hesitantly, eyes narrowed in confusion. "I am Bishop Flagello of the Diocese of Richmond. It's a pleasure to meet you. We have much to discuss."

He was about Cerise's height, but broad and strong-looking with thinning white hair and a ruddy complexion. He smiled at her warmly like a large, friendly uncle.

Her Catholic upbringing surfaced and she felt instantly awed, but stifled it with some success. "Thank you, Most Reverend. I'm . . . a little confused about what we have to discuss, however."

Father Lakaj shut the door of the office and gestured for Cerise and Russell to sit in the two chairs opposite the couch, while he remained standing. Bishop Flagello eased back down onto the couch.

"Please, call me Father Flagello. 'Most Reverend' is so cumbersome in informal conversation. You are Catholic, Dr Davenport?"

"I was raised Catholic." She felt uncomfortable insinuating that she no longer believed, and it annoyed her that her childhood indoctrination still had such sway.

"And now you no longer consider yourself part of the flock?"

She had been questioned like this before, usually by some holier-than-thou who wanted to point out the error of her ways. She never had any qualms about putting them in their place, and it was never difficult considering she knew more about the Bible and Christianity than any layperson— or most clerics, for that matter. But now, face to face with Bishop Flagello in these particular circumstances, she couldn't overcome the feeling of intimidation.

"No. I haven't considered myself Catholic for a long time."

He nodded, his hand on his chin, as if he knew something she didn't. "And yet you became a religious scholar. It's not such a distance from your beginnings, is it?"

"Father, I don't really—"

"Forgive me, Dr Davenport. I don't mean to question your personal decisions. Your faith is between yourself and God, not me."

Cerise glanced over at Russell. He stared down at the floor and held his hands in his lap, looking for all the world like a little boy who'd been caught with his hand in the cookie jar.

"I'm confused about this whole series of events, Father. Could you tell me why exactly Dr Kellar and I are here?"

Flagello nodded slowly. "Of course. Dr Kellar is here because of his expertise with scrolls of this type. I believe he sent you a picture of part of the scroll."

Cerise saw no need to answer.

"Were you able to translate it?"

She caught Russell's movement out of the corner of her

eye, but avoided looking at him. He had told Lakaj that she was an expert in Aramaic, and that meant that Flagello probably thought the same thing. Regardless of how furious she was at Russell, she still trusted him more than either of these men. He had lied to them for some reason, and she didn't think it was the best idea to let them know that just yet.

"I didn't have time to look at it more than a few minutes here and there."

"And were you able to make out anything in these brief glimpses?"

"Father, forgive me, but it seems like you're trying to test me. From what I understand, Dr Kellar has been translating this scroll under your auspices. I think you know better than I do what it contains."

Flagello laughed. "Dr Kellar told me that you are frank, and I see that he didn't exaggerate. Very well. You know of the Q Gospel?"

"Only through inference, like everyone else."

"Dr Kellar thinks we have found it. And what's more significant is that we know the author."

She looked over at Russell. Despite his obvious anxiety, she could see a glint of excitement in his eyes. None of the three men said anything, and Cerise was left with the clear impression that the bishop was building up to a big reveal.

"I'll bite," she said. "Who's the author?"

"It was written by Yeshua of Nazareth, Dr Davenport. We have discovered the Gospel of Jesus Christ, written in His own hand."

Cerise narrowed her eyes. "That seems highly unlikely."

Flagello chuckled. "Of course it is your job to be skeptical. But I am certain that once you hear the evidence you will realize the truth, as your colleague has."

She turned to Russell. "Well? Is that true?"

He nodded. "I know it's hard to believe, but yes, it's true. The scroll was written by Yeshua of Nazareth."

Cerise wanted to smack him. He knew as well as she that a determination about the authorship of this or nearly any other ancient document could only be made after months of study by multiple scholars. Even if the author claimed to be Yeshua—an extremely common Hebrew name of the time—there was no corroborating evidence that supported it. Russell Kellar was one of the most skeptical men she knew; why the hell was he blithely accepting this conclusion? What kind of hold did this priest have on him?

"At the very least, it's unsubstantiated," she said. "Just because the author claims to be Yeshua doesn't mean it's *the* Yeshua. How many Yeshuas might there have been in Nazareth, anyway? Besides, the only autobiography Jesus could have written would have ended before he was crucified. That would mean he knew that he would be arrested, and he would have had to start writing it way before then. But if this text includes Q Gospel material, like in Matthew when Jesus spoke to the Pharisees, then the time frame would be way off. So did Jesus just go home and write everything down at the end of each day? He was kind of busy, especially towards the end."

Flagello said, "Unless He wrote it after His Resurrection."

Cerise stared him in the eye. "With all due respect, Most Reverend, that is utter nonsense. If the author claims that it was written after the Crucifixion, then it can't have been written by Jesus, and I have a hard time believing that you would be taken in by such a blatant ploy. At any rate, dating the scroll would prove it. It would have to have been written after Mark, at least, and probably even later."

"I like your skepticism. A scholar should doubt and question. But we have evidence that the scroll was written no later than 40 AD."

"That's impossible."

"No, Cerise, it's not," Russell said. "I've seen the report. The methodology is solid and the conclusions are supported."

Cerise frowned. "You're saying that this was written before any of the known Gospels, that the author was Jesus himself, and that it's the Q Gospel? To say the least, that is a lot to swallow, Russell."

"You think I don't know that? But I've been working on the scroll nonstop since I got here, and everything I've found supports this thesis."

Cerise didn't know what to say. It was absurd that Russell was buying into this nonsense.

"So why am I here, exactly?" she asked.

Russell said, "I want you to help me continue the translation of the scroll."

Cerise narrowed her eyes at him. "You want me to help translate the scroll?"

Flagello answered. "Of course. It would be an opportunity that any scholar of your caliber would seize. We offer you this opportunity based on Dr Kellar's recommendation. He thinks very highly of you."

She couldn't deny that she was tempted, even if she

thought the claims were irrational.

"You got this scroll from a smuggler named Farouk, right?"

Flagello's smile faltered the slightest bit. "He did have possession of it, yes."

"And now he's dead and you have the scroll."

"I understand how this looks, but I assure you that we had nothing to do with that."

She turned to Russell. "How did you get here, Dr Kellar?"

He looked startled. "What do you mean?"

"How did you get away from the killer at the hotel and end up here?"

Lakaj spoke up. "I picked Dr Kellar up from the hotel. He was frightened from the trauma and he called me. I brought him here."

"How did you know he would be there? For that matter, how do you even know Dr Kellar at all?"

"Bishop Flagello is my sponsor, Cerise," Russell said. "He told me about the scroll and Farouk. I went there specifically to get this scroll."

"So it's just a coincidence that Farouk got murdered when you were there?"

"Why would we have Farouk murdered when we were about to acquire the scroll from him?" Flagello asked.

Cerise had to admit that it didn't make sense, but she didn't trust him or Lakaj.

"Why not go to the police, then? They've been looking for Dr Kellar, and he might have information that could help find the killer."

Flagello said, "The police would take the scroll as

evidence. Such a document cannot be trusted in their hands, I'm sure you'll agree."

He was right. She would never trust the police to take proper care of an ancient document. They just didn't have the expertise to handle something so fragile. The risk of it being irrevocably damaged would be too great.

"So you want Dr Kellar and I to continue translating the scroll here, I assume?"

"Yes," Flagello said. "There is an extensive library here, and I can get any materials you need to examine it more thoroughly. We would open it to more scholarly investigation after some details can be verified to our satisfaction."

"Why not do that now? A few phone calls and we can get a room full of scholars examining this thing."

"We wish to be discreet at the moment. Rest assured, the document will be released in due time. What do you say, Dr Davenport? Will you remain here and assist?"

Cerise looked from Flagello to Lakaj and then to Russell. She couldn't read the expression on his face, but it didn't look like encouragement. More like pleading.

She stood up. "No. I don't want to be involved with this."

She walked to the door of the office. Father Lakaj stood in front of it. Instead of moving out of the way, he looked over to Bishop Flagello. The older man nodded and Lakaj stepped aside.

"Cerise," Russell said.

She turned, her hand on the doorknob.

"Please don't leave," he said.

She narrowed her eyes at him and walked out of the

office.

Cerise caught sight of Jack walking back into the sanctuary as she exited the office. He'd obviously been nearby, maybe listening in on the conversation. She'd ask him what he thought later, but she had no doubt that he agreed with her decision to leave.

What was Russell thinking getting involved with these people? She didn't think Flagello was lying about being involved with the murders—what kind of priest sent an assassin after people?—but there was clearly something strange going on and she wanted no part of it. Couldn't Russell see that? Maybe he did, but his ambition to be involved with this scroll was blinding him. Or maybe he was being forced.

Whatever the case, she'd let the police sort it out. Russell would come to his senses after he was pulled out of this mess, and even though she didn't like it, she'd trust them to make sure the scroll was properly taken care of. Maybe she'd try to make that a condition for providing them with information. She'd ask Jack if that might work and go from there.

Right now she just wanted to get the hell away from this place. She couldn't believe that Russell had let her think he might be dead or in serious trouble when he had been at this fucking church the whole time. Why couldn't he just call and let her know he was okay? She blinked back tears of anger and stormed out to the sanctuary.

Jack was sitting a few rows back, no longer pretending to be praying but instead looking up at the features of the sanctuary. Or at least making it look like he was.

She walked past him with a quick glance in his direction, enough to let him know that she was leaving. Once she was out the front door he'd follow soon after, and they could discuss involving the police.

She got halfway through the sanctuary before the outside door opened.

She froze and stepped back, shaking her head in disbelief as three angels walked inside.

Cerise turned around and looked for Jack. He was in the aisle already, about twenty feet behind her. His pistol was out, and he was pointing it in their direction.

The two old women near the front stood and gasped.

Bishop Flagello's voice came from the open doorway at the rear. "There's no need for that. They are not here to hurt anyone."

Cerise turned and felt another shock when she saw Flagello flanked by three more angels; all six naked, sexless, and more similar in appearance than identical twins. She backed away until she was next to Jack.

Jack leveled his gun at the angels and the bishop while glancing back to check on the three that had just entered. "I can probably shoot all seven of you in about three seconds. And that's what I'm going to do if any of you come closer."

"It won't do you any good," Flagello said.

"I'm not kidding. I will shoot all of you if I have to." He pointed the gun back at the angels in the front of the church. "You three get away from the door."

They stared ahead blankly but didn't move.

The old women stood there clutching their purses, jaws agape in pure terror. They had no idea what to do.

"Dr Davenport, please have your friend put his gun

away before someone gets hurt," the bishop said.

"You aren't going to get another warning," Jack said to the three at the front. "I will not hesitate to shoot you."

Cerise didn't know if she was more scared of the angels or Jack. She had seen that look on his face before, the night he put Chris Clarents in the hospital. And now he was the only thing standing between her and the lunatics who had tried to kill her twice.

She turned to the bishop. "Please, just tell them to back away. We don't want anyone to get hurt."

"The only one who will be hurt is your friend, Dr Davenport. If you value his life, persuade him to put his gun down. Otherwise, I can't be held responsible for what they do to him."

Under his breath, Jack said, "Whatever happens, get out of here and call the police."

"Jack, you don't know what they can do."

"They're not supermen, Cerise. They can't stop bullets."

"I saw one of them shot six times and nothing happened."

"The bullets missed. They're made of flesh and blood. Whatever they are, they can be killed."

"Jack—"

He cut her off with a look before turning to the angels in the front and saying, "We are heading out the front door. If any of you get in our way, you will be shot."

Jack was probably right. Piedmont had missed at Russell's house, and the terror she felt at the time made her misinterpret what had really happened. Maybe she had been wrong about the number of shots, as well. Besides, she had stopped one of them with pepper spray to the face. If they could be hurt by pepper spray, then bullets would cause a lot more damage, wouldn't they?

Jack guided her forward with his free hand on the small of her back. She looked at the bishop once, fear clawing at her insides. He nodded, but not to her, and she turned back around to face the angels in the front.

They moved forward suddenly, and a deafening shot exploded near her ear and reverberated throughout the sanctuary. She cried out, shocked at how loud the gun was.

The old women screamed.

Two of the angels still stood, but another had fallen backwards, a small hole in the center of his forehead. The two stared down at him, their eyebrows lowered and their mouths half open. More than anything they looked confused, the first time Cerise had seen any expression from them. Their faces changed when they looked up, transforming into masks of pure rage.

"Back away now," Jack said, his voice filled with menace.

Cerise glanced at the bishop. He also looked confused, as did the three angels flanking him.

There was movement out of the corner of her eye followed by two more shots. She looked back to see another angel on the floor in the aisle. The remaining angel tackled Jack and knocked him to the ground. The three near the bishop moved forward as well.

"Don't kill him!" the bishop yelled.

The angel on top of Jack had one hand around his throat and the other cocked back to strike, his fingers elongated and tapered to points, as if each finger had become a slender dagger. Before his hand could descend,

Jack shoved the muzzle of the gun in his face and pulled the trigger twice. Cerise screamed as the angel fell, a gaping hole in the back of his head.

Jack rolled to the side and sprang up, already leveling the pistol at another angel speeding towards him. The other two had stepped in front of the bishop in a protective posture.

Cerise was shoved out of the way as the angel rushed past her and grabbed hold of Jack's forearm, yanking it before he could pull the trigger. There was an audible snap followed by a scream of agony, and Cerise felt sick as she saw Jack's arm dangling unnaturally. The gun fell to the floor, and the angel tossed Jack aside like a rag doll. He cried out again as his broken arm hit the floor.

The angel bent down and picked up the gun, momentarily locking eyes with Cerise in the process, then he turned and walked back to the bishop, handing him the pistol.

Cerise got up and ran over to Jack. He had managed to sit up and he was cradling his broken arm against his chest, jaw clenched and face contorted in pain. The jagged edge of one of the bones of his forearm was sticking out about an inch from the skin, and Cerise felt a wave of nausea when she saw it.

She winced and tried to look away from it as much as possible while still keeping her gaze on him.

"We have to get you to a hospital."

He managed to hiss out, "I don't think we're going to get the chance."

She turned and saw the bishop standing only a few feet away, one of the angels next to him. The other two were moving towards the still screaming old women.

The bishop held the gun in his hand as if it was something vile and unholy.

"How did you do that?" he asked Jack.

Jack's expression was a mixture of pain, rage, and confusion. "How did I do what, you sick fuck?"

Flagello ignored the taunt. "How did you kill them?" His voice was filled with sorrow and confusion.

Jack's face contorted further, as if he was speaking to a complete imbecile. "Are you fucking serious?"

"Where did you get this . . . thing?" Flagello held out the gun, obviously repulsed to be touching it.

"He needs an ambulance!" Cerise said.

Flagello looked at her as if he had just noticed she was there. "He killed them." He said it as if the fact of their deaths was just sinking in.

"They attacked us! He warned them to stay back!"

"Dr Davenport, you have no idea what your friend has done."

"Please, he needs an ambulance!"

Flagello turned to the angel next to him. "Take her to the library."

The angel moved forward and grabbed Cerise by the arm. She tried to pull away but his grip was iron. He lifted her up like she was weightless and dragged her away.

The old women stopped screaming. As she was being carried away she saw the two angels with their hands around their necks. The last thing she saw was Bishop Flagello standing over Jack with the gun in his hand.

Chapter Fifteen

The room was large and lined with bookshelves, each one filled, and the musty smell of old books hung in the air. A long wooden table covered by a thin white cloth was set up in the center of the room. An array of instruments for examining ancient documents were laid out on top of it, and an ancient scroll was partially unrolled in the middle.

Cerise glanced over at the angel who had brought her. He stood in front of the door and stared blankly ahead. She didn't think it would take much to goad him into action, however, and she cringed at the fresh memory of what had happened in the sanctuary.

"How long are you going to keep me here?" she asked.

He didn't respond or react, instead continuing to stare as if she hadn't spoken.

She fought the urge to look away. He didn't seem to care if she stared at him, and she would need as much information as possible if she got the chance to call the police. Her cell phone was still in her pocket, and she hoped she might get an opportunity to use it, although she didn't want to do anything to alert him that she had one.

She took a step closer to the angel, her eyes taking in every detail. He was both strikingly beautiful and repulsive at the same time. When she had seen them before it hadn't been hard to note the lack of genitals or the pale white skin and expressionless faces, but having one stand completely still only a dozen feet away made it much easier to examine his features.

The most obvious detail—aside from the missing genitalia—was the complete lack of any body hair other than what was on his head. She saw no evidence of chest, arm or leg hair, and his pubic area was completely bald. There was no sign of stubble, so it didn't look as though it had been shaved. The lack of pubic hair allowed her to see the area where the genitals should be.

Except she saw no evidence of scars or wounds of any sort. The area was smooth and unblemished, as if he had been born that way. For a split-second she wondered if he might actually be a female, but she quickly dismissed that idea. There was no evidence of *any* kind of genitalia, male or female. She had a sudden urge to ask him how he urinated, but she was afraid there might be a limit to his unnatural passivity.

She clenched her jaw. She had thought finding Russell would provide answers. Instead, Jack was probably dead and she was being held prisoner in the musty library of a church rectory. She didn't even want to think about where Amanda might be, and the thought that she might be responsible for Richard's murder was like a millstone around her neck.

The angel suddenly stepped forward and she tensed, wondering what he was going to do. She took a step back and looked around for something she could use as a weapon, while at the same time recognizing the futility of such a gesture.

Instead, he turned and opened the door. Russell entered, followed closely by Bishop Flagello. Flagello nodded to the angel and he left, closing the door behind him. Russell stood next to the bishop, his eyes on the floor.

Emboldened by the rage she felt creeping up her spine, she said, "So are you going to kill me?"

Flagello's face looked pained, as if she had hurt his feelings. "Of course we're not going to kill you, Dr Davenport. Whatever you may think of me, I can assure you that I serve the Church and the Lord. We asked you here because we need your help with the scroll. Finishing the translation is of the utmost importance."

She considered a caustic response but thought it would be counterproductive. But she didn't want him to think she was terrified, either. She was surprised to discover that she was far more furious than anything.

"Is Jack dead?"

Flagello and Russell exchanged glances before turning back to her.

"Your friend is alive," the bishop said. "He will be taken care of soon enough."

"Taken care of?"

"I am not a member of the mafia, Dr Davenport. Your friend was taken to my room and attended to. God's messengers have remarkable healing powers, in addition to their other abilities. Once he is ready, he will be sent home."

Cerise narrowed her eyes. "Your messenger nearly tore his arm off, and you're telling me that Jack is going to be healed and sent home? That's hard to believe."

"It's true, Cerise," Russell said. "I saw it myself. When I left the bishop's room, Jack's arm was almost completely healed."

She stared at him but directed her words to the bishop. "Let me see him, then."

He shook his head. "Unfortunately, I can't. The angels attending him are helping to . . . ease the memories of what transpired today."

"You mean brainwashing him?" She wished she hadn't said it, but it was hard to suppress her rage at what was happening.

If the bishop was annoyed, he didn't show it. "No. His memories will be mostly intact, but if we are to let him go we can't allow him to remember clearly what happened here. He would either return or tell others, and we aren't ready to share our good news with the world as yet."

"Why can't your angel do his memory erasing after I see him?"

Russell's eyes widened the slightest bit.

The bishop said, "I don't pretend to know how His messengers work their miracles, Dr Davenport. Aside from giving me their fealty, they don't communicate with me. I wouldn't deign to ask for more from Him."

"Him who?"

"Him, Dr Davenport. Him."

"Are you saying that God gave you use of his angels?"

"Yes."

She glanced at Russell, but he had no reaction to this insanity. Russell wasn't exactly an atheist—he believed in some vague 'greater intelligence' that oversaw the universe to a degree—but he definitely had no belief in Christianity or any other organized religion, seeing them as artificial constructs rather than divinely inspired truth. She would have expected a knowing smirk or condescending roll of the eyes from him. Instead, he looked like the bishop's nervous lackey.

"That's hard to believe, to say the least."

The bishop nodded. "I understand your reticence. I promise that you will see things differently soon enough."

She felt the hair on the back of her neck stand up. That was the kind of thing you heard from a zealot, not a Catholic bishop.

"What do you mean?"

She was afraid of the answer. How many angels did he have in his service, and what might they do if he asked?

The bishop turned to Russell. "Dr Kellar, would you please wait outside?" Although it was framed as a question, there was no doubt that it was an order. Russell stared at her with a pained look before turning around and leaving the room.

Flagello walked towards her and she took an instinctive step backward.

"Dr Davenport, what can I do to convince you to help Dr Kellar translate the scroll?"

"Are you saying I have a choice?"

He stared at her for a few seconds before calmly sitting down in a folding chair. He waved his hand at another, and she sat as well, fear continuing to worm its way through her body.

He leaned back and folded his hands in his lap.

"When I first went to seminary, I was appalled to discover there were far more than four Gospels. Dozens, in fact. The heretical beliefs they contained made me sick to my stomach. It was detestable to see the words and deeds of the Lord manipulated to serve the whims of sects with their own agendas."

None of this was new information. These non-canonical Gospels had been floating around at the time of the official codification of the New Testament. But only four—Matthew, Mark, Luke, and John—were deemed to be orthodox by Christian leaders at the time. Other versions were repressed and destroyed, their rediscoveries only possible through archeology and other ancient writings like the ones produced by Iranaeus, the third-century cleric. His writings—in particular his *Against Heresies*—mustered a significant attack on Gnosticism, which was seen as a serious threat to the church at the time.

Ironically, it was writings such as these that provided rich sources of information about the very heretical beliefs they condemned.

"I made a promise to myself," he continued, "that I would do everything possible to ensure that no false Christianity would survive to tempt the faithful."

Cerise couldn't contain her objections, although she tried to frame them carefully.

"There are good arguments to be made that Christianity has always been in a state of change and flux. Even Catholic doctrine now isn't the same as it was fifteen hundred or more years ago."

"That is precisely the problem, doctor. The faithful need a unified Christianity—the *true* Christianity—and I have been given a mandate to pursue that goal."

Cerise was struck by how rational he sounded. She would never know just by talking to him that he was delusional. She supposed Jeffrey Dahmer probably seemed rational too—at least until they found the chopped up bodies in his freezer.

She bit back her impulse to engage in argument. This was not an 18 year old freshman in her class, confronted for the first time with ideas that conflicted with a lifetime of indoctrination. Flagello would be well-armed for a theological debate, and it was unlikely he would be rattled by the usual tactics she used.

"I'm sure you can appreciate how hard this is to believe," she said. "Even if the scroll contains what Dr Kellar claims it does, there's still a . . . bit of a leap to angels and holy mandates."

"I understand your doubt. I would doubt it myself if He had not spoken to me."

She felt a spike of fear. He was suddenly more dangerous, and more than anything else she wanted to run out the door. But she knew what was on the other side, although she didn't know if she was more scared of the angels or the bishop who commanded them.

"You really believe that God spoke to you?"

He stood up and walked over to the table, gazing down at the partially unfurled scroll.

"It sounds ridiculous, doesn't it? No doubt you're thinking that I have some sort of mental illness—schizophrenia, perhaps." He turned. "He spoke to me one week ago, after I learned that this scroll was being smuggled into the country. He did not speak in words, but the meaning was clear enough. He sent me images and information so quickly and powerfully that I was overwhelmed. My head was near to bursting with His majesty when I collapsed on the floor.

"I woke hours later and His angels were there, awaiting my instructions. His lingering presence remained in my head, and He bade me to use the angels to protect the church."

"Was Farouk a threat to the church?"

"What happened to him was unfortunate, but Mr Farouk was spreading heretical works for profit. He will be judged for that. I initially thought this scroll was heretical, as well, and I could not let its message be disseminated."

So you had Farouk and two other people murdered to protect your beliefs? It sounds like every rationalization for genocide I've ever heard.

"Thanks to Dr Kellar, we have instead discovered the most definitive and significant document in the history of humanity. So you can imagine that I would very much like to have your cooperation in continuing its full translation."

"And once the scroll is fully translated . . . ?"

"Once we have His actual words, transcribed by His actual hand? You tell me how significant that would be."

"It would be the most important discovery in church history. If it was real."

Flagello shook his head. "I understand your skepticism. But what will you say when I am proven correct, when the world has seen His message?"

Cerise didn't answer, instead shifting her gaze to the scroll. Russell had also said it was Jesus' autobiography, but was that really possible?

"I would ask you once more to work with Dr Kellar to translate this document."

"If I don't help?"

"I can't force you. But I also can't have you interfere

with Dr Kellar's work. You'll stay elsewhere in the rectory while he continues the translation."

"So I'm a prisoner no matter what I decide."

For a moment he looked like he was pondering the thought, probably trying to figure out a way to say that she wasn't being held there against her will.

"Yes. And I'm afraid I'll need you to give me your phone."

Her heart sank. For a second she considered refusing, or maybe dialing 911 before he could get the phone. But she didn't think she could keep it away from him for long, and if one of his angels came in he could have the phone from her in an instant, maybe at the cost of her life.

She also realized that if she didn't translate the scroll she wasn't worth anything to him, and maybe he'd have her killed despite what he said. She didn't think Jack was being 'taken care of'; he was probably dead. After the incident in the sanctuary she could think of no scenario where Flagello would let him live.

She pulled her phone out of her pocket and handed it over, feeling as if she was giving up her last hope to get out of this. He took it with a grim smile.

"Why are your angels after Amanda? What does she have to do with any of this?"

He recoiled slightly, a confused look on his face.

"I'm sorry, but I don't know who you're referring to. They were sent to bring you, no one else."

She nodded, questions filling her head. His response looked real, but she couldn't be sure. Still, if the angels were after Amanda they probably caught her after killing Richard. Unless she was dead, too.

She purged the thought, remembering Jack's opinion that the angels could've killed either of them at any time, and were therefore probably only out to catch them.

Did Flagello really not know who Amanda was? If that was true, then how was she connected?

She shook the thoughts clear; there were no answers at the moment. She stood up and walked over to the scroll. She couldn't deny that she was enticed, and she felt sick knowing that even the murders of multiple people didn't quell her academic interest.

But really, what choice did she have? Agree to help and hope for the best, or refuse and probably be killed. It wasn't much of a choice.

"All right," she said. "I'll help translate the scroll."

He nodded as if it was a foregone conclusion, then opened the door and walked out. An angel replaced him, and the door swung shut while she stared at his emotionless face.

Chapter Sixteen

Jack strained against the duct tape wrapped around his left wrist, while simultaneously trying to keep his right arm still. It was a nearly impossible task, and each time he put more than a token effort into it pain shot through his right arm at the break, leaving him soaked in sweat. He could no longer see the bone jutting out through the skin in his forearm, but that didn't mean it was any better.

After the angel had dragged Cerise away he tried to get up and follow, but was thrown to the ground by the remaining angels. One of them put his foot on Jack's throat, applying just enough pressure to keep him immobilized and gasping for breath, but not enough to kill him.

The priest—Father Lakaj—brought some gauze and hastily wrapped his arm while the three angels prevented him from resisting, but it wasn't necessary. He was well on his way to shock and barely able to stay conscious.

He was only semi-aware as they dragged him out of the sanctuary. His hazy memories of the trip were momentary stabs of intense pain, nausea, and vague impressions of stairs and long hallways. He had no idea how long he had been sitting in the chair when he finally became aware of his surroundings.

A single light bulb dangled from the low ceiling. The

entire room was the size of a bedroom and barren of anything except the chair he occupied. The walls and ceiling were brick, crumbling in more places than they weren't. The floor was uneven stones covered by bits of mortar, dirt, and dust, and many of the stones were cracked and chipped.

The door was made of wooden slats banded by old and rusted wrought iron. Instead of a lock there was a wooden crossbar with slots on either side for inserting it. The door handle was primitive and old-fashioned, and the entire room struck him as something from the 1800s or earlier.

He took a deep breath, sucking in musty, humid air, and tried to assess the situation despite the dizziness and nausea threatening to plunge him back into semi-consciousness.

His arms were duct taped to the rests of a cheap wooden chair that felt rickety under his weight. He tried to move his legs, but a quick glance down revealed they were also attached to the chair with duct tape, and there was another swath of the stuff around his waist, adhering his torso to the back of the chair.

Given time he thought he could probably get out of it, although the broken arm made it much more challenging. He doubted, however, that he would have much time, and his fears were confirmed when the door opened and Father Lakaj walked in followed by one of the angels.

Lakaj stared at him with his arms folded, the angel flanking him and staring straight ahead at nothing. He reached into his pocket and pulled out a gun, holding it in a way that made it clear he knew very little about guns. Jack recognized his Glock.

"Who are you?" Lakaj said.

Jack had seen and conducted interrogations before. When the detainee cooperated freely, things generally went well for him. But that depended on who was doing the interrogating and the purpose behind it. If it really was purely informational, a cooperative attitude went far. If there was an ulterior purpose—like satisfying a sadistic streak—then it would be ugly no matter what.

"Jack Horner. I work for HMDL Security out of Virginia. My ID is in my wallet."

Lakaj pulled something out of his pocket and tossed it at Jack's feet. He recognized his own wallet.

"I know all that. I want to know who you really are."

Jack narrowed his eyes but didn't respond. Lakaj didn't believe him, but he wasn't sure why.

"Are you going to tell me, or do we need to get it from you?"

"I'm not sure who you think I am, but my ID is real. Ask Cerise." He hoped Lakaj would give him some information about Cerise. He had no idea if she was okay or not.

Lakaj scowled and gestured to the angel, who walked over to Jack and put his hand around Jack's right wrist. There was a stab of pain in his forearm and he arched his back as much as possible, letting out a hiss of agony.

"Who are you really?" Lakaj repeated.

The pain died down somewhat, but the angel still had a hold of his wrist.

"I'm not lying. My name is Jack Horner. If you could just—"

Lakaj nodded to the angel, and the little finger on Jack's

right hand was jerked back as far as it could go. He screamed out suddenly, stabbing pain shooting all the way up his arm and into his shoulder, his vision devolving to white-hot flashes.

After an eternity, the pain faded and Jack let his head fall onto his chest, his breathing rapid and shallow.

"Who are you?"

If he knew what the bastard was looking for he could probably concoct some sort of semi-convincing lie, but he was completely at a loss for what he wanted.

Think, dammit!

Lakaj thought he was a threat of some sort, which made sense, but other than coming in and shooting a few of his angels, what was the threat? He wondered if he could stall him and get enough information to make up a plausible lie. If Lakaj thought he was lying the angel would probably move to the next finger, but he didn't have many other options.

Jack lifted his head up. "I was hired, but it was through a proxy. I never saw him face to face."

He steeled himself for more pain, but it didn't come.

"What were you supposed to do here?"

Good question. Kill someone? Protect Cerise?

He had to be careful. He didn't know where she was or what they might be doing to her, or if she was still alive.

"I was just supposed to protect Dr Davenport, that's all."

White-hot pain spiked through his body as his ring finger was forced all the way back to his forearm. He screamed until his throat was hoarse, and only stopped when he ran out of strength to continue.

"You're lying."

Jack's eyes were squeezed shut, his mouth contorted in a grimace, and his head slumped down. His rapid breathing slowed, and he picked up his head and looked Lakaj in the eyes. More than anything he wanted to slam the bastard's head into the brick wall and see his brains spill out.

"Fuck you," he hissed, steeling himself for another broken finger.

"How long do you think you can hold out, Mr Horner? How many broken fingers will convince you that you'll eventually tell me the truth? And even if you can hold out long enough to wear *me* down, *he* will never tire." He nodded towards the angel.

Jack tilted his head and looked at the angel. His face and eyes were blank and he stood completely still, staring ahead at nothing in particular. He turned back to Lakaj.

"What do you want with Dr Davenport?"

Lakaj pursed his lips and stared at Jack for long seconds before answering. "His Most Reverend thinks she can help Dr Kellar translate."

"So your helpers here," he gestured with a quick nod toward the angel, "were sent to bring her back?"

Lakaj didn't answer.

"What about the girl? Why were you after her?"

Lakaj looked surprised. "What girl?"

The reaction was either honest or the priest had been ready for the question and had a prepared answer. Or he was a psychopath, which was entirely possible given the current circumstances. Jack was leaning toward a combination of one and three.

"The six year old that showed up at Cerise's house. Amanda."

"I don't know about any girl."

"If that's true, then—"

"That's enough. Now are you going to tell me what you were supposed to do here, or will you wait until you have no functioning fingers?"

The priest wanted some sort of conspiracy, but what would satisfy him? He'd want to know something about his 'enemies', but Jack had no idea who the hell those were.

"I was supposed to kill the bishop," Jack said.

Lakaj nodded knowingly, and Jack breathed a silent sigh of relief.

"Were you told why?"

"Only that it would interfere with your plan."

He hoped the priest was too much of a zealot to see that the answer was terribly generic. He received his answer when his middle finger was bent back, the pain even more intense than before. He strained at his bonds and sent the chair wobbling backwards, but was unable to focus on anything other than the stabbing agony in his arm and shoulder.

When the pain faded again he could feel the sweat running down his forehead to his nose, dripping into a puddle on the seat between his thighs.

"What plan?" Lakaj said.

He managed to spit out, "I don't know," but just barely. It was hard to think, and he was afraid he would pass out if another finger was yanked backwards.

"Who sent you?"

"I don't know. A . . . a proxy. I got a phone call and a . . .

a deposit to my account." He could barely lift his head up far enough to look at Lakaj.

"Is Dr Davenport involved in this?"

He perked up mentally, but suppressed it. It wouldn't help to let this bastard know he had any connection to Cerise. He would only use it as leverage. He fought down the instinct to lie and say that she had nothing to do with it, afraid that would make the priest suspicious.

"I don't even know her. I was just supposed to use her as a way to get to the bishop. I was told he had her boyfriend here, and I could use that as an excuse to get close."

Lakaj narrowed his eyes at Jack. "Where did you get this gun?"

What the fuck? Why did he care about his Glock? Lakaj held it like it repulsed him.

"I've had it for a few years. I don't remember where I bought it."

"How were you able to kill them?"

He obviously wanted an answer other than 'I shot them', but Jack didn't know what that answer was. Lakaj thought the angels couldn't be killed, and he was trying to figure out how Jack had done it. What answer would satisfy him? He decided to opt for honesty since he couldn't think of a plausible lie.

"I don't know what you want to hear. I shot them. I've shot lots of people, and most of them died."

Lakaj put his finger on the trigger and slowly brought the gun up, pointing it straight at Jack's head. He'd looked down the barrel of a gun before, but it wasn't something he had gotten used to. Despite the haze of pain and weariness, a chill ran through him, but it was not strong enough to force a visible reaction.

At this range the back of his head would be blown off. A day ago he would have welcomed it. Hell, he would have provoked the shit out of this prick just to *get* him to do it. But now? He still wanted it, but the thought that he had failed yet another person under his care made him sick to his stomach.

Jack closed his eyes.

The echo of the gunshot was deafening in the small chamber, but aside from the stabbing in his ear drums he felt no additional pain. He opened his eyes.

Lakaj was pointing the Glock at the angel, but he had no wound that Jack could see.

"Do you understand?" Lakaj said.

Jack narrowed his eyes. "You didn't shoot him."

Lakaj sneered and the gun went off an instant later. The muzzle was only a few feet from the angel's chest; there was no way he could have missed. And yet he still stood, completely unharmed, as if the priest hadn't fired the gun at all.

"Blanks. You reloaded the clip."

Incredibly, Lakaj laughed. "Yes, I guess you would think that, wouldn't you? That this was some elaborate ruse. That would be a lot easier to swallow than the truth."

"What's the truth, father? All I see is a priest and a naked man with no balls." He knew it was stupid to antagonize Lakaj, but he was finding it harder and harder to contain his rage.

"You really don't know what you've stumbled onto, do you?"

Jack didn't answer, but a creeping unease wormed into his gut.

Lakaj leaned in closer, bringing his face only inches away. "Do you really believe that he is nothing more than a mutilated man? Can't you see him for what he truly is?"

"Tell me what you think he is, father."

"He has been sent to us so we can better serve Him."

"Him?"

Lakaj grabbed his chin and forced his head to the side, putting the angel fully in his field of vision.

"Do you deny the evidence of your own eyes? You are in the presence of an angel of the Lord!"

Jack yanked his head away and glared at the priest, his jaw clenched.

"You're insane."

Lakaj scowled and drew back, his head shaking. He put the gun in Jack's face once more, but only held it there for a second before allowing it to drop down slowly.

The gun fired and Jack felt as if someone had smashed his foot with a red-hot hammer. He cried out in pain and tried to pull back, but the chair kept him in place.

"Do you still think I loaded your gun with blanks, Mr Horner?"

Jack was too lost in searing agony to process the words, and before he could make sense of them his eyes closed and his head fell down to his chest.

Chapter Seventeen

Cerise looked up from the scroll as the door opened, expecting to see the bishop walk in. She scowled when Russell entered instead, closing the door behind him.

"Are you all right?" he said.

She could barely contain her rage. "Go to hell, Russell."

He stepped forward, one hand out, but she folded her arms and stared at him icily.

"I'm sorry I brought you here; it was the only way to keep you safe."

She felt an overwhelming urge to slap him, and would've done it if he was any closer.

"Have you lost your mind? How am I safer here, Russell? We're being held by a lunatic who thinks God has given him angels! How do you even know him?"

Russell sighed. "He sponsored a few of my trips in the past. He—"

"You work for him? Jesus Christ, Russell. That man is insane."

"A few days ago I would've agreed. But what I've seen is too far beyond a normal explanation. I think we need to consider that Bishop Flagello might actually have talked to God."

She stared at him, unsure how to respond. This was the

man who she had seen regularly demolish fundamentalists and evangelicals in theological debates. He had once so infuriated a Pentecostal preacher that the man had actually been reduced to tears. And now he was telling her that God was talking to some middle-management cleric in Virginia?

"I-I don't even know what to say. Do you really expect me to believe this?"

He opened a folding chair and set it in front of her. Cerise reluctantly sat, and then he opened one for himself and sat down across from her, their knees almost touching.

He leaned in, his voice low. "The ones that attacked you in the church? They came after me, too."

"At the hotel?"

He looked surprised for a second, but it faded quickly. "I suppose it's been on the news, hasn't it?"

Cerise nodded. "What happened?"

Russell briefly told her about the attack.

"The person chasing you in the security video," she said, realization suddenly dawning, "it was one of them, wasn't it?" She gestured towards the door.

He nodded.

"Amanda thinks they're angels, too."

"Amanda?"

She told him how Amanda had shown up on her doorstep, and how the angels had attacked her at both her house and his.

"The pepper spray hurt him?" he asked.

She nodded.

Russell folded his arms and further narrowed his eyes, clearly leaving something unsaid.

"What is it?"

He looked up. "When I was in the hotel with Farouk, his bodyguard shot one at point-blank range multiple times, but he was completely unharmed. Farouk's bodyguard—Zeev—was a trained killer. There's no way he missed at such close range."

"Then he had a bulletproof vest on or Zeev missed. There are lots of possible—"

"No, Cerise. I was there. The man was completely naked, just like all the others we've seen. He killed Zeev and Farouk with his bare hands, and then he came after me."

She cringed as she remembered the horrible way Detective Piedmont was torn apart.

"So how," he asked, "did pepper spray hurt one of them? And how did your friend kill three when Zeev couldn't kill one?"

She had known it didn't make sense, but didn't want to acknowledge it. He was right—if bullets didn't hurt them, then why would pepper spray? And why did Jack's gun work when Zeev's and Piedmont's didn't? She had no reason to believe his gun was anything special.

"I don't know."

He stroked his chin for a minute. "Has there been anything else like this?"

She suddenly remembered the car starting without the key and explained what had happened.

"You were terrified?"

"Yes."

"Just like when you used the pepper spray, right?"

She nodded. "Do you think that's the answer? They can be hurt when you're afraid?"

He frowned. "Zeev shot the archon in the hotel, and I'm sure even he was afraid on some level, but nothing happened. It must be something else."

She sighed. "Maybe we need to look over the scroll. If this is all connected, it's possible there might be answers there."

Cerise stared down at the fragmented pieces of vellum scattered across the table. The scroll was mostly intact, but pieces had broken off when it had been unrolled. Russell had begun arranging them to match probable parts, but as with any ancient document, it was slow going.

Russell said, "The bishop thought this was a Gnostic scroll, and he was going to destroy it. He wanted me to verify it first to make sure."

"Part of his holy crusade?"

"He was afraid he might be wrong and he'd end up destroying something valuable."

"And that's when you decided it was the Q Gospel, among other amazing revelations?"

He nodded.

"I don't understand how you could come to a conclusion like that with such little time. No one could translate a document like this so quickly, not even you."

He looked up from the scroll and frowned. "Cerise, I made it up."

She didn't know whether to laugh or cry.

He smiled. "It was all I could think of. If I had told him what I really thought it was, he would have destroyed it and . . . had me killed, I think. He wanted to get rid of any connection to it. I'm sure that's why he had Farouk killed."

Cerise suddenly blanched. "Oh my god."

Russell moved closer, a hand instinctively on her arm. "What is it?"

She sat down, suddenly dizzy and nauseous. "Richard . . . that's why Richard was killed."

He frowned. "Richard Burgoyne?"

She nodded.

"Richard's dead?" He sat down across from her, visibly shaken. "How?"

"I'm not sure. I called him and his son told me he'd been murdered."

"You think it was—"

"I gave him a copy of the fragment you sent me. That has to be it." She gasped, her eyes wide. "It's my fault. Oh my god, it's my fault. If I hadn't given him that . . ."

Russell reached across and put his hand on her knee. "You couldn't possibly have known. It's not your fault."

She nodded unconvincingly, her eyes filling with tears.

He got up and put his arms around her, drawing her close. A while later she pulled away gently, wiping her face with her sleeve.

"I'm okay," she said. She stood up and smiled weakly. "You said you didn't tell the bishop what the scroll really is."

He nodded slowly, his eyes downcast.

They stepped closer to the table.

"Like you said, I haven't had time to do more than a cursory look, but some features jumped out at me right away, almost like they were waiting for me. I'm not sure anybody else would've noticed them, but—"

"Humble as ever."

He smiled. "Not because of my utter brilliance, I assure you. But it just so happens that these are Gnostic."

"That's why he called you in the first place."

"I think so," he said.

"But if you've worked with him before, why do you think he would have killed you? You obviously had some measure of trust."

"Something's changed. He's not the same person he was before."

"You mean he wasn't a megalomaniac with delusional fantasies before?"

"I'm glad you're keeping your sense of humor."

She sighed. "Defense mechanism. How else am I supposed to deal with all this?"

"Let me show you a few things I noticed about these texts."

"Wait. Just to be clear, you made up all the stuff about the Q Gospel and Jesus' autobiography, right?"

He hesitated. "Not exactly."

"What do you mean, not exactly?"

He paused. "I don't think this has anything to do with the Q Gospel, but—"

"But you think this is Jesus' autobiography?"

He just stared at her, his eyebrows raised.

"That's impossible."

"Not if you think about the Sepphoris hypothesis."

"It's wishful thinking with no concrete evidence to back it up."

"Forget about Sepphoris for now," he said. "It works as a hypothesis, but you're right that there's no concrete evidence yet. There is some good textual evidence here for it being His autobiography."

He pointed to a fragment towards the middle of the table, careful not to get his finger too close.

"Look at this section here. I'm fairly sure it says, 'I was taken down after two days and put in a shallow cave.' And here," he pointed to a later section, "it says, 'they had fear to see me alive.' There's a partially obscured reference to crucifixion here," he indicated an earlier section that was too damaged to make out completely. "Along with some of the earlier features, I think there's a strong argument to be made that the narrator is referring to his own crucifixion and resurrection."

"There's no way to verify the identity of this narrator."

He nodded. "You're right, but consider how the features line up with the crucifixion story in Mark. As far as I can tell—and it's not far yet, I'll admit—it lines up quite well." He pointed to another section. "Here is where Jesus cries out, 'Why have you forsaken me?' just like in Mark."

"That doesn't prove anything."

He reached under the table, pulled out a bound report, and handed it to her.

"Farouk had the scrolls analyzed. Check out the conclusions."

She flipped towards the back of the report and scanned through the conclusions.

"Is this right?" she asked.

"I know some of the researchers. They worked on the Judas Gospel. I don't think this was faked. There's no way that Farouk or any layperson would be able to fabricate a report like this. The only other possibility is that he paid them off, but I don't think that's realistic."

Cerise put her finger on a series of dates. "These dates predate Mark. Is this for real?"

"I think so. This may very well have been Mark's source."

She glanced down at the fragments, processing the ramifications.

"But that doesn't mean they were written by Jesus. It could easily have been written by someone who witnessed or heard about the event, maybe one of the original apostles. I wouldn't even put it past Paul to do something like this."

"Let's assume for the sake of argument that Jesus did write these."

"That's quite an assumption."

"Just bear with me for a minute," he said. "If we assume He wrote these, then we have to accept one of two corollaries: either He wasn't dead when He was taken down from the cross and was later revived, or He did die and actually rose from the dead."

"I don't like either of those assumptions."

"But which one is more likely to be true?"

"I'd say neither, but since I'm going along with this for now, it would have to be the first one since people don't actually come back from the dead. But it's not realistic—nearly impossible—that he'd survive crucifixion. The Romans were experts at crucifying people, and they wouldn't have cut him down unless they were sure he was dead."

"I agree, but it's a possibility. So if Jesus woke up after being crucified, He might naturally assume He rose from the dead, and even if He didn't He might be persuaded to believe it by His followers. At the very least, He might be encouraged to write it down. Maybe at that point He thought about the long-term impact of His return. He might have realized He could be a more effective messiah if He had thwarted the Romans' attempt to kill Him."

"That," she said, "is a hell of a lot of speculation to get to the conclusion that Jesus wrote this."

He folded his arms. "Fair enough. I agree it's a stretch, but it actually doesn't matter who wrote it. What's important is what it says."

"Okay. So aside from being similar to Mark, what *does* it say?"

He pointed towards another fragment.

"Look at this word, right where He asks why He is being forsaken."

She did, but she could barely make out letters. She was completely out of her depth.

"What about it?"

"In this other section I think these are sayings like in the Sermon on the Mount. There's a few 'you should do this' sort of things. But if you look at the way He says 'you' over here, there's something kind of striking."

Cerise looked at one section then the other, but it was too much to take in. "I don't see what you're getting at."

"Right, of course not. Sorry. Do you remember how Aramaic is gender-specific?"

"Yeah. There's a first person masculine and a first person feminine, right?"

"Yes. Note how 'you' is written here," he pointed to the section with the 'sayings', "and how it is written here." He moved his finger over to the other section where Jesus was asking 'why have you forsaken me?' "Do you see how they're written differently?"

"I think so."

"This first one is masculine, but the second one—where He is asking why He is being forsaken—is the feminine form."

She narrowed her eyes and examined it closely. "Are you sure it isn't just a mistake?"

"I don't think so. If you look at the structure of the letters, you'll see some slight differences, just enough to mark one as masculine and one as feminine."

She thought she saw it, but it was difficult to say anything for certain about a 2000 year old document.

"This one," he indicated the sayings, "is masculine, which is what you'd expect since He's speaking to a general group. This other one, however, is feminine."

"So who's he talking to? According to Mark Jesus was talking to God."

"Presumably. But of course God wouldn't be feminine."

Cerise agreed. "I don't understand why that 'you' would be feminine. It has to be a mistake."

"I don't think Jesus is talking to God there."

"Who else would he be talking to?"

Russell looked up from the scroll. "I think He's talking to the Christ entity."

"What?"

"Remember the Gnostic belief that Jesus Christ was two entities: Jesus the man and Christ the divine spirit?"

"Yes."

"The Gnostics liked Mark because it supported their belief in this duality. When Jesus asks why He's being forsaken, the Gnostic argument is that Jesus the man is talking to the Christ entity as He is being abandoned to die. But they weren't concerned with Jesus as a material being because they believed the body was a trap for the divine spark."

Cerise said, "That explains his plea before he dies; Jesus the man thinks the Christ spirit is abandoning him. But why would he use the feminine gender?"

"Exactly! He wouldn't if He was talking to the true God! Even though the Gnostics thought the true God was unknowable, they still referred to God as a 'He', maybe for simplicity sake or maybe an inherent cultural bias—there are arguments for both. But they would never refer to the true God in the feminine."

"That doesn't answer the question. Why would the Christ entity be referred to as feminine?"

"Think about it: the divine sparks that inhabit the material bodies of the Gnostics came from Sophia's attempt to comprehend her creator. Wouldn't it make sense that the sparks themselves would be referred to in the feminine?"

Cerise glanced down at the fragment, more for somewhere to avert her eyes than any attempt to discern what it said.

"So these spirit forms are all women?"

"No, of course not. They're genderless entities. In fact, Sophia would likely be genderless as well. Although the Gnostics thought of themselves as transcending the material world, they couldn't help but fall prey to its prejudices and cultural memes. Even they wouldn't have argued that they were immune to it. That would only happen once they were freed from their mortal shells."

"I guess I can buy—for now—the notion that someone around the time of Jesus' death wrote this 'autobiography,' although I don't believe for a minute it was Jesus himself. Where do these naked angels and this crazy bishop fit in?"

Russell pulled his glasses off and ran his hands through his hair. "The bishop thinks they're angels, but I don't think that's exactly right."

"Well, I'm so relieved to hear that you don't think they're exactly angels."

He ignored her sarcastic tone. "The God of the Old Testament—Yahweh—created angels to serve as intermediaries between humanity and heaven. The Gnostics didn't disagree with this, but of course they thought that Yahweh was a false god. In their dogma, the angels are more like oppressive enforcers defending the status quo.

"The angels—the Gnostics called them archons—were basically Yahweh's desire for control made into corporeal form. They're essentially just an extended part of him, rather than independent entitles of their own."

"You think the bishop's naked angels are archons?"

"In a nutshell, yes."

She wasn't sure if this theory was any less crazy than them actually being angels.

"I don't see how that changes anything. You're still asking me to accept that there's some higher power out there who sent down these—call them angels or call them archons, it's all the same—to serve the whims of this crazy bishop."

He stood up and walked over to the fragment. "The explanation is here, Cerise. Jesus was a Gnostic! Or at least

Jesus the man interpreted the Christ entity in a way that led to this Gnostic version of what happened to Him. He—or whoever wrote this right after His death—was possibly the originator of the Gnostic sect, which means that *Gnosticism was the original Christianity!* A sect that's been dead for more than a millennium was closer to getting the true version of God than any church or religion in the history of the world!"

She didn't know what to think about Russell's theories. If the dating was accurate there was a compelling case to be made that Gnosticism predated orthodox Christianity. She wasn't sure what the result would be, however. In the back of her mind she couldn't get rid of the idea that Jesus might have written it himself, although every rational bone in her body rebelled against the idea as nothing more than speculation.

But nothing they discussed did anything to change the fact that they were being held prisoner with no way to escape.

"So what," she said, "do we do? We're still being held here, and there's still at least one angel outside our door, and probably more nearby."

"We can't let the bishop know the real contents of the scroll. If he discovers it's Gnostic, he'll destroy it and have us killed."

"He's bound to find out. Besides, he won't just let us go after the scroll is completely translated, although how long will that take with just the two of us?"

"I think I can keep stalling him for a few more days, maybe a week. But we've got to figure a way out by then."

Cerise looked around the room but there was only one door. The ceiling was plaster and the room was heated with an old radiator, so there were no ducts to access, if that would have even been possible.

"The only way out of here is that door," he said.

"Have you been anywhere else besides this room?"

"Only a bathroom and a small room with a cot and no windows. And an archon was always nearby."

She frowned. Archon seemed like a better term for them than angel, but regardless of what they were called, there would be no getting away from one in the tight confines of a hallway or room.

"Do you think it would be possible to sneak out in the middle of the night?"

He shook his head. "I couldn't sleep the first night I was here. After the archon led me to the room with the cot, I opened the door every hour or so. He was always there, facing the door in the exact same position. I don't think he moved an inch the entire night.

"I think they're more like automatons than living things. They have their purpose, and they single-mindedly follow it."

Cerise stifled her irritation and walked over to the door. She stood there for a moment before grasping the handle and opening it wide. An archon stood there, facing her, his hands down at his sides and his stare blank. If he was even aware of her existence he didn't show it. But she had no doubt that if she tried to leave he would stop her.

For a brief second she considered testing him to see what he would do, but the thought of his skin touching her made her nauseous. The bishop wouldn't want to risk killing her or Russell, but that didn't mean these archons wouldn't hurt them. She suspected there were many ways she could be harmed and still be able to work.

It was even possible they might kill her. Despite what Russell said, there was no assurance that these archons were under the full command of the bishop.

She shut the door and returned to the table.

"Do we just sit in this room and stare at these fragments until the bishop finds out you've been lying to him?"

"We work on the false translation for him and I'll also continue doing the real translation."

She waited, expecting him to say more.

"That's it? Work on the fragment? And then what? Hope he doesn't have his archons kill us?"

He suddenly looked ten years older. "That's it. I have no other ideas. I think all we can do is go along with this for now and hope we can find an opportunity to call someone or get out of here."

She wanted to argue, but she couldn't think of even one alternate plan that might work.

Was this it? Were they going to end up like Detective Piedmont or one of the other victims when the bishop found out that they were lying?

She had a hard time blotting out the memory of the poor detective getting ripped apart on the front lawn of Russell's house.

Chapter Eighteen

Cerise followed the archon to the foot of a long, narrow staircase. The entrance to the sanctuary was further down the hall. She considered bolting towards it, but one glance at the pale, thin figure in front of her quickly changed her mind. She doubted she could get five steps before he caught her, and what then? She had no problem envisioning him snapping her neck like they had done to the old women in the sanctuary.

The archon started up the stairs and she followed, hoping that at the very least he was leading her somewhere where she could lay down.

There was a door at the top of the stairs and a short hallway leading to an even narrower set of stairs going up. From where they were in the building she guessed it probably led up to the bell tower.

The archon opened the door and stepped aside. The hall was mostly dark, but a little light from a bulb further down partially illuminated the room beyond, although Cerise would hardly have called it a room.

It was only ten feet across at most. Along the far and right walls were metal utility shelves with a cornucopia of different items scattered amongst them—light bulbs of various sizes, books, folded tablecloths, candlesticks—all of them covered with a layer of dust. An old cot was to her left against the opposite wall.

There were no windows, and the only potential source of light was a single bulb with a long string dangling down just above her head.

She stood at the threshold, desperately hoping she wouldn't be forced to go in. The archon held the door open and stared at her, so still he could've been a statue. She wondered what might happen if she took a step back towards the stairs, but realized it would be ridiculous to think she could refuse to enter.

He stared at her, unblinking and stone still, while she worked up the nerve to step into the claustrophobic little storage room. It wasn't long before the weight of his pale eyes on her overrode her reluctance, and she stepped into the room and pulled the string on the bulb, the door closing behind her simultaneously.

Exhausted, she sat down on the cot and put her head in her hands. She was grateful to be too tired to think about anything other than lying down and sinking into a deep sleep. The amount of energy it would take to stand up and pull the string on the light bulb was more than she was willing to expend, so she eased her body down onto the musty cot and immediately fell asleep.

She dreamed that the room was shaking and someone was telling her she needed to leave before the ground opened up and swallowed her. She opened her eyes and nearly screamed when she saw a face only inches away from hers. She pushed herself as far away as the cot and the wall would allow and scrambled to a half-sitting position.

"Hi, Cerise."

Cerise rubbed her eyes before sitting fully upright. "Amanda?" she said, attempting to discern whether or not she was still in a dream.

The girl smiled and nodded.

Cerise glanced over at the closed door. "How did you get in here?"

Amanda shrugged.

Cerise stood up, clearing the last vestiges of sleep from her head. She had no idea how long she'd been asleep, but she felt marginally better as the fog began to lift.

She grasped the handle and opened the door up a crack, instantly shutting it when she saw the archon's face. She backed away, afraid he was going to burst in, but the door remained closed.

She turned back to Amanda. "What are you doing here?"

"I wanted to come help you."

Cerise was still too shocked by the girl's appearance to form any relevant questions. Instead, she stared at the girl's half grin for a full minute before finally deciding to sit back down on the cot. Amanda sat next to her.

"Are you okay?" the girl asked.

"I . . . I guess. I'm not hurt or anything." She turned her body to face Amanda. A chill went through her; how could a six year old girl be so terrifying? "What happened at Richard's house?"

"That old man with the big house?"

She nodded.

"I didn't want to stay there, so I left."

"You left? Where did you leave to?"

"I just left."

Cerise felt the hairs on the back of her neck rise. She thought she should ask more questions, but doubted she'd get anywhere. And she wasn't entirely sure she wanted to know the answers, anyway.

"I know where your friend is."

Cerise perked up. "My friend?"

"Jack."

Cerise's eyes got wide and she felt another chill

"How do you know about Jack?"

"I just do."

Cerise had to fight the urge to throw open the door and barrel past the archon outside. Instead, she tried to focus on the fact that without Amanda's help, she'd likely be dead.

"Where is he?"

"It's like a basement, but not really. It's kind of small, and they used it a really long time ago to help people escape."

"I don't understand."

"People who didn't want to be slaves any more. They used to come here and the church people would help them get away."

"You mean the Underground Railroad?"

"I don't think there's any trains there."

It made sense. The church was old enough to be part of the Underground Railroad, and it was in a good location. Thousands of slaves had been hidden in churches and other 'stops' in Virginia and other border states before heading to the North. If Amanda was right, there was probably a hidden room somewhere below.

"Do you know how to get to this basement?"

She nodded.

Cerise looked over at the door.

"He's still there," Amanda said.

"Will he let us leave?"

She shook her head.

Cerise stood up and looked around the room before she began shuffling items around on the shelves. She ran her hand across all the exposed wall surfaces, looking for some sort of irregularity.

"What are you doing?" Amanda asked.

"Just looking for something."

She continued around the small room, finally standing on the cot and running her hands along the ceiling while Amanda watched her with a perplexed look on her face. Finally, after touching every bit of wall, ceiling, and floor she could reach, she sat back down on the cot, defeated.

"You didn't find it?"

"No, I didn't."

Amanda sat down next to her.

"What were you looking for?"

"A way out." But she hadn't found anything. The walls and the ceiling were all solid plaster, and the floor was hardwood planks. If Amanda had gotten in through some hidden door, Cerise had no idea where it was.

"We could go to the in between place."

"The in between place?"

"It's a place where I go sometimes. We could go there and the angel wouldn't see us."

"How . . . how do you get there?"

"I just close my eyes and think about it. I think you might be able to go, too."

Cerise's hands were shaking and she shoved them in

her lap. "Is that how you got here? From the in between place?"

Amanda looked down and nodded slowly, her face etched with guilt.

"Can you tell me more about this place?"

Amanda's face scrunched up again and then relaxed. She looked up at Cerise. "They're hurting Jack."

Cerise's eyes went wide. "Who's hurting him?"

"The bad man in black."

"Father Lakaj?"

Amanda shrugged.

Cerise looked over at the door, wondering if she could take the archon by surprise.

"I can take us there."

Amanda held her hand out. With only a few seconds hesitation Cerise grasped it, her stomach a knot of worry and fear. If Jack was still alive she had to help him if she could.

"Close your eyes and pretend you're floating."

She expected Amanda to chant or say something, but instead the girl was eerily quiet. If Cerise didn't have a hold of her hand, she wouldn't have even known the girl was there.

Abruptly Amanda pulled her hand away and Cerise opened her eyes. They were still in the storage room. Amanda was pressed up against the far wall, terrified. Cerise jerked her head the opposite way and felt her stomach contract.

The door was wide open and the slender archon filled the doorway, his fingers elongating to an obscene degree, the ends tapering to points.

Amanda screamed, and Cerise was reminded that even though Amanda terrified her, she was still just a little girl.

The archon moved into the room. Without any thought of how suicidal it would be, Cerise launched herself from the cot and grabbed him around the midsection with both arms.

It was like tackling a marble pillar. The archon's flesh was cold and hard, as if he were carved from rock instead of made of flesh. His skin was unyielding and inflexible, and her fingers couldn't get any grip. She clung as hard as she could with her arms and tried to wrench him backwards, but she was unable to move him the slightest bit.

He grabbed a fistful of her hair and pulled backwards, ripping her off of him as easily as if he was ripping off a days-old band-aid.

She screamed and instinctively grabbed onto his wrist, attempting to lessen the searing agony of her hair being pulled out by the roots. He tossed her to the side and let loose his grip before taking a step toward Amanda, but he was halted by Cerise's death grip on his wrist.

Both of her hands were wrapped around his forearm, and she attempted to dig her fingers into his rock-like skin. He swung his arm back and forth to dislodge her, but she held on fiercely; the only result was him flinging her back and forth in the small space.

Unable to free himself from her grip, he turned his attention to Cerise. He reached over with his free hand and grabbed her by the throat, his fingers digging into her neck so quickly and so tightly that she was forced back against the shelving. She let his arm go and grabbed the other, attempting to pull his hand from her throat.

He moved closer, bringing his face only inches from hers. His grip relaxed the slightest bit, allowing her a quick gasp. The metal shelves dug into her back but she couldn't get any leverage to push away.

He held his face in front of hers for long seconds. His eyes were pale blue and without life, but she had the distinct feeling that he was studying her, almost like a scientist studies a moth before he impales it on a pin.

She continued to hold his wrist but didn't struggle as long as he was letting her breathe. Amanda's screaming had died down, and Cerise was able to see her out of the corner of her eye, huddled and cringing against the far wall. Her attention was brought back to the archon as his grip slowly tightened and she felt her air flow cut off.

She dug her fingernails into his forearm as she tried to get some purchase with her feet. She finally managed to get one foot up on a shelf, and she shoved her other knee into his groin. He gave no indication that he had even noticed.

Her vision began to go black at the edges and she saw bright flashes of light. She realized she was about to lose consciousness and attempted to push herself to the side, hoping desperately that she could get loose that way, but the archon's hold on her didn't waver.

A sudden movement caught her eye, and the archon's grip on her throat loosened just enough for her to take a quick, painful breath. Amanda was suddenly next to the archon and she had something gold in her hand—was it a candlestick? She was hitting him with it, an intense and angry look on her face.

"Let her go!" the girl yelled again and again, each word

punctuated with a blow from the candlestick, although the only effect seemed to be getting his attention.

Cerise's hands were still on his forearm, although her grip had slackened, allowing her to notice the strange texture of his skin even more than before. It was like nothing she had ever touched before, and more than anything it felt lifeless—no warmth, no pulse of blood through veins and arteries, no . . . muscle?

She felt herself delving below the surface, seeing just below the archon's skin. It was the same way she had seen into her own arm when it was broken—the fracture, the network of bone cells suddenly spurred to intense, rapid growth—except the archon's arm looked nothing like hers.

The substance under the skin was uniform and made of the same material as the skin itself. She saw no network of blood vessels and capillaries—no blood at all, in fact—no bones, no ligaments or tendons. Instead, the entire mass of the arm was nothing more than one solid—

The vision disappeared as the archon pulled his arm away. Cerise's breath returned as she fell to the floor, and she was shocked to see him backing away from her. Even more surprising was that his face finally registered an emotion, although she almost didn't believe what it was.

Amanda continued to hit him with the candlestick, but he still took no notice of her. His wide eyes were fixated on Cerise and his mouth was open in an undeniable expression of fear.

She pushed herself away from him, but was only able to get a few more inches of space up against the metal shelves. Her movement, however, spurred something in him, and he backed out of the room quickly, not bothering to shut the door. She could just see his torso and head disappear as he ran down the narrow stairway back to the first floor.

"Do you think I scared him away?" Amanda asked, incredulous.

Cerise put her arm around her. "You definitely did."

The girl looked up at her. "For real?"

Cerise smiled. "For real. I don't think he'll be back." She wasn't lying that he wouldn't be back, but not because he was scared of Amanda and her candlestick. Cerise had seen the fear in his face and knew that she was the cause. She didn't know why, but it had happened right after she saw inside him.

She remembered the attack in the sanctuary and envisioned Jack shooting the three archons.

"There was no blood," she whispered.

"What?"

Amanda stared at her, her face questioning.

"My friend . . . shot some of the bad angels. They didn't bleed."

"Angels don't have blood?"

She could still see the inside of the archon in her head.

"No, I don't think they do."

"That's weird. How come?"

She ignored the question. They needed to find Jack.

"Do you think you can find the place where they're keeping my friend?"

"Uh huh."

She smiled and nodded before standing up and taking the girl by the hand. They walked out of the small room, eyes alert.

Chapter Nineteen

Amanda knew exactly where to go. She led Cerise through the rectory and down to the basement. In a back storage room there was an old door that looked conspicuously out of place. It was made of wooden planks with bands of rusted metal to keep them in place, and it had no latch, just a wooden handle.

"He's in there," she said.

"Is there anyone else in there?" Cerise asked.

She mused to herself that she didn't even consider asking how Amanda knew any of this. She didn't like the fact that she was beginning to accept the insanity of these events as normal. The certainty of the rational universe had been upended, and she was scared of what it might mean for humanity and for herself.

"I don't think so," Amanda said.

Cerise nodded, grasped the handle and slowly pushed the door open.

The room was dark, the only illumination coming from the weak light of the storage room. Someone was slumped over in a chair. She couldn't see his face, but she could tell by the hair and clothes that it was Jack.

Cerise moved into the room, Amanda at her side. She knelt down and felt for a pulse, and recoiled when she discovered she was kneeling in a small puddle of blood. She ignored her disgust and put two fingers on his carotid artery. She panicked when she failed to find a pulse, but forced herself to stay calm and press deeper. She breathed a sigh of relief when she finally felt it. It was faint, but there.

He was duct taped to the chair, and she fumbled through her pockets for something she could use to cut him loose. She pulled out the keys to the BMW and tested the edge.

"Jack," she said. "Jack, can you hear me?"

He didn't stir.

She touched his face gently, but pulled back when she felt a tug on her sleeve. She turned to see a strange look on Amanda's face, a mixture of fear and confusion.

"What's wrong?" Cerise asked.

"Somebody's coming."

Urgency and terror welled up in her gut.

"Who?"

Amanda's gaze met her own, the look on the girl's face transforming into calm resolution.

"Angels."

Cerise glanced back toward the open doorway.

"How long until they get here?"

"Not long."

Cerise turned back to Jack and began sawing at the duct tape around his arm, hoping the movement would wake him.

"Amanda, start pulling on that tape on his other arm."

When the girl didn't comply Cerise looked up. Amanda was back in the open doorway.

"I need your help!" she said.

"They're gonna be here real fast."

"I know! That's why I need you to help me!"

Amanda just stood there, an intent look on her face. "I can make them chase me."

Cerise's eyes got wide. "No! Just come here and help me with this tape!"

But the girl didn't move and continued to stare into the previous room. After seconds that seemed to drag on, she said, "I'll be right back," and then ran the way they had come.

"Amanda! Come back here!"

Cerise got up and chased her. She ran through the basement and to the stairs leading up, but saw no sign of her. She continued up the stairs more slowly, afraid she would be seen or heard. At the top she opened the door and peered into a long hallway, but still didn't see Amanda.

She stood on the top stair for a few seconds before cursing and retreating back down. There was no way she would be able to find Amanda quickly, and every second she spent looking was time lost. If the archons showed up before she freed Jack they would probably both be killed. She had no illusion that what had happened with the archon upstairs would be repeated with a group of them.

Back in the room she knelt down and continued sawing at the duct tape with her key. Once she was partially through she was able to rip off large swaths of it. She managed to get one arm free and was rewarded with a groan of pain.

"Jack!" she whispered. "Wake up!"

She didn't wait for him to respond before starting on the other arm. As she sawed through the tape he moaned and gasped, finally lifting his head and opening his eyes.

"Cerise?" His voice was weak and confused. "What are you doing here?"

"Trying to get you loose. We don't have a lot of time."

He looked around and held his free arm up. His hand was shaking and he couldn't move his fingers.

"Shit," he hissed.

"What is it?" She paused and looked behind her, praying she wouldn't see archons filling up the doorway.

"They broke my middle finger. How am I supposed to flip them off?"

"I'm glad you can keep a sense of humor, but if we don't get you out of here soon we're going to be in a lot of trouble."

"You need to get out of here. I can't walk. That fucking priest shot me in the foot."

She ripped through the tape on his other arm and pulled it off, a little more carefully than the first one now that he was awake. He winced in pain but said nothing while she started working on his uninjured leg.

"I won't be able to stand up, much less walk. You need to get out of here and call the police."

"I'm not leaving you here."

"You have to. There's no way I can make it, and you can't carry me. Even if I could walk I'd just slow you down and get us caught."

She paused and looked up at him, realizing he was right, but also knowing she wasn't going to leave him here to be tortured or killed. She put the keys in her pocket and stood up, looking around for a light. She found the bulb overhead and pulled the string.

The room was entirely made of brick. The mortar was crumbling or broken nearly everywhere, and most of the bricks were in bad shape. She had no trouble believing this room was used as a stop on the Underground Railroad.

She walked over to the door and closed it, discovering a wooden crossbar and slots to place it against the door. Even though the door was old, the wood was thick and sturdy, and the crossbar would keep anyone out for a little while. She doubted it would keep the archons out for more than a minute, but it was better than nothing. At least there'd be advance warning when they arrived, although the advance warning of a door being splintered apart by evil angels was maybe not ideal.

"That's not going to do much," Jack said.

Cerise ignored him and knelt down to examine his foot.

His shoe was crusted with blood where the bullet had entered. She gently touched the top of it with both hands, careful not to press down.

"What are you doing?"

She didn't answer, instead remembering how her wrist had been healed in the car. *No*, she corrected herself, *how I healed it.*

Even with his hands and arms free Jack was useless to do anything other than watch.

Cerise put him out of her mind and stared at his foot. The shoe was a casual brown loafer. Although ruined by the bullet, she could tell it was expensive and high quality. The leather was soft, and as the ridges and imperfections became more and more obvious under her fingers, she began to see the individual layers that comprised the hide.

The top was covered by a thin, nearly imperceptible

layer of dye coating the surface and filling the peaks and valleys. Underneath there were pressed layers of cells—dozens of them—each microscopically thin.

She frowned as fear and panic rose in her chest. It quickly became overwhelming, and just before she pulled her hands free there was a sudden, violent blow, and a weakness throughout her body.

She fell back, sweating and panting, trying to dispel the horror.

"Are you all right?" Jack said.

She looked up at him, suddenly brought back to the present.

"Yes, I'm . . . fine."

He stared at her strangely. "What the hell happened?"

She got back to her knees. "Nothing. I just . . . I just thought I saw something." His disbelief was palpable, but she ignored it. "How long did that take?"

"How long did what take? All you did was touch my shoe and then fall back."

She narrowed her eyes. "Right away?"

"You touched it for maybe a second or two and then fell back. Are you sure you're okay?"

A second? It had seemed so much longer. She had seen not only the skin of the animal, but the animal itself, both as an outside viewer and as if she was actually in the animal's skin. It had been a calf, only two years old, and in the final moments of its life it had felt confusion and panic, then pain and sudden weakness before it was overcome. She had felt the skin being separated from muscle, dried, tanned, and stretched. It made her ill but she didn't have time to think about it.

"I'm fine."

She touched his shoe again, willing herself past the leather. There was a brief flash of intense emotion, but she was able to move past it. As when she had seen her own broken wrist, she could see the wound in Jack's foot from the outside. She was drawn into it like a passenger on a miniature tour, passing through the burned and cracked skin, amidst a tangled web of split and destroyed capillaries pooling blood where they had been blown open. Muscle fiber was ripped and shredded and bones were splintered, sending miniscule shards ripping through the tissue.

She focused first on the bone, just as she had with her own injury, willing the broken ends to send out a latticework of fibers and rejoin each other. It was harder than with her own injury—the ends were not directly against each other due to the force of the bullet—but there was an ease in the coaxing of the cells that had been absent the first time.

She next began weaving together the strands of muscle. They came together more easily, although she encountered splintered pieces of bone embedded throughout. She wrapped her consciousness around them, noting the individual cells and seeking similarities to the surrounding tissues before dissolving them into their microscopic components, causing them to be reabsorbed for muscle, blood, and other elements.

As she wound her way through his injured flesh, she continued spurring any damage to heal itself. Blood vessels were rebuilt and connected, bits of cartilage and ligaments regrown. When she finally exited she was tired but satisfied, knowing the wound would be almost completely healed in a manner of minutes.

Jack's eyes were wide and incredulous. "What did you do?"

"I . . . fixed your foot."

He looked down at it and watched as he flexed it.

"The pain is almost gone," he said. "How the hell did you do that?"

"I don't know, exactly. How bad is your arm?"

"I think they must have set the bone; it's not sticking out anymore, although it hurts like bloody hell. They broke my fingers, too." He held up his swollen, useless hand.

She reached up and touched it, weaving damaged tissues, shrinking swollen tendons, and then did the same for his arm while he stared at her, uncomprehending.

Jack flexed his fingers and arm.

"How did you do this?" It was the first time she had ever seen him so awestruck.

She began tearing at the duct tape binding his legs and torso.

"We have to get out of here," she said.

As if waking from a daze, he suddenly started helping her rip the tape off. When he was free he stood up and took a small step away from her.

It was probably an unconscious gesture, but they both knew that something had changed within her. She had wondered in the car if Amanda had somehow healed her wrist, but now she knew the girl had nothing to do with it. She had pointed out the path, but it was Cerise who had taken the first steps, and now there was no going back.

The splintering of the door jarred her awake. They both looked over to see a pale hand reaching in through a hole it had just punched through the door. It grabbed hold of a plank and pulled, ripping off a chunk of the door. The blank face of an archon stared back at them.

"Get behind me," Jack said, instinctively stepping in front of her and scanning the room. He grabbed the wooden chair and smashed it to the floor repeatedly until one of the legs broke off. He picked it up and stomped down on the chair, breaking off another leg.

Cerise backed up against the wall. Her fingers brushed against it and she turned and looked. Halfway down the brick ended, and in its place were wooden boards. She knelt down and placed her hands on them, noting the dampness and rot.

"Jack, over here! I think there might be a tunnel behind these boards!"

He scrambled over and examined it while the archons continued to rip away pieces of the door. Cerise didn't think they had more than a couple of minutes before they would be inside.

"Look out," Jack said. Cerise moved out of the way and Jack kicked at the boards. They split instantly, and he bent down and ripped open a hole big enough for them to crawl through.

"Quick! he said, motioning for her to go through the opening. She only hesitated long enough to hear the next plank pulled from the door before she plunged into the darkness, hoping she was right about this being an old Underground Railroad tunnel.

She moved forward quickly on her hands and knees, feeling her hair touch the ceiling occasionally. It was pitch black, and she could feel her face go through silken webs every few feet. The floor of the tunnel was stone, but she could feel her hands getting coated with dirt as she crawled, terrified she was going to plunge into a pit in the darkness; or worse that the tunnel would narrow and she'd be stuck there. She would have turned back despite the archons but she could hear Jack just behind her, his heavy breathing filling the darkness.

"Keep going!" he hissed. "I think they're almost through!"

She moved faster, feeling things scamper across her face and hands and fighting the urge to scream, knowing she would break down if she did. It would be the leak in the dam that would send the waters rushing forth, and that would mean that she, Jack, Amanda, and Russell were all dead. The girl's face appeared in her mind, crystal clear, and she focused on it. If they didn't get away now she'd never find Amanda, and as terrifying as the girl was, Cerise couldn't stomach the thought of anything happening to her.

She struck her head and cried out, her willpower suddenly crumbling. She scrambled back until she hit something behind her, and she began flailing and kicking as it grabbed hold of her legs.

"Cerise, stop! It's me!"

She stopped struggling and brought herself back to some measure of control.

"Something hit me," she whispered, her hands wrapped protectively around her head.

"It was probably a root or something. We've got to keep going! I think they're in the tunnel!"

She didn't know if she was more afraid of the archons behind her or the unknown in front.

"Cerise, we've got to move!"

The fear and panic in Jack's voice stirred her forward, but she didn't move as quickly as before. She pawed the space in front of her before crawling forward, and she hadn't gone far when her fingers brushed something hard.

"There's something up ahead."

"Is it the end?"

Some of her fear evaporated when she realized he might be right. She tentatively reached her hand out, flinching when she hit the hard surface, but forcing herself to keep her hand steady. It was hard and slightly damp, but it didn't feel like dirt or stone. She ran her hand down the surface to where it met the floor.

"It feels like wood."

"Let me see if I can shimmy past you."

She pressed herself up against the side of the narrow tunnel while Jack slid past her. Her body was pressed up against his, and she was embarrassed to discover that she felt a tingling despite the horror of their circumstances.

"It feels like a door but I can't feel any handle."

"Let me get—"

Something grabbed her ankle and she was yanked backward. She screamed as she was pulled back the way they had come, arms and head bouncing on the floor and side of the tunnel.

"Cerise!"

She felt Jack's hand grab at her, but she was pulled out of his reach. In rapid, intermittent bursts, she was dragged back through the tunnel, the grip on her ankle never loosening. Dirt flew into her mouth and eyes, and she coughed in rhythmic spasms as she was pulled back to the room.

She heard Jack call her name, but it seemed distant and weak, and she could not concentrate on anything other than the dirt stinging her eyes and filling her mouth and throat. Finally the movement stopped and the grip on her ankle released. She rubbed the dirt out of her eyes and got to her hands and knees.

Three archons stood over her. One reached down and grabbed her shirt, hoisting her roughly to her feet. She pulled away and was surprised when he let her go, although there was nothing that could be construed as fear on any of their faces.

She was in the middle of the room, and she took a backwards step towards the tunnel. The two flanking archons stepped to the side, opening up a clear path to the door. The middle one walked around her, cutting her off from the tunnel.

Why don't they just grab me?

She felt like she was being herded toward the door, and she wondered what they would do if she refused to move the way they wanted.

Jack backed out of the tunnel and got to his feet. None of the archons acknowledged his presence.

"Stay away from her," he said, his voice low and menacing.

One archon continued moving around Cerise, drawing closer. Jack's hands were up and he was crouched, like a tiger ready to pounce.

The difference in their sizes was comical. Jack was over six feet tall and probably weighed about seventy pounds more than she did. The archon was half a head shorter than she was and looked as though he weighed less than a hundred pounds.

But Jack could not punch through solid wood or rip a man apart with his bare hands. He knew how to fight—she would never forget what he had done to that foolish, drunken student—but he was no match for even one archon, much less three.

"Jack, don't." Some of her fear fading, she spoke to the archon circling behind her. "We'll go with you."

"I'm not going to let you do that, Cerise," Jack said.

She frowned. "There's nothing we can do. You're just going to get yourself killed."

"They're going to kill us anyway."

She looked over their blank faces. "I don't think so. They would've done it already." She held out her hand. "Let's just go with them."

He stared at the archons for long seconds, and she had no idea whether he was going to take her hand or attack them. She was surprised and relieved when he dropped his guard and shuffled over to her, grasping her hand.

"Are you sure about this?" he said.

"No, but I don't see an alternative where you don't get killed, do you?"

"Probably not. I just don't like the idea of giving up so easily."

"If we can get out of this alive, it'll be worth it."

He nodded and relaxed somewhat, and they walked between the two flanking archons, the third herding them from behind.

Cerise realized her mistake when the archon next to Jack curled his lip the slightest bit. But she wasn't quick enough to do anything other than watch as the archon shot out a backhand almost faster than she could register the movement. The resounding crack as it connected with Jack's head was like a gunshot, and she could only watch as he flew into the wall and crumpled to the floor.

"No!" she screamed, and without thinking she reached out and grabbed the archon's shoulder, sinking her fingers as deeply into his flesh as she could.

She felt it again, the delving below the surface. And this one was like the other—solid, gray, with no blood, muscle, or bone. It was as if they were sculpted from clay. She realized what it reminded her of: *"And the Lord God formed man of the dust of the ground . . ."*

The archon tried to pull away but couldn't get loose. The other two hesitated for a moment before stepping forward and grabbing her, one on each arm. They tried to pull her away, but to her surprise they couldn't move her.

Fear splayed across their faces as clearly as if they were human. They tried to pull their hands away, realizing their mistake, but it was too late—Cerise could see and feel inside their bodies as well. She was not surprised to see the identical structure as the first archon.

They tried to pull back, their faces becoming more and more animated as they . . .

Animated . . . ?

The revelation struck her, and the archons increased their activity, now desperate to get away from her. She tightened her control, sending herself even deeper inside them, seeing them for what they really were.

There was no individual thought. There was barely anything that she recognized as consciousness, and none of it was centered in the brain—which was nonexistent—or any other part of the body. Instead there were impulses, commands, understandings to do or respond to certain things. These understandings suffused their entire bodies, were present in every speck of the material the archons were made of.

The barest hint of emotion lay buried, but she felt it from time to time as she weaved her way through them. She experienced jealousy, anger, hatred, and others, but nothing that could be described as positive.

She continued deeper and deeper, eventually touching upon the faintest memory of an intelligence, the leftover remnant of whatever it was that had shaped them. They had been created by something, but she couldn't grasp what it was. And then it was gone, once more buried, leaving her to wonder if she had only imagined it.

It hadn't been their own intelligence; these things had never possessed that. They had been formed, and she was surprised to discover that the material of their bodies was recognizable. It was something she had only seen once before, in a college chemistry class.

The professor had shown them a video of two roughly circular clouds of what looked like a cluster of bees, and asked the class what they thought they were seeing. For a few seconds no one said anything. One student raised her hand and said she thought it was a picture of molecules.

"Close," the professor had said. "They're actually gold atoms."

Cerise's jaw had nearly dropped. The idea that you could see an atom was a revelation to her. This was not some theoretical illustration or diagram, this was the actual thing viewed through an electron microscope. She was staring at the matter of the universe.

The electron clouds inside the archons were visible, and as she drew back she could see the connections between the atoms as they flew around each other. She didn't know what any of the atoms were, but the fact the archons were made of the basic building blocks of matter was undeniable. These supernatural beings were made from matter, not from some heavenly material that existed only on a higher plane. Whatever had made them had joined atom to atom, molecule to molecule, and connected them together to form a human-shaped body with no mind.

And if they could be formed, then they could be unformed.

She willed the connection between two atoms to break, and as one atom spun away from its parent molecule she did it again and again and again, sending hundreds, thousands, *trillions* of atoms spinning away from each other. She repeated the process, seeing molecules explode as if she were detonating bombs everywhere she went.

She finally left the archons' bodies and allowed them to release their grip on her. Their eyes were wide and their skin rippled and seized as if a colony of ants was eating them from the inside out. Holes opened as pieces of them dissolved like dust being blown from a statue. Fingers crumbled and fell away as the molecules continued separating, an ever-repeating chain reaction of chemical bond dissolution that slowly claimed the archons' bodies bit by bit.

Cerise backed away as they continued to fall apart in front of her, their eyes and mouths wide open and silently pleading for an end to the suffering. None of the three made a sound as they crumpled to the floor, their eyes glued to her as she watched them slowly disintegrate.

She was torn between relief and sympathy. Even knowing what they were—semi-mindless automatons created to serve a master's whim—she couldn't completely reject the notion that they were alive in some sense. She felt no satisfaction in seeing them reduced to the piles of pale gray in front of her, as if someone had dumped several large ash trays onto the floor.

Carefully avoiding their remains, she moved over to Jack and knelt down, her hands feeling for a pulse. He was alive, although he had blood running from his nose and ears, and his breathing was shallow and quick.

Without thinking about it she entered him again, noting how easy it was to send her consciousness into another person. She found the cracks in his skull, the broken blood vessels, the swelling brain tissue, and sped up their regeneration. Before she pulled free she willed a thought into him, hoping it would override his own natural instinct to protect her. She no longer needed his protection—if she ever really had—and she didn't want him to go back into the church and confront the bishop or Father Lakaj.

She stood up and looked down at him, feeling a curious sadness for what might have been, and an acute sympathy for the loss of his family.

She took a deep breath and walked out of the room. Amanda and Russell were somewhere above. She had to find them and get them out of the church before she confronted Bishop Flagello. She had no idea what she would do when she found him, but she discovered that she was no longer afraid.

Chapter Twenty

Jack opened his eyes and the world slowly came into focus. He was lying on his side on a stone floor, but he couldn't remember where he was or how he had gotten there. He put his hands underneath him and started to push himself up before a wave of dizziness dropped him back to the floor.

When it finally passed he pushed himself back up again, but more slowly, until he was sitting with his back against the cold brick wall.

The room looked familiar. There was a broken chair in the middle and several piles of what looked like ashes scattered around. He remembered smashing the chair, but he didn't remember seeing any ashes.

He and Cerise had crawled into a tunnel and—

Where was Cerise?

He crawled to the tunnel entrance but he couldn't see beyond the first few feet. He remembered going in and then crawling out backwards.

He suddenly remembered the angels, and the scene came flooding back to him. The last thing he could recall was walking next to Cerise with three angels surrounding them. Then he woke up on the floor.

Leaning back against the wall he ran his hands across

his face. When he dropped them he saw blood on his palms. He felt his face again, noting the blood under his nose, and also finding blood on the side of his temple and from his ears. He wasn't currently bleeding, however, and he couldn't find any injuries. He had a mild headache, but nothing that would indicate a concussion.

So why do I have blood on my face?

He considered that it might not be his own, but then quickly rejected that. There were clear remnants inside his nose and ears. There was a trace of blood on the wall near him, as well as on the floor. He reconstructed his position from when he woke up and then glanced again at the wall.

Somehow he had smashed his head into the wall and then fallen to the ground.

He tried to remember what had happened after he stepped next to Cerise, but it was a blank. He had taken a few steps before noticing that one of the angels was looking at him, and he seemed to have a sneer on his face. That was the last thing he remembered before waking up on the floor.

That fucker hit me!

He stood where he thought he had been when he had been struck. The spot where he had hit the wall was about ten or twelve feet away, and about two feet from the floor. Since he had no memory of the blow, he was probably knocked unconscious right away, but he was apparently hit hard enough to send all 195 pounds flying across the room.

Jesus, how strong are these things?

He had discounted a lot of what Cerise had told him as hysteria: ripping through the metal roof, knocking down the door, crashing through plate glass. But calculating the trajectory of his headfirst trip to the wall made him realize that she probably hadn't been exaggerating.

Any blow that could toss a two hundred pound grown man across a room would have broken bones, and the header into a brick wall would have been even more damaging. And yet he felt fine. The ache in his head was already fading, and while the blood on his face was alarming, he didn't feel any accompanying symptoms.

He should be dead or at least severely injured, not walking around reconstructing how his head had violently met a brick wall. Cerise had done it, of course. She had healed his hand, arm, and foot in seconds, and while he lay unconscious she had done the same thing to his head.

He moved toward the tunnel and peered in. It was pitch black, and he had no idea if it even led anywhere, but he dropped down to his hands and knees and entered anyway. For a few brief seconds he wondered why he was going this way; it would certainly have been much easier to just go through the door. But the cold, claustrophobic darkness beckoned him, although he couldn't explain why.

The end of the tunnel seemed closer than before. Jack sat back on his haunches and ran his fingers over the wood, eventually locating a metal handle. It was like an old cellar door, and he guessed it led outside. He pushed against it but the door didn't budge.

Repositioning himself, he leaned his shoulder against the door and pushed again, bracing his feet against rough stones in the tunnel floor. The wood of the door cracked, but he wasn't sure if the door had opened somewhat or if he had simply strained the planks. He pushed again, throwing his entire weight against the door and pushing as hard as he could. The door cracked again, although he felt it from the middle rather than the edges.

He paused, sweat dripping down his face and back. The door wasn't just stuck or rusted shut; there was something behind it. It was an old tunnel, probably unused for decades or longer. He suspected it probably had something to do with the Underground Railroad, which meant it was somewhere around 150 years old. If it led to the grounds around the church like he suspected, it might be covered with hundreds of pounds of dirt. How the hell was he supposed to get it open, especially half-crouched in the dark with no tools?

He considered turning around and heading out of the tunnel. As long as he didn't run into any angels, he didn't think he'd have any problems. Lakaj still had his gun, but shooting a man in the foot while he was tied to a chair was a lot different than shooting him while he was coming at you. Besides, the priest handled the gun like an amateur; Jack was certain he could disarm him before he would be able to get a clear shot.

He could not, however, force himself to crawl back out of the tunnel. Instead, he began prying at the wood with his fingers, digging them into the crevices between the planks. He worked his fingers in and began pulling at the boards, skin and nails tearing as he did so.

He had no sense of time passing in the darkness of the tunnel as he continued pulling and clawing at the boards, loosening them millimeter by millimeter, his fingers finally touching cold, moist earth between the cracks. His guess that the door was buried had been right, although he wasn't satisfied to know that he had an indeterminate amount of dirt to dig through before he would emerge from the tunnel.

A board was pulled loose, and he ripped it off and set it aside before grabbing for the adjacent plank and yanking that one loose as well. Once the first one had been torn off, the ones surrounding it were easier to grasp.

He traced his hands along the inside edges of the door and found that he had about a three foot by three foot opening, although it was probably more accurate to call it an impenetrable wall of dirt rather than an opening.

He still couldn't understand why he didn't just turn around and leave the tunnel. Every instinct told him that he needed to go back through the room where Cerise had freed him and find her. The angels had taken her from the room—or at least he assumed so after he had been pummeled—and he should be looking for her instead of wasting his time trying to get out this way.

But no matter what he told himself, he could not force his body to actually leave or even stop digging. He had grabbed one of the torn planks and was using it as a shovel to cut through the packed dirt. He felt more and more frustrated with every swipe, but it was as if he wasn't in control of his own body.

He continued to dig as the dirt cascaded down, falling into his eyes and face, and then down to the floor around him. He ignored it, the digging becoming a ritual as he let go of his attempt to make his body do what he wanted.

Images of his wife and daughter flashed through his mind. His daughter giggled as he chased her through the house, his wife smiling from the couch as she watched them. He caught her and threw her over his shoulder, running around the couch while she bounced and giggled in delight, finally dumping her down next to his wife and mercilessly tickling her while she begged him to stop, and then begged him to do the whole thing again.

He felt her tiny hand in his as he walked her across the street or from aisle to aisle in the grocery store. He felt her arms encircling his leg whenever a loud truck passed them on the street, or around his neck as he lifted her out of the backseat. He heard her high-pitched scream of delight when he tossed her high in the air and caught her as she plummeted to the ground.

And then the sound of rending steel and breaking glass, a sudden blow that sent the world spinning just long enough to sink the inevitable realization deep into his gut. He saw himself turn around, watching the events unfold as if they were on a screen, praying that he wouldn't see what he already knew was there.

In the millisecond before his daughter's crumpled and broken body registered, he said a thousand prayers that it would be different this time; that somehow none of it had ever happened. He swore he would never speak a word of it, would never even question the shift in reality, if he could go back and change that one thing. It would be a simple task for an omnipotent being. His daughter could've remained quiet instead of calling out to him, he could've kept his eyes riveted on the road instead of turning, or the other driver could have hit the brakes instead of slamming into their car. There were a million possibilities, and he would've been happy with any decision that would have left her alive and intact, including trading places with her.

It would be a secret pact between himself and God. The

event would never have happened, he would never have needed to be pulled from the mangled door of the car by half a dozen cops and EMTs as he screamed in anguish. He wouldn't watch from the backseat of a police car as both of their bodies were taken away under sheets. Time would be reset and everything would march forward with just that one little difference.

It would be inconsequential to the universe. One little girl would live instead of die, and the world would continue to move forward much as it did before. He would tell no one about what God had done, would not even think of it himself, not even in gratitude. He would continue his life as he had before, purging the memory so completely that it would cease to exist.

The plank got caught on a tangled mass of roots, and Jack was brought back to the utter bleakness of reality. Gritting his teeth he doubled his effort, ignoring the dirt coating nearly every inch of him and his cramped thighs and sore arms. The roots grew thicker and he attacked them with ferocity, stabbing and dragging the plank again and again until the tightly packed dirt grew looser. Finally the tip burst through, and a single ray of pale light stabbed into the tunnel, sending a wave of relief and satisfaction through his body.

He paused only a few seconds before he continued ripping through the soil and roots, widening the hole. It only took minutes to create a passage large enough for him to crawl through, and he squeezed his head and body into the hole and exited onto the tall grass of an open field across the street from the church.

The immediate surroundings were a mixed bag of

stores, houses, and apartments, all radiating from a square of sorts that centered on the church. Sleeping cars dotted the edges of the streets as active ones sporadically drove past. The street was otherwise empty and quiet.

He needed a phone. It must be late, possibly past midnight if the frost on the grass and lack of activity were any indicators. He needed a plausible story that would get the police inside the church, but he wasn't sure what that would be. Even if the police got into the church, they wouldn't be able to find Cerise and Russell without searching, and there'd be no probable cause to do that.

The smart thing would be to head back into the church and find Cerise and Russell by himself, but the unspoken imperative to get help was too strong to override, although he didn't understand why.

He narrowed his eyes as he stared at the church. Even if he did get inside, he doubted he would get far before the angels descended on him. He didn't think he'd get away with just being captured this time; they would probably rip him apart right there.

He scanned the cars on a nearby street, noticing an old Ford truck in a pool of shadow under a broken street lamp. He hadn't hotwired a car in years, but the process was not complicated or difficult if you had the right tools. All he needed was a screwdriver, and there was a chance there might be one in the truck. He crossed the street and headed towards it.

The F-150 was an early 1980s model and not in the best shape. He leaned against a street lamp and looked around. All of the windows in the nearest buildings were dark, and the street was deserted.

He moved to the truck and looked into the bed—empty—and then through the driver's side window. The bench seat was ripped in multiple places, duct tape covering large gashes. The ashtray was filled with cigarette butts, and ash was scattered across the floor. A haphazard pile of newspapers and magazines covered the passenger seat, and there were empty cigarette packs and crumpled wrappers on the floor.

He glanced both ways before smashing the driver's side window with a hard elbow. He reached in, opened the door from inside, and then slid in, closing the door behind him.

The glove box popped open with the press of a button, and he leaned over and pulled out a crowded stack of old McDonald's napkins, a rusty pair of pliers, a small plastic baggie of marijuana, various dirty pens and pencils and other odds and ends, but no screwdriver or anything similar. He closed the box and reached under the seat, his hand meeting hamburger wrappers, desiccated french fries and old ketchup packets, but nothing else. He sat up and wiped his hand on the old napkins before swearing under his breath and opening the door.

He slipped out quietly and saw movement out of the corner of his eye. Before he could turn completely he was hit on the side of the head, and he crashed to the ground. Someone grabbed his shirt and yanked him to his feet, slamming his back against the truck.

"What the fuck you do to my ride, asshole?"

A large, bearded face glared at him. He recovered from his daze enough to see huge arms connected to a large torso.

"I asked you a question, mother fucker." The statement

was punctuated with another violent slam against the truck.

Jack gathered his wits enough to fumble out a weak, "Sorry." The beard was not impressed.

"Sorry? You're sorry you smashed my window?" The punctuation came in the form of a fist in his gut. He doubled over, his breath gone, but was forced upright again.

"I should fucking kill you right now, you piece of shit. I'd be doing society a favor getting rid of a useless, dirty fuck like you."

Jack put his hands up above his head in a clear gesture of surrender. He could barely breathe much less speak, but he managed to squeak out a somewhat audible, "Please."

"Please? Please kick your ass is what I'm gonna do."

Jack opened his mouth to say something and then his right hand came down, fingers splayed out, and jabbed the man in the eyes. He cried out and let go of Jack's shirt, his hands instinctively flying to his face.

"Goddammit! You fucking asshole!"

Jack kneed the man in the groin with enough force to break a wood plank. He let out a pained gasp before crashing to the ground, one hand over his eyes, another covering his testicles. He was curled up in a fetal position on the sidewalk, quietly moaning.

Jack knelt down and felt the man's pockets, finding his keys and phone. He took both and hopped back in the truck. The engine started immediately and Jack drove off, leaving the man still groaning on the sidewalk.

Chapter Twenty One

The library door was closed and there were no archons in sight. Cerise had no idea if Russell was there or not, but it was as good a place to start looking as any. She turned the handle and pushed it open slowly.

The room was dark and quiet. She ran her hand along the wall until she found the switch. Fluorescent lights hummed to life illuminating the table, but there was no sign of Russell.

The scroll was the reason for all this. A lifeless piece of vellum possibly inscribed with the words of a Jewish peasant who'd lived 2000 years ago had caused the deaths of half a dozen people, and would possibly cause more. Despite its historical value, she wanted to light it on fire and watch it burn. Instead, she shut the light off and pulled the door closed.

She leaned against the door, unsure what to do next. Russell was probably squirreled away in some storage closet like she had been, but she wasn't sure how to go about looking for him. She couldn't just wander through the church and rectory; archons might be looking for her. She had eliminated the ones in the basement, but that didn't mean she was safe. She might be able to repeat what she had done before, but she wasn't certain.

As she continued through the rectory she found empty offices and a few storage rooms, but nothing else. The sanctuary was up ahead, but the memory of how the archons had attacked her and Jack in there made her cringe.

Voices drifted into the hallway from the sanctuary, but she couldn't make out who was talking. She paused to listen and was surprised to hear someone chanting a Latin mass.

She peered around the corner. Bishop Flagello was dressed in full vestments on the dais while he led the ritual. Russell and Father Lakaj knelt at the railing as if they were about to receive communion. A dozen or more archons stood behind the bishop, so still and so white that she would've guessed they were statues if she didn't know otherwise.

She watched in awe for a few minutes before working up the nerve to walk around the corner. The bishop saw her and paused, his mouth open in surprise, before smiling with what looked like genuine warmth. The archons looked over at her in unison, like the rehearsed response of a Greek chorus. Their faces registered the slightest expression of something that looked like confusion. Or was it fear?

Russell and Father Lakaj looked behind them, and they both stood up when they saw Cerise standing there.

"Cerise!" Russell said. "What are you doing here?"

She felt a stab of hot anger at him, but before she could respond the bishop spoke up.

"Dr Davenport, I'm so glad you could be here for this miraculous event. Please join us." He motioned towards the railing where Russell and Father Lakaj stood.

She didn't move, unsure of what to do. Something very

strange was going on, and she had no desire to find out what it was.

"I . . . would like to leave." She stammered, "and take Dr Kellar with me."

The bishop's smile didn't falter. "If you knew what you were about to witness, you wouldn't ask to leave."

She glanced at Russell. His face was plastered with indecision.

"What am I about to witness?"

The bishop's smile grew wider, an expression of pure joy.

"I would like to tell you with all my heart and soul, but I don't think you'd believe me. It's something so incredible that I can scarcely believe it myself. Can I ask you to trust me that this is something that you—as a religious scholar and a human being—will regret missing?"

She scanned the motionless archons staring at her. Despite their rigidity they looked as if they might leap into action at any moment. Would she really be able to stop them like the three in the basement? She doubted it.

"It would be hard to trust you after being kept here."

His smile faltered the slightest bit. "It was an unfortunate necessity after the . . . incident with your friend. But you haven't been harmed in any way, have you?"

Was he serious? Did he really think that just because she didn't have any broken bones she wasn't harmed? She would have PTSD for years if she was somehow able to get out of this alive.

"I just want to take Dr Kellar and leave."

He stared at her for long seconds before responding.

"Of course. I think you'll regret not staying, but neither you nor Dr Kellar are prisoners."

She wasn't sure she had heard him correctly. Was he really going to let them leave?

"I can understand why you might not believe me," the bishop said, reading her expression. "But I can assure you that no one will harm you or try to stop you. You are truly free to go if you so desire."

She stared at him, pondering what to do. The bishop walked down the few steps of the dais and drew closer. Cerise tensed.

"You've spent almost your entire academic life studying Christianity, haven't you, Dr Davenport?"

Cerise didn't answer, but it was true.

"And yet you believe in none of it. Can you explain that dichotomy?"

She'd heard this argument before—it wasn't sophisticated—and she had demolished the asker on more than one occasion. Bishop Flagello thought highly of himself and his intellect, but having a middling rank in the Catholic hierarchy didn't make him a genius in religious scholarship. Maybe his claim to have talked to God had puffed up his self-importance. She imagined he had probably been fairly insufferable before, and now that he had gone insane he was probably worse.

Still, she didn't want to argue with him. There was no swaying a lunatic or a zealot. But she was afraid he might send the archons after her if she didn't cooperate. Just because he said he would let them go didn't make it true.

"I study the human element of religion, the things that people have done and said in the past. The spiritual realm," she almost said 'supernatural' but decided it would have a negative connotation for the bishop, "is not my area of expertise."

He smiled and nodded—a condescending gesture. "You're avoiding the question. Why are you so fascinated by Christianity if you don't believe its tenets are real?"

The bishop desperately wanted her position to be untenable and weak. He wanted her to admit she had some sort of unconscious need for the supernatural, and that her academic study of Christianity was a smokescreen for her real need to believe in the faith.

It would've been simple to lie and tell him she had doubts, that maybe her role as 'atheist scholar of religion' was a facade, a role she played. But despite all she'd seen, she was more sure now that the God the bishop envisioned was not real. Whatever or whoever had animated these archons was no benevolent deity.

"Because of people like you, father, who insist with perfect certainty that only you have the answers, who ignore all rational and logical evidence in favor of what you want to be true. Because woeful, blind acceptance of a ridiculous set of made-up stories is fascinating to me."

The bishop's face soured immediately, the condescending smile vanishing as his eyebrows lowered and his lip curled. Before he could respond, however, Russell said something to him that she didn't hear. The bishop nodded, although his expression remained. Russell walked over to her.

"Are you all right?" he asked.

"That's a stupid question, Russell."

He recoiled slightly, his eyes wide.

"I'm sorry. I know this has been hard." She opened her mouth to say something, but he held up his hands. "Just hear me out, please." She curled her hands into fists at her side, but didn't respond. She'd listen for now. She was curious—in an angry way—about why he looked like he was suddenly in league with the bishop.

"Something very big is about to happen here, Cerise," he said, his voice low. The bishop stared over at them, but she didn't think he could hear the conversation. "I think everything will change after this."

"You sound like a zealot. What do you mean, 'everything will change'?"

He drew the slightest bit closer, his voice lowering even more. "The bishop thinks God is sending a messenger here, someone—something—that will help him usher in a new age."

She glanced past him at the bishop, Father Lakaj, and the assembled archons. She didn't believe God was sending anything, but she couldn't deny something seemed poised to happen. There was a current in the air she couldn't ignore. She would never have noticed anything before, but things felt . . . different.

"Are you making decisions based on the beliefs of a lunatic?"

"Can you really tell me that you think nothing is going to happen, that everything you've seen can be explained away?"

"No, but just because I can't explain it doesn't mean that God is real."

"You're right, and I don't think that. But . . . I think something *is* coming, Cerise."

"Something? What the hell do you think is coming, Russell?"

"These archons—they're not serving their own purposes. They're here for something else, some greater entity. Not the God that Flagello believes in, but something else."

"There are no gods, Russell. They were invented by humans and you know it."

"I can't believe that any more. Not after what I've seen. Maybe it's not a god in the way humans have always conceived, but it's still some kind of higher being, something so far from humanity that we might as well call it a god."

She narrowed her eyes. "You sound like you know what this thing is." When he didn't respond, she said, "Oh my god, you think you do, don't you?"

"The scroll, Cerise. I don't think it's an accident that I was sent to see it, and that it survived the attack at the hotel. I think this higher power is using the bishop, making him think the archons are his to command. When this thing comes, I think he'll be cast aside. His agenda won't be the same."

Cerise took a step back, but Russell's hand shot out and grabbed her wrist, pulling her close.

"It's Ialdabaoth, Cerise. I think we're about to see Ialdabaoth."

She tried to pull away, but he only tightened his grip and leaned in close. "Russell, let me go!"

His breath was hot on her cheek. "Don't you understand? We're about to be visited by the God of the Old Testament! Don't you see how staggeringly important this is? We are about to witness the creator of the material universe!"

She stared at him, unable to comprehend what had happened to him in only a few days, but they were interrupted by a low and silent rumble that pierced their bodies as if they were standing directly under a jet turbine.

Chapter Twenty Two

Jack let his head fall onto the steering wheel. The truck was at a four-way stop, but there was no traffic around so he let his eyes close for a few seconds, suddenly exhausted. He jerked his head up and opened his eyes when he heard the police siren. The red and blue lights were flashing in his rearview mirror.

"Goddammit," he hissed under his breath.

His eyes ached, and he guessed he had fallen asleep for a few minutes, just long enough to be lingering at a stop sign when the cop showed up.

The officer was still in his cruiser, and Jack half-considered flooring it and driving away, but dropped the idea. He wanted to gauge how reasonable the cop was first; there was a chance he might convince him to go check out the church.

He glanced once more in the rearview mirror, hoping the cop was going to exit, but he just sat there with his eyes down on his computer. He lifted up his handset and said something before putting it back down and finally exiting the car and walking to the driver's side of the truck.

"Is there a problem, officer?"

He had one hand on the grip of his service pistol, ready to pull it out quickly, which was a bad sign. A cop wouldn't approach like that without a reason, and a routine traffic stop was not one.

"Step out of the car, please," he said.

Jack hesitated, feeling his stomach sink. "Have I done something wrong, officer?"

"Step out of the car now, please."

He was young—probably in his mid-twenties—and looked nervous. It might very well be his first major confrontation, and he was likely thinking about what he would do if Jack didn't cooperate.

Jack pushed the car door open slowly before stepping out. He kept his hands where the cop could see them and moved carefully.

"Could you tell me what the problem is, officer?"

He knew what the problem was: he was going to be arrested for carjacking, and there was nothing he could say now to get the cop to the church. He'd be hauled in, booked, and tossed in a cell, and then he'd be less than useless.

The officer's hand curled around his pistol, probably an unconscious motion, but Jack noted it. If he did anything suspicious, the gun would be out in a split second.

"Turn around and put your hands on the truck."

Jack did as he was told. Faint sirens sounded in the distance.

"Spread your legs apart."

He felt his legs, torso, and back frisked.

"I'm going to grab your right wrist now. Don't resist."

He would be cuffed any second, and then he'd be totally screwed. He felt the cop grab his wrist and twist it—not roughly, but with the amount of force he'd been trained to use at the academy—and then he brought the arm down behind his back. As the handcuff was locked around his wrist he bent forward suddenly, touching his forehead to the side of the truck, and kicked out behind him, aiming for the man's lower leg.

He hit something but it was a glancing blow, and instead of the cop falling to the ground as he hoped, Jack lost his balance and was smashed into the side of the truck, the cop twisting his arm with enough force to send a spike of pain up his arm.

Completely off balance, he was helpless to prevent the cop from grabbing his other wrist and yanking behind his back.

Before the other cuff was locked a low, deep sound vibrated through Jack's entire body, as if the world's most powerful bass had suddenly released one long note. Jack felt it as a wave that insinuated itself into his body and vibrated every molecule. For the brief second it lasted, he knew nothing but the overwhelming feeling of immersion in something he did not understand.

And then it was gone and his knees began to buckle. As he sank to the pavement, he twisted enough to see the cop dazed and teetering, looking as if he might collapse at any second.

He kicked out on his side, sweeping the officer's leg at the calf. Taken completely unaware, the officer crashed to the ground. Jack was up in an instant, ready to kick the gun out of his hand before he could get a shot off, but there was no need. The man lay still, arms sprawled out and unmoving.

Jack knelt at the officer's side and pulled out his pistol,

expecting him to move at any moment. He remained still, and Jack grabbed the keys to the handcuffs. As he was unlocking his wrist, he noticed the small pool of blood gathering under the man's head.

Jack checked for a pulse. It was faint, but he was only partially relieved that the man wasn't dead. He must've hit his head on the pavement when Jack swept his legs, and a head wound like that could have serious consequences. He needed a hospital.

The sound of the sirens was louder now. The officer had probably called for backup after noting the stolen truck, and they were on the way. He stood over him, unsure of what to do.

The sound wave that had hit him—he thought of it as sound, but that only touched the surface of the experience—had come from the direction of the church. Something was happening, and while he had no idea what it was, he knew he had to get back there as quickly as possible.

And what am I supposed to do once I get there?

He had no idea, but he did know that the officer needed an ambulance as soon as possible.

He went back to the truck and grabbed the flannel shirt on the bench seat. Gently lifting the man's head he put the shirt underneath, hoping his weight on the flannel would put enough pressure on the wound to slow or stop the bleeding.

He ran to the patrol car and picked up the transmitter.

"There's an officer down on—" he glanced up, looking for a street sign, "Parkwood. It dead ends at some warehouses about half a block away. Send an ambulance."

He dropped the receiver and popped the trunk before getting out of the cruiser, ignoring the confused response from the radio. There were several flares in the trunk, and he lit them and tossed them around the officer before jumping back into the truck and driving away.

Jack was sure someone would get there in time, and there was nothing else he could've done. He tried to put the image of the injured cop lying in the street out of his head as he turned around and headed back to the church.

Chapter Twenty Three

Cerise and Russell both turned toward the dais. The bishop was smiling beatifically, tears streaming from his eyes.

"Do you feel it?" he said. "Do you feel the Holy Spirit?"

Cerise wanted more than anything to call him a lunatic, but she did feel it, or at least she felt a presence so alien and unearthly that she couldn't just dismiss it. Could Russell be right? Or even worse, was the bishop right? Were they about to see God?

Russell let her wrist go, but she couldn't move.

"This can't be happening," she whispered under her breath. She turned to Russell. "We have to get out of here. Whatever is about to happen can't be anything good, not if it has anything to do with those archons."

Russell's face was nearly as enraptured as the bishop's. He couldn't tear his eyes away from the unseen presence on the dais. "Don't you understand, Cerise? We're about to see something that no human alive—maybe no human ever—has seen. We have a responsibility to see this!"

She leaned closer to him, grabbing his arm. "It's not what you think, Russell. It's not some benevolent deity. Whatever this thing is, it doesn't mean anything good for us!"

He turned to her with a wild, maniacal look in his eyes. "We're about to witness the greatest event in human history, and you want to leave because you're scared? Who in their right mind wouldn't be scared right now! But think about what is going to happen next, Cerise. We will be facing and addressing the entity that created the universe!

"Can you begin to comprehend this opportunity? This isn't some made-up story about a burning bush or some myth about Creation. This is real! Imagine how this will change history!"

Cerise stared at him aghast, letting go of his arm and pulling back. But he didn't allow her to leave completely. As she stepped back and slipped her arm away from him, his hand shot out and he grabbed her arm right above the elbow, digging his fingers in.

"Let me go, Russell!"

He pulled her closer, his wildness making him stronger, more insistent. He had never been a physically big or strong man, and she was shocked at his iron-like grip. No matter how much she struggled, she couldn't break it.

"Think, Cerise. Think about what this means for humanity. We'll finally be able to know where we came from—where *everything* came from! We won't wander about in the dark, constantly trying to find our way. Now we'll know for certain!"

She pulled again, but it was no use. She opened her mouth to protest again, but something was happening on the dais, and they both turned to see it.

The bishop was glowing.

The glow was faint, but there was no mistaking it. His appearance was luminescent, as if his face was no longer made of skin, but delicate glass. As she watched the glow increased in intensity, spreading out like a halo, and Cerise couldn't avoid the automatic association of halos with angels and Jesus.

"Do you see it?" Russell said. "It's happening. It's happening now."

"How do you know it's what you think? You're making assumptions that have no basis in reality!"

His face went blank for an instant, and she had the feeling she was looking at the man she knew before, the contemplative intellectual who examined every problem thoroughly before making a conclusion. But it was gone seconds later, replaced by someone she didn't recognize.

"I know enough to be able to identify God when I see Him."

His certainty was chilling. Russell was never certain that he had all the answers, even when he had thought and researched more about an issue than anyone else. But he spoke about what was happening with the bishop as if there was no room for doubt.

"Listen to yourself. You're saying you know without a doubt what's happening here, but you've never accepted a claim without evidence. That's not who you are!"

He sneered and pushed her away. Surprised by the sudden assault, she tripped and fell.

"You don't know who I am," he said. "I won't waste my time when you refuse to accept that we are about to see Ialdabaoth."

The way he said Ialdabaoth this time triggered a memory—she had heard someone else say it recently, but who? Her eyes went wide when she realized who it had been.

"I Hold The Bath," she whispered, one hand over her mouth. "Oh my god. *Amanda knew.*" What other names had she used?

She opened her mouth to say something but stopped short, the shifting of the bishop's halo commanding her attention. She glanced at Russell, noting the wide eyes and broad smile, and then over to Father Lakaj. He did not look as spellbound. His eyes were narrowed and he took several steps back from the dais, clearly anxious about what was happening.

The bishop was taller than before, and it took her a second to realize his feet were no longer on the floor. The halo was taking on a shape that mimicked the bishop's own, forming arms and legs as if he were floating in a fluid suit of amber. She could still see his body within, but he didn't look as though he had control of his limbs. Only the whites of his eyes were visible, and the expression on his face was not rapturous. Instead, his mouth was half-open and he looked catatonic.

The names suddenly came to her: Yes We and A Done Eye. They were absurd, but they made sense if she put herself in the frame of mind of a child hearing an unfamiliar word. She whispered the names out loud, wishing she had seen the connection before. She'd heard both names thousands of times. Yahweh and Adonai were nothing more than transliterations for the God of the Old Testament.

She considered turning and running out the door, but she couldn't leave Russell there. Whether he was correct that this was Ialdabaoth or not, it was something to be feared. He might have been right that it should be witnessed, but she didn't think it would do much good if the only witnesses were killed.

She looked back at the motionless archons, seemingly in thrall to the haloed bishop, and realized she wasn't powerless. She had seen what they were, had known them so completely she could break them down atom by atom just by willing it. Could she do the same to this entity?

The bishop's halo expanded. It still looked like fluid, but the shape was lengthening and forming something that more closely resembled a human body. It took on definition—indentations on the arms, legs, and torso where muscles would run under the skin, vaguely formed hands and feet, an ellipse around the bishop's head.

The humanoid shaping continued from there, and Cerise was unable to tear her eyes away. There was further definition—rounded cavities where the eyes would be, a broadening of the shoulders. The entity grew taller, larger, taking on the outline of a perfectly proportioned male.

The amber shell surrounding the bishop—who floated inside like an insect caught in a sudden spurt of tree sap—towered over them and was much like an idealized copy of the pale white archons standing silently behind it.

Cerise shook free of her daze and grabbed Russell's arm. She forced herself to look away from whatever the bishop had turned into and concentrated on sending her consciousness into Russell as she had done with Jack.

As before, she felt her point of view shrinking as she passed through skin and bone until she was floating in the encephalic fluid surrounding his brain. She was simultaneously aware that she still clung to his arm in the church, but she ignored it, afraid that fear of the bishop entity would distract her.

She shrank further, entering his brain and traversing a path of neural connections and synapses, a cob-webbed series of thoughts and memories. Some glowed brighter than the sun while others were dark. As she observed, new links were created, strands of fiber linking with electric rapidity as pulses flew across to other connections and split, going down multiple paths to eventually disappear deeper into Russell's mind.

She wasn't sure if she was seeing his actual brain or some sort of representation that her own mind had concocted, but she did know she could affect it, just as she had affected Jack's body before.

As she delved deeper she reached a section where the neurons and synapses were forming more slowly, and when they did form they pulsed with black light. She touched one tentatively and recoiled; she couldn't explain what it was other than it felt alien. Whatever was wrong with Russell was situated there.

She reached out again, prepared to weave together damaged cells and molecules, to purge whatever corruption might be there. There was a stabbing pain in her head, as if someone had driven a spike into her skull. Her consciousness was thrown back into her own body and she fell to the floor, all connection with Russell suddenly broken.

Her hands on her head trying to quell the pain, she looked up to see Russell's body hovering in the air in front of the entity, as if he was dangling on an invisible string. Russell floated closer to the entity, arms and legs hanging lifelessly. She couldn't see his face, but there was a tremor in his voice as he addressed the being.

"Are . . . are you God?"

The entity was a luminescent, golden creature of intense beauty and majesty, but it still seemed incomplete. It did not have eyes, but there was a distinct movement of its face, as if it was sizing Russell up as he floated in the air not ten feet from it.

There was no voice, but it communicated somehow, a wave of feeling that indicated something she could only describe as overwhelming amorality. It felt like the forceful projection of a personality that was beyond humanity, an arrogance justified in its complete superiority. She felt an overwhelming desire to worship this being.

A part of her was able to resist, and she forced her head up so she could look at its face. Its attention was not on her; she was only caught in the periphery of its focus on Russell, and she wondered if she would be able to even think on her own if it focused on her instead.

Some of the entity's hold on her loosened when one of Russell's shoes fell off his foot and hit the floor. The other followed soon after.

His clothes hung loose on his frame, and she was shocked to see the few exposed bits of flesh—his hands, the back of his head and neck—shriveling, the bones visible through the paper-like skin. It continued, as if the meat of his body was being sucked out, leaving only the husk.

Finally, too quickly for her to fully register what was happening, his body caved in upon itself, his clothes falling into a crumpled pile on the floor.

She stared at them, unable to comprehend that all that

was left of Russell Kellar was an empty set of clothes.

It is one who knows.

The voice was more than sound. It buffeted her with force, penetrating her body and boring into her, leaving a residue of fear and awe that paralyzed her.

It must rejoin.

The power of the voice decreased, and Cerise was sure it had been done on purpose to communicate with her. The fear was still there, but it had lessened to the point where she could move, and more importantly, respond.

Her voice was shaky and she wasn't able to stand up, but she managed to weakly say, "A-are you . . . Ialdabaoth?"

We serve that which it calls Ialdabaoth.

It moved its translucent head the slightest bit, seeming to look beyond Cerise. The features of its face were more defined than before but still looked unfinished. The bishop's body hung suspended inside, as if he were the puppet master instead of the puppet.

She got to her feet and took a tentative step forward. She felt like a little girl facing an unreachable, unreadable father, terrifying in his absolute power, unpredictable in his response. She had to claw down an overwhelming desire to drop to the ground and cower.

"Why did you kill him?" she asked, hardly able to believe she could actually address it.

It was not one who knows.

"Russell?"

It didn't respond, but she thought she understood. She was 'one who knows' but Russell was not. It only took her a second to realize that 'one who knows' meant Gnostic and she paled. Was Russell right?

"What do you mean that I must rejoin?"

The self is fractured. It must be made whole.

She shook her head. The Gnostics thought that a piece of Sophia resided within them—a divine spark that had once been a part of the true God. The knowledge, the *Gnosis*, of what they really were would free them from the material world so they could transcend their bodies and reside with the true God. Their bodies were nothing more than vessels for their true selves.

Was it all true? Was she a Gnostic? She glanced down at Russell's clothes. If he was not, did that mean he was nothing more than flesh and blood?

She had scoffed at the notion of a soul before, but now, knowing she may very well have one and that Russell might not, she was left cold. What kind of universe imparted immortality to some but not to others? And what kind of god presided over such a universe?

It must rejoin.

The entity towered over her, waiting for a response. She stepped closer and held her hand out, eyes briefly flashing to the row of archons still on the dais. Ialdabaoth or one of his agents had animated them and sent them for her, and she had been able to destroy them by knowing what they were.

Whatever this golden entity was—god, angel, or demon—it was made of *something*. She would send her consciousness into him just as she had done with the archons, and once she knew what he was made of, she would rip him apart atom by atom.

Chapter Twenty Four

She realized her mistake as her fingertips brushed the entity. A flood of images and feelings ripped through her, a torrent that set every nerve on fire and filled her head to the point where she felt like the pieces of her skull were being pushed apart to accommodate the overload of information. She squeezed her eyes shut but the images weren't just visual, and she was helpless to prevent them from overpowering her.

The deluge slowed eventually and the pain lessened. Images and feelings continued, but they were slower, more manageable. She opened her eyes and took in a vast emptiness that surrounded her on all sides.

The blank canvas stretched to the edge of infinity, but it wasn't the black emptiness of space. It didn't register in her vision so much as in her mind. It was the total absence of anything, a void where the universe should be. She couldn't put the experience into words or even coherent thoughts; there was nothing more than an understanding that the empty expanse existed and that she was witness to it.

A sudden explosion sent waves of space rolling past her, tsunamis that carried the blackness of space. Random particles flew past her at velocities that couldn't be comprehended. She saw the mass of the universe unfold to the edges of reality in the span of time it took to blink.

As the waves faded, swirling clouds of gases and particles began to coalesce. More clouds were created as the particles and gases were drawn into orbits around each other. The blackness filled with these conglomerations, and they began to crash together in silent collisions that formed even more massive concentrations of coalescing particles.

Stars were born and they drew other bodies to them. Some were absorbed while others collided, sending streams of matter scattering for hundreds of millions of miles, only to be trapped by the gravity of passing bodies. Others were caught in orbits that circled their stars wildly, eventually slowing to form ellipses that continued predictably traveling around their parent stars.

Sections of the universe calmed and cooled, and in those sections, life arose. Cerise watched the births and deaths of trillions of species on billions of worlds. The process repeated itself over and over again for billions of years, some species surviving for millennia, others dying out in days.

But it was the entity at the center of the explosion that would forever be imprinted on her consciousness. For a fraction of a second before reality was initiated, she had perceived a vast and terrible intelligence; a being of such unimaginable power that it made the golden entity seem like an amoeba in comparison. This entity had been the catalyst, the prime mover. It had set the machinery of the universe into motion; everything that existed did so because of its will and desire.

Her lack of belief was no longer relevant. She had seen the evidence that God was real, and in that microsecond of perception she had nearly lost her mind. She was left with a vague impression of the scale of its existence, a faint memory of something beyond all normal understanding.

And then she was back in the church, her fingers still brushing the golden entity, her body so weak she could barely stand.

It knows.

"What did you show me?"

The truth.

She wanted to question it, to argue as she always did, but she couldn't. She *had* been shown the truth, or at least a piece of it, and it would be a waste of time to deny that there was some greater intelligence out there—that this intelligence was, for all intents and purposes, God.

But it was a God that few would recognize. It wasn't a fatherly deity promising a reward to the faithful. It wasn't an anthropomorphized representation with a long, white beard and flowing robes. This was a being that could not be described by human language or concepts; it was power and time and energy, and it was both utterly terrifying and infinitely captivating.

Her rage had dissipated. The underlying reasons remained, but they were subsumed by the realization of what the bishop entity was comprised of. Unlike the archons this was not simply an amalgamation of atoms and molecules animated with a rudimentary intelligence. It was a piece of the godhead, and she understood how the attempt to know a supreme being had fractured the Gnostic goddess, Sophia, into various parts. She understood because one of those parts was within her.

She was staggered with the implication.

"What . . . what do I need to do?" she asked.

Release itself and rejoin.

She would die, or rather her material form would die, but was that relevant anymore? Did it matter that her body would be gone when her essence, her spirit, would continue? Whatever it was that animated her material form would live on within the godhead. She wondered if her own identity and consciousness would survive or if she would be completely absorbed, but it didn't matter. What could matter in the face of what she now knew?

She closed her eyes, searching inside herself for the connection between the material and the spiritual. Her muscles became more relaxed than they had ever been in her entire life and she fell to her knees, the link to the bishop entity the only thing keeping her from completely falling to the floor.

Her anger at what had happened to Russell seemed so irrelevant now. He didn't have the spark within him, and his death erased him from existence. She thought she should be sad, but couldn't manage to feel the actual emotion. His time was over now, and he was a temporary being, while she was eternal.

A formal declaration of submission wasn't necessary, but she craved the symbolism. All she had to do was set free the divine spark inside her and she would join with God. In the back of her mind, one sliver of defiance screamed at her to refuse, but she ignored it. It was nothing more than fear of the unknown. As Russell had said, who wouldn't be afraid when faced with something of this magnitude? Soon all fear would be gone and she would literally become one with the universe.

She imagined the spark as a ship and her body as the dock, and one by one she released the moorings, the ship becoming more and more free with each untethering of a line. Her body felt lighter and lighter and she wondered if she was only imagining it, but she continued casting off lines and accepting the sensation, real or not.

The ship was nearly free and she began unwrapping the final rope, purposely slowing down the experience to savor the last few moments before her transformation. She was equal parts fear and anticipation, and she accepted both, realizing that nothing could be more terrifying than meeting the creator of the universe, and that nothing could be more sublime.

The universe shook suddenly and the image was gone. She fell backwards, hitting the hard wooden floor underneath, and she looked up. The bishop entity stood just in front of her, but her fingers were no longer in contact with it. Its attention was on something behind her.

Her thoughts were muddled and she shook her head to clear it. She had reached out to touch the entity and she had experienced something, but she couldn't grasp it. It felt like a rapidly fleeting dream—the more she tried to remember, the quicker it receded.

She was left with an impression that some truth had been twisted and perverted, and that she had been close to . . . dying? That wasn't it exactly. Somehow it had been even worse.

She scrambled away from the bishop entity but it paid no attention to her. It took a step forward and she saw an undeniable expression of rage on its face. The look jarred her, and a few scattered memories surfaced.

Some other being was trying to . . . absorb her? And it tried to convince her to allow it by insinuating that within her was a missing piece of itself.

It was a lie.

Somehow she knew Ialdabaoth was trying to gain something it had not originally possessed. She didn't understand how she knew this fact, but it was more true to her than anything she had ever comprehended.

But why did such a powerful being need her to submit? Why didn't it simply take what it wanted?

She didn't know, but she realized that the proximity to the bishop entity had allowed its master to access her. Ialdabaoth wasn't on this plane; maybe that was why it couldn't simply take what it wanted.

She had been within seconds of giving her soul away to something posing as God. Maybe it was the creator of the universe, but Ialdabaoth had only its own selfish motives and interests. How had the Gnostics been so accurate in their understanding of it?

Another revelation suddenly occurred to her: if Ialdabaoth was real, did that mean there *was* a true God that it had been derived from? A Gnostic God who was not understandable and who lived in a spirit realm?

She craned her head around to see the gaping hole in the front of the sanctuary. Whatever had caused the damage, it had saved her. The bishop entity—she began to think of it as an archangel—was Ialdabaoth's link to this plane, and it was not simply animated material like the archons. She could not understand what it was and dissolve it as she had done with the archons.

She wouldn't make that mistake again.

Chapter Twenty Five

The truck clipped the curb doing fifty, Jack gripping the wheel with white knuckles as he was jostled across the bench seat. He slammed on the brakes and skidded to a stop on the stone plaza leading to the front of the church. He threw the door open and jumped out without bothering to kill the engine or take the keys, and dashed to the wide front doors.

He yanked on them several times, already knowing they'd be locked, before running toward another set of entry doors to the right. They were locked as well, and he cursed under his breath while he backed away to see if there was another way he could get in.

Stained-glass windows above flanked a large rose window, but none were low enough for him to reach. Given time he'd probably be able to climb up to them, but time was not something he had much of at the moment.

He remembered that the rectory was connected to the church, and it was just around the side and past the sanctuary. He doubted the doors would be open, but they were probably a lot less secure than the several hundred pounds of solid oak at the front of the church. Even if the door was locked, there were likely to be windows low enough for him to reach, and it wouldn't take much to kick them in. Unless they were barred, of course, but he didn't want to think about that at the moment. It would be a lot better if they were just alarmed—a break in would send the cops, which was exactly what he wanted.

He rounded the corner and stopped short. The rectory was only a few hundred feet away, and the windows and doors didn't have bars on them. He could've kicked in the door or smashed in any of the windows with ease, except he had no idea how he was going to get past the dozen archons that stood on the sidewalk as if they had been waiting for him the entire time.

Their faces were impassive, but all eyes were locked on him. He instinctively reached for his Glock before remembering he didn't have it anymore. He didn't think it would have done him much good anyway.

When Lakaj had shot one point blank with no effect, Jack realized that these beings—whatever they were—couldn't be stopped with something as simple as a gun. But why had he been able to kill three of them before? It didn't make any sense.

At the moment, however, he was more concerned about what they were going to do. They made no move towards him; they looked like they were waiting for him to do something first. He was certain they wouldn't let him past, but he didn't know if they would actively pursue him.

He had his answer when they began to move forward at once, as if they shared a collective consciousness. Jack turned and bolted for the truck, glad he had left it running. He rounded the corner and ran full out, afraid that at any second he'd be grabbed from behind and pulled down, disappearing under a mass of wiry, pale flesh.

He got to the truck and scrambled around to the driver's side, catching a quick glimpse of movement in his periphery but afraid to give it his full attention. He threw the truck into reverse as he got behind the wheel and floored the gas. The truck lurched backwards just as two of the archons leaped onto the hood. Jack turned the wheel and swerved hard to the left, sending one sliding across the front of the truck and onto the ground. The other grabbed hold of the still open driver's side door and began trying to climb over it and into the cab.

The rest of the pack was close, but he was more concerned about the one about to get into the truck. He slammed on the brakes and the door swung in, bringing the archon even closer. He shifted into drive and floored the gas again, grabbing the door and slamming it shut with as much force as he could manage.

The door shut with a sickening thud; the archon's hand was caught where the top of the door met the roof, twisting the fingers into unnatural angles. But instead of crying out in agony as any human would have done, he was silent and expressionless, and he used the leverage he had gained from having his hand wedged into the door to smash his other fist through the window.

Shattered bits of glass sprayed into the cab, and Jack brought his arm up in front of his face. The archon grabbed his sleeve and pulled Jack over to the door.

Jack's foot was still pressed down on the accelerator, and he tried to pull himself free while the truck swerved off the plaza, into the street, and eventually slammed into the side of a building. The sudden stop sent Jack's head into the windshield, and the pain was like a white-hot dagger in his skull. Through the haze of blood dripping down his face he saw that the archon had been thrown forward, losing his grip on Jack's shirt while still dangling from the hand that was caught in the door.

Jack reached over and pulled on the handle, and the archon's hand slipped free. He fell to the ground and Jack put the car in reverse and backed away before the creature could regain his wits and come at him. He spun the wheel and ended up back on the street, only a quarter mile or so away from the church.

The pack of remaining archons was just ahead, standing between him and the church, but not otherwise moving. They might not come after him—although the one he'd just gotten away from might be pretty pissed—but it did him no good to be left alone; he needed to get to Cerise. It might be too late already, and every second he sat there made it more and more likely that she would be killed.

Out of the corner of his eye he saw the archon he had dumped running towards him and he gunned the engine. The truck took off, heading straight for the pack of archons standing in the middle of the road.

He wanted more than anything to run over them and hear the thud of their bodies hitting the pavement. Even though it made sense that a 4000 pound truck could easily mow down a dozen thin, naked angels, there was no logical sense to the things he'd witnessed. As the truck drew closer and they stood their ground, he knew with almost complete certainty that the truck was no match for these creatures.

Some part of him wanted to see what would happen out of grim curiosity. Would they remain frozen in place like concrete pillars, the sheet metal of the truck crumpling around them and folding up like an accordion? Or would they leap onto the truck at the last minute, fly through the window, and rip him apart before he could blink? Maybe they'd sprout wings and whisk the truck up into the air for all he knew.

He smiled for a second with the absurdity of the image before turning hard to the right and avoiding the center mass of them with a screeching of rubber. The truck felt like it went up on two wheels, although he might have imagined it. There was a harsh sound like metal ripping through metal, and the truck hesitated for a brief second before pulling forward.

Jack looked in the rearview mirror and saw that one of the archons had grabbed hold of the side of the bed and another held onto the rear. He swerved hard the other way, aiming for the church and hoping he could whip them off, but both clung with what looked like very little effort, their hands digging into the metal.

The rest of the group followed but were too far behind to catch up. Maybe they'd thought he would plow into them and the sudden turn had thrown them. It was comforting to realize they might not be all-knowing, even if it didn't make much difference with the two in the back about to pounce on him.

He straightened the truck and floored the accelerator again while the glass in the back of the cab shattered and he was grabbed from behind. He probably would have been pulled out and killed if the front of the church hadn't been so close.

The truck hit the few front steps and was launched into the twin oak doors at sixty miles per hour.

Chapter Twenty Six

Cerise gasped at the sight. Something had crashed through the front of the church, splintering the front doors and sending the rear pews scattering, although it was hard to see how extensive the damage was through the cloud of dust and debris.

The archons on the dais suddenly moved, making their way to the front doors. Before they could get there some of the rubble shifted, and two additional archons emerged from beneath piles of broken masonry. Despite the dust covering them, they looked and acted unhurt. They dug down, pushing away loose bricks and shattered beams before ripping out the broken windshield of what she could now identify as a truck of some sort. They pulled out a limp and bloody body, tossing it to the rubble-strewn floor of the church before backing away, looking as though they were ready to leap into action at any second if needed.

Cerise's eyes went wide when she recognized Jack, but she was pushed aside by the archangel, the bishop a helpless captive inside. Flagello made eye contact with her for the briefest of seconds, and the misery in that glance was enough to fill up the Old Testament. Then he was past her and the archons, and all she saw of the bishop was a floating mass within a translucent golden shell.

She heard a cough behind her and turned, startled to see Father Lakaj still standing by the dais. He had Jack's gun in his hand, but the shock and awe on his face was so intense that she didn't think he was even aware of the pistol. It was the expression of a man who had seen the face of God. She wondered what he would say if she told him that the God he worshipped didn't even exist.

She turned back to the archangel. Jack's limp body was hovering in front of him just as Russell's had been. His eyes opened, looking around as if he didn't know where he was. This was going to end the same way it had with Russell if she didn't stop it.

"Please don't hurt him," she said, self-consciously afraid to raise her voice much louder than a normal speaking volume.

If the archangel heard her there was no acknowledgement.

Jack's expression changed from confusion to fear as he realized his predicament.

She stepped closer. "Please! Don't hurt him! I'll do whatever you want!"

Again there was no response and she panicked. She couldn't bear to see the life drained from him right in front of her, not after all he had done to help her.

Anger overshadowed fear and she moved even closer.

"You can't do this! What kind of a God would allow this? Let him go!"

She wasn't sure if the archangel would respond, but other than physically assaulting it—for what little good that would do—she had no better idea how to get its attention.

She grabbed a standing metal candelabra near the dais

and turned. She stopped when someone grabbed her arm from behind.

"Put it down," Father Lakaj said.

She turned to see him behind her, now more aware of the gun in his hand. She frowned, unsure of what to do, but kept hold of the candelabra. The archons watched impassively.

He raised the gun and when she saw his eyes, she had no doubt that he'd actually shoot her.

"I won't let you commit sacrilege."

She pulled her arm out of his grip. He didn't resist, but he also didn't drop the gun.

"It's not God. It doesn't even serve the God you know."

He sneered the slightest bit. "I will shoot you before I allow you to do this."

"Are you insane? Didn't you see what it did to Dr Kellar? To the bishop? Do you think Flagello wants to be part of this? This isn't any kind of Second Coming! It's not here to save anyone!"

Lakaj's face remained as impassive as one of the archons. "Put it down now."

Cerise felt a chill go through her with the realization that this priest would shoot her if she didn't do as he said. She glanced over at Jack, still suspended in mid-air, his mouth and eyes open wide. She turned back to Lakaj and sent her consciousness towards him, hoping she didn't need to physically touch him.

She felt herself slide into the muscle fibers of his hand, feeling the tension from his grip on the pistol. There were no injuries there, nothing but pristine flesh, but she went deeper anyway, desperate to get control of his hand. When she had healed injuries before she had coaxed those parts of the body to speed themselves up, but there was nothing to coax. She was on a mission to destroy, not heal.

She traced several individual fibers, seeing the red blood cells transmitting oxygen, seeing the individual molecules. She could sense the electrical connection between the atoms, charges tenuously grasping each other in a rigid ballet of microscopic complexity, structures building upon each other and falling in fractions of a second.

As she drew closer, delving deeper into the miniscule universe of molecules and atomic links, she was able to discern the paths of electrons despite their impossible velocities. She began releasing them, sending nuclei scattering about, watching massive chains of molecules disburse in a chaotic chain reaction that began ripping muscle fibers apart.

She pulled out, noting the look of pain and confusion on Lakaj's face. The gun shook in his hand, although it was still pointed at her. He might be able to pull the trigger but she didn't think he'd be able to hit her with his increasingly shaky aim.

"What did you do to me?"

She turned her back on him and walked quickly down the aisle, the candelabra held in both hands like a samurai sword. Lakaj shouted at her to stop but she ignored him, less worried about getting shot than what the archangel was doing to Jack.

She stood behind it, awe and fear coursing through her at the thought of what she was about to do. When her fingers had brushed against it she felt the tie to the bishop.

It was using him as an anchor to travel from its own plane to this one, but the transference was incomplete. If she could stop it, she thought there was a chance the entity would be sent back.

Jack's silent scream moved her to action, and she swung the candelabra hard at the bishop's head with only the slightest hesitation.

The candelabra hit the entity and went through with virtually no resistance, but it stopped before reaching the bishop. She pulled but it was completely fixed in the glowing body, just inches from the bishop's head.

She tried to release her hands, but they were stuck to the candelabra, and she hung there, now painfully aware of how futile her plan had been.

"Let me go!" she screamed, terrified but also furious.

The candelabra was released and Cerise stumbled and fell backwards. The archangel's form was becoming more solid, the bishop inside becoming less distinct, although she didn't know if it was because he was being absorbed or if the outer shell was becoming more substantial.

She stood up and swung the candelabra back over her shoulder, knowing it would do no good but needing to lash out at something. She let it fly towards the bishop again, the hesitation she'd felt earlier now gone with the knowledge that she probably wouldn't be able to reach him.

As she made contact there was a loud crack and a sudden hot pain in her shoulder. It was completely overshadowed, however, by what she saw within the archangel's shimmering outline.

The bishop's head exploded, sending blood, brains, and skull fragments into the semi-solid interior of the entity.

Jack fell to the ground as if the invisible strings that held him aloft were suddenly cut. The gore floated inside the golden shell of the archangel, looking for all the world like a multi-colored jello salad with suspended bits of fruit cocktail.

She recoiled at the sight and nearly retched, her hand going instinctively to the pain in her shoulder. She pulled it back when she felt wetness and was further sickened by the blood on her palm. She looked behind her; Lakaj stood with the pistol pointed in her direction, a look of horror on his face.

He was slowly shaking his head, silently muttering the word 'no' over and over again. He dropped the gun and fell to his knees, his face slipping down into his hands.

The bishop—or what was left of him—had sunk lower inside the archangel, his feet touching the floor where previously they had been floating several feet above. Despite the gore and winding streams of blood, she could see the bishop more clearly than before as the archangel grew more and more transparent. The remains of the bishop finally slumped to the floor, and the golden outline of the archangel completely dissipated.

Cerise ran over to Jack, kneeling down to see if he was still alive. There was a faint heartbeat and shallow breathing, but she didn't think he would last much longer without help.

She turned to Lakaj. "Father!" she hissed. "Call for an ambulance!"

The priest didn't respond.

"Father Lakaj! We need an ambulance right now!"

He brought his hands down and stared at her,

unadulterated hatred twisting his face.

"You did this," he said, his voice low and menacing.

She was taken aback by the pure hate emanating from him.

He got to his feet and stared at her across the sanctuary. He looked as though he wanted to tear her apart with his bare hands. She quickly scanned the floor for the candelabra and calculated whether or not she could reach it before he rushed her, but he turned instead, running past the dais and back to the rectory.

Cerise turned back to Jack. He was covered in blood, and she had no idea where to even start. She put her hands on his chest and closed her eyes, but she couldn't focus.

"Jack!" she hissed, leaning in closer. "Can you hear me?"

He opened his mouth and she leaned down closer to him.

"Are you all right?" he said, his voice barely audible.

"I'm fine, but you're a mess." Tears squeezed out of the corners of her eyes and dripped onto him.

"I . . . I don't think . . . I don't—"

"Don't talk. I'm going to fix you." She closed her eyes and tried to focus, but she was too exhausted. After long seconds willing her consciousness to see inside him with no result, she gave up and opened her eyes. He was still staring at her.

"I'm going to call an ambulance. I'll be right back."

She started to stand, but he grabbed her wrist with surprising strength and pulled her back down.

"Stay." His voice was barely above a whisper.

"I have to get help. I'll be right back."

He didn't release her wrist. "It's . . . it's too late."

Panic rose in her chest. "It's not too late. I just need—"

"Cerise," he said, his voice weaker. "Don't go."

She knelt back down even though every instinct in her body was screaming at her to get help. Tears flowed full force as she bit back a sob and held his hand.

"Jack, I'm so sorry for getting you into this. I never . . . I didn't know—"

"Do you think I'll see my daughter?" His eyes stared out at something she couldn't see, and she knew he would be dead soon. Before she could respond, there was movement out of the corner of her eye. She looked up quickly, prepared for Lakaj to attack her, but instead of the priest a small girl stood there, a crooked smile on her face.

"Hi, Cerise."

She stared at the girl silently for long seconds before finally managing a weak response. "What are you doing here, Amanda?" It was a distillation of every question she had about who this girl was and why she was here, about how she fit into these events.

"I came to see him," she said. She knelt down near Jack's shoulder, put her hand on his forehead, and smiled down at him beatifically.

"Hi, daddy," she said.

Cerise's eyes went wide, but neither Amanda nor Jack noticed. Jack shifted his gaze to the girl.

"Lauren?" he asked.

Amanda nodded and stroked his head, looking down at him with more affection than Cerise had ever seen.

"It's me, daddy." As if guessing his thoughts, she added, "It's not a dream."

Confusion clouded his face. "But you . . . ." He didn't finish the thought, but it was clear what he was thinking.

"Cerise needed help, so I came back. I knew we could help her."

Cerise broke from her stunned daze. "I . . . I thought your name was Amanda?" It felt like a stupid question, but she was so shocked she didn't know what else to ask.

The girl smiled at her. "Amanda is my middle name, so I didn't lie. I just didn't tell the whole truth."

"Lauren," Jack said. "It's really you, isn't it?" His voice was thick and choked.

"It's really me, daddy."

He held his hand up to her face and caressed her cheek.

"I'm so sorry." Tears flowed freely down his face. "I'm so sorry I hurt you."

She smiled at him, a look of pure love and forgiveness. Cerise had never seen such an angelic expression on a human face before.

"It wasn't your fault, daddy. It was an accident. Mommy and me aren't mad at you."

Jack reached up and touched her face before letting his hand drop. His eyes were closed and he was still, his breath coming in shallow rasps.

Cerise wanted more than anything to get up and run away, but she had to know the truth. "You died, didn't you?"

The girl nodded. "I knew daddy could help you so I came back."

"Are you . . . are you a ghost?" She felt the hairs on the back of her neck standing on end.

Amanda screwed her face up and thought about the

question. "I don't think so, but I'm different now."

"I don't understand."

The girl looked suddenly sad. "We have to save daddy."

Cerise frowned. "I can't go inside like I did before. I don't know what to do."

Amanda held her hand out and Cerise took it after a split-second's hesitation. Her skin was warm and soft, but Cerise couldn't completely suppress her fear.

"Do like you did before with your arm."

Cerise sighed and closed her eyes, trying to send her consciousness outside of herself. Her concentration wavered at first, but then she was able to overcome her initial block. As she moved through Jack's injuries she saw torn muscle fiber, shattered bones, and ruptured blood vessels. Forgetting that she was holding the hand of a girl who had died in a car accident weeks ago, she began speeding up the healing process, watching old tissue repair itself and new tissue grow where necessary.

She continued until she could no longer focus, then she opened her eyes, the girl smiling at her while holding her hand over Jack's chest.

His eyes were still closed. The damage was more severe than it had been before, and it would take time for him to heal completely, but he would survive. He looked contented, as if he had put something to rest.

Amanda released her hand and stood up.

"Wait! Where are you going?"

Her smile was warm and sad. "I have to go now. My daddy will help you." She paused for a second before adding, "Will you tell him that me and mommy are okay?

That we forgive him?"

Cerise nodded, a fog of confusion refusing to lift.

"There's lots more like us, Cerise. I'm going to see some of them. But you have to help the rest."

Cerise frowned. "What do you mean, 'like us'? I don't understand."

"You're special, Cerise. Me too, but I didn't know it till after I died. I think that's why I could stay around for a while. But I have to go now. It's getting hard to stay here."

"I don't know what I'm supposed to do. Are those bad angels coming back?"

"I don't know, but the others like us, they're not safe. You have to go help them."

She opened her mouth to ask another question, but the girl was gone. She didn't have time to think about it, however; the sirens in the distance gave her the more pressing concern of how she was going to explain the crashed truck, the dead bishop, and the various other bits of chaos around her.

She put Jack's arm over her shoulder and tried to rouse him.

"What?" he said, clearly dazed.

"We have to go now."

He was able to stand, and she led him towards the rectory. The archons were no longer there.

He stopped her. "Russell?" he said.

She shook her head slowly.

"I'm sorry."

She walked into the rectory with his arm over her shoulder. A row of chairs were set outside one of the rooms, and she eased him into one of them.

"Why are we stopping?" he asked.

"I need to get something. I'll be right back."

"Cerise!" he hissed as she walked towards the library. "What if there are more of those archons?"

"They're gone."

"How do you know?"

She smiled. "I just do."

She was back in two minutes with a Solander box under her arm. He looked at her strangely but said nothing, and the two of them exited the rectory and walked down the dark city street just before several police cars pulled up in front of the church.

Chapter Twenty Seven

The elevator doors opened into the lobby of the hotel, and Cerise walked across the tile floor to the clerk at the desk. He was young—maybe twenty—and looked bored, although she couldn't fault him for that at 5 am. He mildly perked up as she smiled at him.

"Can I help you, ma'am?"

"Could I get some extra sheets and towels?"

"I'll have them sent up to you in a few minutes. 403, right?"

She nodded.

"Also, I need a Bible."

He cocked his head. "Did you check the nightstand?"

"There isn't one. I looked everywhere it might be."

He looked like he didn't believe her, but he reached underneath the desk and put a Gideon Bible in front of her.

"Does that work?"

"Yes, that's great. Thanks."

She turned and walked back to the elevator, feeling childish for lying to him. There had of course been a Bible in the room, but she wanted a second one so they could both have a copy for reference, and she wanted to avoid any questions about why she wanted two. She'd had enough confrontation and didn't want to explain herself to anyone.

She got back to the room and slipped in quietly. Jack was sitting in a chair by the window, staring out at the airport lights across the freeway. She walked over to the chair opposite him and sat, pretending to look out the window.

"Someone's going to bring up some sheets and towels in a few minutes."

He nodded absently, still intent to gaze out the window. His injuries had healed enough that they were no longer life-threatening, but she had still needed to rip up some sheets and towels for bandages. She could see where the blood had soaked through the portion of the sheet she had used to bandage his head.

"How are you feeling?"

"Like shit, but a lot better than before. I don't feel like I'm being stabbed every time I breathe anymore, although my head still hurts like a bastard."

"I could get some aspirin or Motrin."

"No, it's okay. I think I deserve to feel some of this, anyway." He turned to face her. "Was it really her, Cerise?"

She nodded. "I don't know how it could be, but it was. Without her help I think we'd both be dead."

"She wasn't a ghost. She was flesh and blood. I felt her hand on my head." His voice was calm, but there were tears in his eyes.

"I don't know exactly what she was, but I think you're right. She wasn't a ghost. It's like she was . . . waiting around, like she had a mission. She said we were both special, but I don't know what she meant."

It wasn't entirely true, but she couldn't say what she

thought out loud. It would make it real, and she wasn't sure she wanted to accept what it meant. Accepting that there was a supreme being was difficult enough; to contemplate why she had been singled out threatened her sanity.

But it was worse to begin pondering the consequences of these revelations; some had this spark and some didn't. Those who did—Cerise, Amanda, others—could access knowledge on some level, and could use that knowledge to change things.

As she watched the planes taking off, she knew she had only touched upon a very basic understanding of what she could do, how she could change the world around her. Even her view of the things around her was different. The air was no longer an invisible and intangible abstraction, something to be assumed and taken for granted. Now it was alive with swirling masses that no one else could see, entire universes of microscopic water droplets and the multitudes of bacterial life within them, each tiny life also an amalgamation of smaller things.

She saw these things as if they were superimposed over the world she knew, although she could look past them if she wanted. They didn't disappear completely, but they were relegated to the background, and if she tried hard enough she could pretend they weren't there at all.

She had finally seen the spark in Amanda, just before she disappeared. They *were* alike, although Amanda had left to—to what? Go to Heaven? Join a collective of other spirits? Cerise didn't know and she was afraid to find out the answers. But she did know that she would now be able to recognize others like her, others that had the divine spark within them, even if they weren't aware of it.

More than anything she wished it wasn't true. Did this make her immortal? Not her physical body; she knew that could die. But what about her consciousness? Would that transcend her physical frame? Even more upsetting was the notion that only those with this spark might live on. The rest—like Russell, Jack, nearly everyone she had ever known—were they nothing more than flesh and blood?

The thought would have made perfect sense to her only days ago, but after learning there was some sort of spirit dwelling within her, something distinct from her physical self, she felt nauseous. Would Gnostics like her be the only ones who would survive death? The Gnostics from the first century would have reveled in the notion, but she was horrified by it. Who was she to survive indefinitely while the rest of humanity turned to dust?

She shook her head, trying to dispel the thoughts.

"She wanted me to tell you that it wasn't your fault, Jack, and that she and your wife forgive you."

Jack nodded, the tears flowing down his cheeks. He turned to look back out the window.

"Where do you think they are?" he asked.

"I don't know if it's a place, but your daughter seemed content. That has to mean something."

He sighed and wiped his face with one hand.

"I can't go back, Cerise."

"Can't go back where?"

"I can't go back to my old life. There's nothing there for me. I need something to give my life meaning. I had that with my family, but now that's gone."

"Jack, I—"

"I'm not asking you to marry me or anything, so relax.

We're way past that."

"I didn't think you were going to ask me to marry you, jerk."

He smiled. "Just wanted to set the record straight. You're not as adorable as you were ten years ago."

She relaxed a little in the easy banter, recognizing his attempt to move forward.

"I assume you're not going to become a priest or anything."

"Nothing that requires so much studying. But I do have something in mind, something kind of in my field."

"Like what?"

He looked around the room, finally settling his gaze on her.

"Do you think this is over?"

"Do I think what is over?"

"Don't bullshit me, Cerise. You know what I'm talking about."

She sighed. She didn't want to think about it; she already knew the answer.

"No. It's not over."

He nodded. "That's what I thought. Lauren—well, she didn't tell me exactly, but I sort of understood from her that these things—angels? archons?—that they might come back. And that there are worse things."

"There are."

"If these archons are coming back, you're going to need someone to help you, someone who knows how to drive a truck through a church, for instance."

"Jack, it's not that simple. I—I can't be responsible for you getting killed. You almost didn't make it. You don't have any idea of the magnitude of what we're dealing with. I can barely comprehend it myself. Besides, you can't stop those things."

"I seem to recall killing three in the church."

It was true, and she still didn't understand how it had happened. The archons had looked surprised themselves. It didn't make sense with what she now knew about them. They weren't human or even any kind of animal. They were animated beings with a hive mind.

"Besides," he continued, "I have the feeling that my stunt with the truck helped you, at least a little bit. Am I wrong?"

She looked down. "I can't—"

"Listen. As much as you're pretending you're an expert on this, we both know it's not true. All your knowledge about the Bible will only get you so far. You need someone to help you; someone who isn't worried about niceties. Think about it—what will you do if you get arrested or held by the police? They're going to be on the lookout for you, especially with the bishop dead. And we have no idea what that bastard Lakaj is doing. For all you know, he could be telling the police that you murdered the bishop right now. You need me to help you navigate this stuff."

She knew he was right, but he made it sound so easy, as if they could just 'team up'. He didn't know that God—or whatever she had glimpsed during the creation—might be pissed at her.

She stared out the window, suddenly thinking of Russell, and the thought of what would come next terrified her. Her old life was over for all intents and purposes. She couldn't just stroll into class and pick up where her last lecture had ended.

As scared as she was, she couldn't deny there was also a spark of excitement. She stood to learn more about the nature of the universe than anyone who had ever lived. And what about 'the others'? Amanda told her there were more like her and that she needed to help them. If archons and archangels were coming for them, she couldn't just let them be killed, or absorbed, or whatever it was Ialdabaoth wanted them for. She couldn't let that happen, and she knew Jack would stay by her side no matter what.

She held out her hand and he took it as he stood up next to her. They stared out at the airport as the first few airplanes took off into the early morning darkness.

About the Author

Mike Vasich teaches English to gifted and talented students in suburban Michigan. He regularly sows the seeds of discontent and scrupulously avoids any work which forces him to stand up or lift anything heavy. He is busily at work on a sequel to any book which happens to be selling well.

Author's Note

I owe a debt to Professor Bart Ehrman, upon whose very accessible and entertaining books on early Christianity I heavily depended for the information in this novel. I sincerely hope I can buy him a beer some day.